PHIL TOMKINS

ONCE
a Soldier

Even Parachute Regiment training couldn't
prepare him for the ordeals he would face -
on and off the field of battle

PHIL TOMKINS

ONCE
a Soldier

Even Parachute Regiment training couldn't
prepare him for the ordeals he would face -
on and off the field of battle

[signature]

June 2014

MEMOIRS
Cirencester

Mereo Books

1A The Wool Market Dyer Street Cirencester Gloucestershire GL7 2PR
An imprint of Memoirs Publishing www.mereobooks.com

Once a Soldier: 978-1-86151-175-1

First published in Great Britain in 2014
by Mereo Books, an imprint of Memoirs Publishing

The address for Memoirs Publishing Group Limited can be found at www.memoirspublishing.com

The Memoirs Publishing Group Ltd Reg. No. 7834348

The Memoirs Publishing Group supports both The Forest Stewardship Council® (FSC®) and the PEFC® leading
international forest-certification organisations. Our books carrying both the FSC label and the PEFC® and are
printed on FSC®-certified paper. FSC® is the only forest-certification scheme supported by the leading
environmental organisations including Greenpeace. Our paper procurement policy can be found at
www.memoirspublishing.com/environment

Typeset in 11.5/16pt Goudy
by Wiltshire Associates Publisher Services Ltd. Printed and bound in Great Britain
by Printondemand-Worldwide, Peterborough PE2 6XD

www.philtomkins.com

Cover designed by Max Vitali

*'A killer story, with a strong emotional core, plus powerful themes
that will touch hearts and a believable protagonist'*

Kaye Jones - History in an hour

*'A mixture of human interest, military history and good
old fashioned emotion'*

Hugh Grant - A game of soldiers

Also by Phil Tomkins
TWICE A HERO

For Maree, with love and thanks.

Grateful thanks to Chris Newton, Editor, Mereo Publishing, Mary Berry for copy editing, and to Annie Wittles and Caroline Tomlinson for proof reading. To graphic designer and family friend Max Vitali for another splended book cover and my youngest son Philip for his help on IT.

CHAPTER ONE

IRELAND

The last thing the recruit soldier expected as he sat on his bed polishing his belt brasses was to see a fellow recruit run through with an eighteen-inch bayonet. Travis, the youngest in the billet, stared at the unreal scene. *This can't be happening. God! Will it be me next?*

As the bug-eyed, crazed attacker struggled to pull the weapon from his victim, four other recruits threw themselves at him, unclipped the rifle from the bayonet and forced him to the floor. He screamed and lashed out with his fists and feet until one of the men knocked him unconscious with a blow that burst his lip. The wounded youth slumped to one side with the bayonet still lodged in his body. A tide of blood soaked into his bedding, forming an ever-widening crimson pool on the barrack floor.

Snapping out of his fear, Travis grabbed the pillows from his bed. Running to the injured recruit, he pressed them into the wounds in an effort to stop the flow of blood.

There was no sleep that night for Travis. The medics were quickly on the scene, followed by the Military Police, who arrested the attacker and took the rest of the billet's occupants away for questioning. The barrack block was now a crime scene, and the witnesses had to spend the night in the guardroom cells.

Lying on a cot in a two-man cell waiting for his turn to be questioned by the Redcaps, Travis was in turmoil. He was shaking like a leaf and shit scared.

Some soldier I'm going to be if I can't stand the sight of blood. How the hell did I end up in this mess?

As the last thought entered his head, another pushed it out.

Because I had no bloody choice!

He lay there in the darkness, recalling the moment he had handed over the forged letter of consent to his under-age enlistment. The recruiting sergeant sized up his skinny frame and boyish looks and jokingly asked him, 'Are you sure it's the army you want to join and not the Boy Scouts?'

Well, I made it, he thought. *I've been accepted into the military and out of the clutches of my vicious stepmother and a miserable life at home.*

He thought about the last five years of meagre food, worn-out clothing and wet feet in shoes beyond repair; the cold winter nights roaming the streets until the small hours of the morning waiting for his parents to return home from their regular late nights out; the continual hostility of his stepmother, both mental and physical, and the total indifference of his father.

I'm going to get over all the upset and get stuck in and make a decent soldier. I'll prove to myself that I am not cowardly and weak like my father.

For then, recruit training came to a halt. Travis spent long, tedious hours at the general court martial. It appeared to be a straightforward enough case to him. A whole section of soldiers had witnessed that terrible night. But the army had to have its day in court. The fact that the attacker had had a mental break-down had no impact on the letter of military law.

Unknown to Travis his father was also in camp, putting forward a case to have his son discharged from the army as an illegal entrant. The result of this came to light a week after the court martial had ended.

'Left, right, left right. Halt. Remove headdress.'

Travis stood at attention in front of his Company Commander.

'We have been informed by your father that you are an illegal entrant to the Irish Army, in that you enlisted whilst under age of consent and without parental permission while using a forged document. Therefore you are, as of now, discharged from the Army. Your Platoon Sergeant will make all the necessary arrangements for return of kit, pay etc. You are dismissed. March him out, Sergeant Major.'

'Replace headdress, about turn, left, right, left, right...'

His father and stepmother were waiting for him as he stepped down off the bus in Dublin from the army camp in Kildare. His father handed him a brown paper bag which held his work clothes and boots.

'Go back to the camp and find your real father' he said. With those words, his parents turned their backs on him and walked out of his life. Before he lost sight of them, he shouted, 'My mother must be spinning in her grave right now. I'm the bloody image of you, you lying fecker!'

The bitterness and hatred in his voice at his father's final act of betrayal was almost tangible. There and then he vowed that it would be a freezing day in hell before he ever made contact with, or spoke to, his father again.

A stab of panic hit him as he realized that he was on his own and would have to fend for himself from this day on. Fighting his feelings, he knew he had to sit down somewhere and make plans for the future.

This was the 1950s, and the serious state of unemployment in Dublin and elsewhere brought mass sit-downs in O'Connell Street in the city centre by thousands of unemployed people waving placards begging for work. Travis had to skirt one such human road block to get to the Rainbow Rooms, a favourite meeting place for him and his girlfriend Melissa in happier times. Shocked at what he had just seen and working his way through a ham sandwich and a pot of tea, he looked at his options.

Travis reasoned that he hadn't a snowball's chance in hell of getting a job there. His only option seemed to be to emigrate. His army pay should get him to London, where he had some mates, and he should have a few bob left over to cover himself for a week or so. But what would he do if he couldn't get work? He would be in deep shit.

Sod it, he thought, I'm in deep shit already. I've got to do something to dig myself out.

So, his mind made up, he went to a movie to kill some time. Then, to save money, he spent the night shivering in the doorway of a warehouse in Dublin Docks. Next morning he bought a one-way ticket to Liverpool and joined the end of a long, slow-moving queue at the North Wall to board the B & I (British and Irish) boat for the twelve-hour voyage to Liverpool.

The boat sailed that evening. Standing on the after-deck looking at the Irish coastline fading in the distance, his only regret was not being able to contact Melissa. He would write to her and explain all when he got settled.

It was the only time Travis had ever been on a ship. Heading out into the Irish Sea the wind got up, the rain lashed down, the ship heeled and rolled and he had his first taste of seasickness. The crossing was quite dreadful and the passengers travelled in absolute squalor, with next to no facilities. There was nowhere to lie or sit except on the open deck or down in the hold, a heaving mass of suffering humanity, foul smelling and awash with vomit.

He chose to settle down on the deck, which was littered with empty Guinness bottles which rattled and rolled all night long. Between that and the biting cold, he got little or no sleep. In the grey light of a winter's morning and as the ship docked, Travis whispered to himself, 'welcome to Merry England'. He wondered if he had made a big mistake in leaving Ireland.

CHAPTER TWO

ENGLAND

Finding his way to Lime Street Station, Travis boarded the train for London in the hope of finding some of his Irish friends living and working there. The journey was another ordeal to overcome. It was a long and dirty trip, with black soot from the engine blowing back through the open window into the compartment and coating his face, hands and clothes. Although he was young and fit, he arrived in London a total wreck.

After washing his hands and face in the toilets at Euston Station, he went about finding his mates. He got an enthusiastic welcome from his friends, and one of them took him in and let him share a room with him.

Next a job – plenty of those in the big city. Travis never looked back. He worked hard, played even harder, and had never had it so good or enjoyed such happiness every weekend out on the town with his pals, seeing the sights of London and drinking copious amounts of alcohol.

That is until, after a six-month spell, his call-up papers for National Service dropped through the letterbox.

'Not a problem' his friend Mick Callaghan told him. 'All you have to do is go home to Dublin. Have a short holiday and come back and register for work as Joseph Travis, or whatever the hell you want to call yourself. Then my boyo, you're on for another six months call-up free work. We've been doing it for ages.'

'I don't know Mick, I did a short stint in the Irish Army and enjoyed it and I'm not afraid to take the plunge again. But not yet, I'm enjoying life at the moment.'

'Whatever you do is all right with us. The very best of luck to you, but you're a daft bastard to give the army a second thought.'

Right or wrong, Travis decided to make his way to his designated recruitment office in Acton, London, to be greeted by a Sergeant of Engineers.

'What can we do for you, young sir?' said the Sergeant.

Travis handed him his call-up papers and asked, 'What are the conditions of enlistment and the weekly pay?'

'One pound eight shillings a week' the Sergeant said.

'I don't think I'll join your army, thank you.'

'It's against the law to try to dodge National Service and you could end up in prison.'

'Not me, I'm Irish, and I have the option of going back home. There's no call-up there.'

'What's your problem son? It's a good life in the modern army.'

'Maybe so, but it pays bloody silly money.'

'Look lad, instead of serving eighteen months' National Service, why not sign on for three years' Regular Service? The pay's three pounds three shillings a week.'

Despite himself, Travis was showing interest. 'That's a lot better than one pound eight.'

'Better yet, if you join the Parachute Regiment you'll get

another two pounds two shillings, which would bring you up to five pounds five shillings a week.'

'Now you're talking. But, who the hell are the Parachute Regiment when they're at home?'

'They're the élite of the British Army and they go into battle by aircraft and by parachute. If you think you have the balls to jump out of a plane, this could be the mob for you. Last but not least, they are the highest-paid troops in the British Army.'

Travis' grandmother had told him his dad had been a crap soldier who had spent his career as a waiter in the officers' mess. He couldn't soldier if his life depended on it. He had also been a moral and physical coward. If Travis could do this, it would prove he was a better man than his father.

Much impressed with what was on offer and the opportunity to test himself to the full, Travis signed on the spot. He spent his first night in the home of the British Army, Aldershot, with forty or so other hopefuls all bedded down in double bunks in a draughty barrack block. He found difficulty in sleeping due to the sobbing of some of the young lads on their first time away from home.

This started the whittling-down process of the new recruit platoon. Despite his previous army training, he found the weeks of Para Basic to be gruelling in the extreme. With no respite, it went from one phase to another.

There was drill, map reading, fieldcraft and weapons training. There was cross-training in learning how to handle a rifle, sub machine-gun, light machine-gun, pistol, rocket launcher (anti-tank weapon) and mortar. The Paras worked on the principle of 'slick skills produce quick kills'. Weapons training was followed by a scary trip to the grenade range, where each trainee had to throw two grenades, then duck as the base plate of the grenade and pieces of shrapnel came winging back at the thrower.

Radio and radio procedure, battlefield first aid and guard duties and day and night exercises were interspersed with the military side of training. This was the tough, physical aspect, with ten-mile runs and route marches carrying full kit. The Paras call the ten and twenty-mile runs 'tabs' (Tactical Advance to Battle). They placed considerable stock in a future Para being able to sustain the pace, complete long, forced marches and arrive at his destination ready for battle.

On Travis' first tab, he came down with the biggest blister on his right foot he had ever seen. During a quick break, the accompanying medic lanced it and left him to struggle getting his sock back on. When he stood up the pain was indescribable. In no time at all, he was well back from the main group. He broke down and cried from the pain and cursed every member of the training team to hell and gone.

You bunch of heartless bastards. You don't give a monkey's whether I live or die. It's all right for you feckers in lightweight trousers and maroon singlets, posing in your red berets. God, I just want to die. What the hell am I doing here anyway?

One of the corporals dropped back to encourage Travis to keep going and help him catch up with the main bunch. *Bloody hell, one of the evil sods is coming back to bollock me. Drop dead, you feckin' arsehole, just leave me alone!*

'Come on Travis you can do better than that, I've watched you, you have the balls to do this. All you need is the belief. Try and up the pace a little. Come on, you can do it.'

It's all right for you, you smug bastard. I'd like to see you with a feckin big hole in your heel and a bag of bricks on your back. See how bloody tough you would be then.

When Travis failed to up his pace, the corporal's mood changed. 'OK Travis forget it, you're done. Break off and I'll bring up the

Land Rover and get you a cushy ride right out of the Regiment. Just pack it in, you bloody wimp.'

Sod you, you gobby bastard, I'll show you who's a wimp.

Lost in his own mind-numbing world of pain and fatigue, he started to get used to the pack filled with bricks and gradually the pain from his blistered heel began to ease. With a supreme effort of will he was in among the pack, while others dropped back and some dropped out. This helped his confidence. Now all he had to do was make the time set for the course.

Finally, his nightmare ended. He had made it on time and could get some proper medical attention to set him up for the next tab.

Travis' favourite skills lesson was the radio. He could disassemble and reassemble the various sets better than any weapon he had to learn. Unfortunately, his instructor deemed him unsuitable to become a radio operator because of his accent and poor pronunciation. He would say 'tree' for three, 'tirty' for thirty and 'turd' for third. In the years ahead, this problem would come back to haunt him.

Interspersed with the basic training was Pre-Parachute Selection, or 'P' Company. This was a series of rigorous physical tests, the toughest course, after SAS Selection (Special Air Service), in the British Army, designed to determine if a recruit had the right mental attitude and qualities to succeed in the Parachute Regiment. Travis and his fellow hopefuls had to show the right amount of aggression, initiative and self-reliance for the next stage, parachute training.

The proud history of the regiment was drummed into the recruits during sessions on regimental history. The drops on 'D' Day in Normandy and Arnhem, Holland, where the Paras had had to hold a bridge across the Rhine for forty-eight hours and the remnants of a single battalion had held it for three days and nights.

Ten thousand Paras dropped into that cauldron and only two thousand came out.

Luckily for Travis, he found that his pride and self-belief helped him to build the right mental attitude to face the seventy per cent failure rate for potential Paras. He believed that if he was ever going to prove himself a better man than his father, selection for the Paras would be the ultimate test of balls, brains and physical fitness.

This was tested to the extreme on a forty-four foot high structure of scaffolding poles, loose planks, ropes and nets call the Trainasium. The whole contraption swayed like a willow in the wind. Having arrived at the top of this monstrosity he had to do a 'look Mam no hands' shuffle across two parallel bars on top of this nightmare.

Success on the Trainasium was followed by the 'Log Race', which he felt should be renamed the 'Telegraph Pole Race'. Along with seven other victims and carrying a long, heavy pole with the aid of toggle ropes, a three-foot length of thick rope with a loop at one end and a toggle at the other, he had to race along a mile and a half course, up hill, down dale, through mud and shale, all the while harassed by the PTIs (Physical Training Instructors), armed with hockey sticks, which they applied to the backside of any dawdling recruit.

Before Travis and his team got their breath back they were into 'milling', a toe-to-toe style boxing match or, as it turned out, a slugging contest. If the recruit ducked or dived at any time during the match or, in fact, failed to complete or qualify to the highest standard in any aspect of the tests and training, he would be out of the regiment. Should he or any of his fellow recruits fail, for any reason, they would be back-squadded to try the whole torturous trail again. If they were unlucky, and had been transferred in from another arm of the forces, they would be returned to their previous unit, or if not, into civilian life again.

Travis and the remaining recruits were not allowed see or speak to the rejects. The system was to spirit failures away from the platoon before their fellow recruits returned from some training stint. In effect, the rejects were not given the opportunity to influence the mindset of the remaining trainees, or knock their confidence in any way. There was just an empty bed space where their erstwhile friend used to sleep, never to be heard from or seen again. It was rumoured that rejects were sent to a Siberian salt mine and truth to tell, Travis never met a former reject for the rest of his life. He had the sneaking suspicion that there might be some truth in the old story.

When the going got really hard, he thought back to his schooling under the nuns at his convent school. The old gits had put the fear of themselves first and the fear of God second into their five to seven-year-old charges. The sisters looked angelic as they glided around the classrooms as if they were on castors, with their rosary beads wrapped around their waists and their bunches of keys. In fact, they were awful, nasty old biddies. He remembered the swish and crack of their bamboo canes and the cries and screams of the kids being thrashed in the classrooms and corridors. More often than not, he was one of them.

The convent was a great preparatory school for the next step of his education with the Christian Brothers, or bastards, as the boys called them. In the main, they were a bunch of sick sadists in religious uniform. 'Discharged from the Gestapo for extreme cruelty,' as one lad in the class remarked. Travis didn't have to do anything wrong to be lifted off the floor by the side locks of his hair, or his 'louse ladders' as his Gran called them. This punishment would leave him with a swollen face and in pain for the rest of the day.

At other times he was beaten across the knuckles with a drill stick, a long, half-inch thick piece of dowelling wood. This would leave him in agony for hours, until the swelling went down. In the meantime, his stepmother would attempt to rearrange his face with her ivory-backed hairbrush - her preferred weapon.

On an early morning cross-country run, Travis was moving well and had just got his second wind when the squad came to a barbed-wire fence. Since he was leading the pack, he held the open strands as his mates ran through. As the last man cleared the obstacle, Travis made to follow him. Unfortunately the wire snapped back, gouging a deep cut in the palm of his left hand. With blood pouring out of the wound, he attracted the attention of the PTI, a corporal in charge of the run. 'Close up you dozy little man and keep that bloody hand away from your PT kit!' he shouted.

When Travis returned to barracks, his injury was ignored and he was ordered to change into uniform and get back on parade double quick. Wrapping his dirty boot-polish cloth around his hand, he did as ordered. It was late evening before he was allowed to attend the medical centre. The duty medic was asleep on the examination table and well hacked off at being woken up. He reluctantly slapped a gauze dressing and bandage on the wound.

Next morning Travis had a lump under his left armpit the size of a golf ball; he had blood poisoning. He was driven to the military hospital by the duty driver and was dismayed to find himself admitted for an operation to draw off the poison. The following day the operation went ahead. The nurses tried to have him up and walking as soon as he came to, but the toilet was as far as he could go.

One afternoon during recovery he visited the snooker room, where he started to chat with a fellow patient who was in a wheelchair.

'Which unit are you in?' Travis asked.

'The Paras' the soldier replied.

'What battalion?'

'I'm just a recruit.'

'So am I.'

'Well we were! I don't know about you, but I'll be glad to get back into civvy street, I don't think I would have passed selection.'

'What do you mean about us and civvy street?'

'Don't you know? Once you get an injury which leads to being hospitalized, that's you out of the Paras.'

It was as if someone had kicked Travis in the guts. After all he had been through, to lose out because of a little barbed-wire fence. Head down, he slunk back to his bed, his dream shattered. Pulling the covers over his head, he wept silently.

Late that afternoon he was issued with a bottle of beer, which was common practice in the hospital, and he was glad of it as it helped him to sleep that night. The ward housed fourteen patients, three of them from the Guards Division. They were old soldiers, hard cases and heroes to a young boy-soldier patient who hung on their every word.

The guards decided to run a lottery. Every patient had to put his name in a beret and the first name to be drawn would get fourteen bottles of Guinness. The guardsmen banked on one of them winning the prize, which would give two of them four bottles and six for the winner.

The boy soldier won, and some time later he went mad with the drink and started smashing up anything and everything that wasn't nailed down. It took two hefty male medics to restrain him, and he was never seen or heard from again. That was the end of the free bottles of beer. However, the fracas helped to cheer Travis up a little bit.

Next day he was discharged and with his arm in a sling, he made his own way back to his barracks. Reporting to the training wing office and feeling like a condemned man, he was greeted by the duty sergeant.

'Yes Travis, I've got a note here about you. You have an interview with the Terminator. Just wait here and I'll find out if he will see you now.'

The Terminator, Travis thought, how very apt. Seconds later, 'Right Travis, you're on. It's the third door on the left, knock, wait to be called in and don't forget to salute the officer on entry and exit.'

Travis, his heart in his mouth, walked slowly down the corridor. Knocking on the OC's door he got a curt, 'Come.' Opening the door, he marched in smartly and saluted.

'How is the arm, Travis?' the Training Major asked.

'Good sir, getting better fast.'

'Glad to hear it. Now, what are we going to do with you? Let me see.'

Travis was filled with dread as the officer shuffled some papers and started to leaf through them.

'Well, Travis, it appears that you have worked hard and have potential. So… (long pause) we've decided to back-squad you to a platoon with only a few weeks to run, as you were near the end of your course when you had your accident. Report to the sergeant of 42 platoon, who will put you on light duties until you can dispense with the sling. Is that understood?'

Travis, his heart and his mind flooding with joy, mumbled, 'Yes sir, thank you sir.'

'Carry on Travis, and good luck.'

'Thank you sir.'

'I wonder whether you will thank me after you have been through the next few weeks' the officer replied.

A salute, an about turn, then out the door and down the corridor, this time walking on air.

'If you think you're going to have an easy time Travis, you have another bloody think coming.' This from his new Platoon Sergeant. 'You will attend every parade and take part in every lesson and exercise that you can do with one arm. Where you can't, you will act as billet orderly, looking after the barrack room and keeping it clean, and tidy, understood?'

'Yes Sarge.'

That was how it was, he was given no favours or help from anyone and he never asked for any. The old saying that 'many are called, but few are chosen' just about summed up the finale to Basic and P Company.

Travis was one of the few. His name was called out in front of his peers. He had passed. He felt special, he had proved that he could push himself beyond normal limits, a self-knowledge that he believed would affect the rest of his life. However, he still had to get through Parachute Training School, which was next on the list, to prove himself.

His passing-out parade was a particularly proud event for him, but he was rather envious of his mates, surrounded as they were by their excited and loving families. No matter, he thought, the army is my family now.

Along with the rest of the survivors of pre-Para Selection, he was bussed to Jump School with the words of the reviewing officer ringing in his ears: 'Never give in - never, ever, in anything great or small. Never give in, except to your convictions of honour and good sense. Never yield to fear, to the apparently overwhelming might of an enemy, real or imaginary.'

Travis on the parade ground stood as straight as a ramrod, battledress pressed with razor-sharp creases, boots polished to a mirror shine, crowned with the coveted Red Beret, the silver parachute winged badge of the regiment glinting in the early-morning sunlight. He listened to the address and thought, The man was right; from now, on that would be his motto. Now all he had to do was to get through Parachute Training School.

CHAPTER THREE

PARACHUTE TRAINING SCHOOL, ENGLAND

Travis' time with the Royal Air Force at Abingdon in Oxfordshire proved to be the most enjoyable part, if not the scariest, of his final training to be a Paratrooper. Firstly, the tough army discipline he had come to expect was left at the gates of the RAF Station. Now it was down to him and any balls he had left after selection to go through with parachute training and to fling himself out of what he hoped would be a good aircraft. Secondly, the food was excellent, in contrast to the army cooks or 'slop jockeys' and their ideas of how food should be cooked.

The potential Paras looked with disdain at the Erks, the lower ranks of Crabair, as they called the RAF, but they had the highest regard for the PJIs, the Parachute Jump Instructors, who were affectionately known as the 'nursemaids in blue'. To Travis and the rest of the trainees, they were a very special breed of men.

On the first day of their course, they were herded into the camp cinema and formally greeted by the Commandant. His welcoming speech was followed by a film outlining various phases of the course.

When it ended there was a deathly silence from the prospective Paras. The showing left Travis, who was scared of heights, worried witless that he would fail at the first hurdle, the balloon jump, or before that, on some of the most lofty equipment and fittings he had to master.

In command of Travis' 'stick' of eight trainees was their own personal nursemaid, an RAF Flight Sergeant PJI, a real hard, sarcastic bastard. He looked like a guardsman on parade; uniform immaculately pressed, cap with the peak cut back so that it rested on the bridge of his nose, which forced his head back. He looked most imposing. The other PJIs had a more fatherly arm-around-the-shoulder way of treating their students, but Flight Sergeant Ellison harangued his stick with a bellowing voice which could be heard in every corner of the training hanger. His mantra was 'Knowledge Dispels Fear', but as time went on, Travis came to believe it should have been 'Fear Dispels Knowledge' as the more scared he became, the less he remembered.

Another of the Flight's pieces of advice was to the effect, 'If you leave the aircraft and something goes wrong with your chute, don't panic. You have the rest of your life to sort it out'. The consensus of the stick on that piece of tutorial wisdom was 'Bollocks'.

Travis and his fellow students would be in the hands of this martinet for the next month as he endeavoured to teach them the theory and practice of parachuting; how to land with your elbows tucked in, knees and feet together, leaning backwards, forwards and sideways, in line with whichever way the wind was blowing at the time. This included the parachute roll, designed to distribute the shock of landing from the feet to the calves, thighs, hips and shoulders. The practice of this became an everyday ritual where, instead of press-ups for punishment if you goofed off, the offending student had to execute twenty parachute rolls.

Then on to exiting the aircraft, using mock-ups of a plane's fuselage. This was followed by evasion techniques; how to use the four webbing straps which, in a non-steerable chute, could only be used to spill air and hopefully slip away from an incoming fellow Para who might become entangled in your rigging lines. One of Travis' stick summed up this unholy trinity of exit, flight and landing as, 'The bloody fear, fright and panic of parachute training.'

Mostly their time was spent on the ground learning how to fall correctly from ever-increasing heights, with a bewildering array of equipment best suited to an aerial act in a circus. Ellison was an endless nightmare to Travis, who appeared to have no coordination when it came to the contortions of parachute training. The Flight Sergeant christened him 'Rock Iron' to add insult to injury.

Travis and his mates began their progress upwards from a contraption called the 'fan', up near the hanger roof, to the 'knacker-cracker', a thirty-foot high tower that looked like a big crane from a construction site. Except for a trip up Blackpool Tower during a holiday break from work in London, this was the first test of his head for heights. It had taken him an age just to walk to the rail of Blackpool Tower and look over. This time, there was no rail and he would have to jump out into space.

Already scared and shaken from his long climb up, Travis pulled his helmet over his eyes and waited for the tap on the shoulder and the command to 'GO!' When it came he literally fell off the platform. Then, hurtling down at a great rate of knots, his fall controlled by another pulley and fan system, he landed in an ungainly heap on the ground. Step one over, and a rollicking from the PJI over his exit and landing, but he had done it.

Next on the agenda were the regulation eight parachute descents required to qualify for their wings, two jumps at eight hundred feet and six at a thousand. The first two were from a barrage balloon with what looked like an open-topped horse box hanging underneath it. On the fateful day, Travis and three other trainees in his stick were the first to jump, with their own PJI as their dispatcher. As the steel cable tethered to the balloon started to pay out from a drum on the back of the conveyor vehicle and started the slow journey up to eight hundred feet, Ellison challenged them to sing all the way up. 'I'll give each man a pound note if you are still singing when we level out at eight hundred,' he said.

The challenge was duly accepted. Travis and his mates started to sing the old Para song, which was sung to the tune of 'John Brown's Body' or the 'Battle Hymn of the Republic'. With considerable gusto they belted out, 'Glory, glory, what a hell of a way to die.' Three choruses were followed by a verse, and there were many verses, such as, 'They scraped him off the tarmac like a lump of strawberry jam'. Again three choruses, followed by, 'and he ain't going to jump no more.'

At about six hundred feet the PJI remarked, 'Beautiful day gentlemen, with a wonderful view and lots of spectators. Take a look down at your audience.' The singing stopped abruptly. The PJI had won his bet.

Travis was the first to jump. Called forward, he shuffled carefully to the exit, thinking, *Here I go again, sticking my neck out, trying to prove I am a better man than my father. I must be bloody mad, or thick, or both. But, if I refuse it'll scar my soul for the rest of my life. I've got to do this.*

The helmet's all-encompassing chin-strap chafed his skin, and his testicles were in the vice-like grip of the parachute cross-straps. Uncomfortable wasn't the word for it, but he was as ready as he ever would be.

The PJI shouted, 'Stand in the door!' A pause, then 'GO!'

Travis jumped out. As he cleared the door the PJI shouted,

'Come back.' Like a right idiot, Travis tried - he had fallen for an old instructor's joke. He dropped straight down for about two hundred feet before his chute opened and developed, leaving his stomach back in the balloon cage, his legs floating up in front of his face and his baggy combat trousers flapping in the wind. The whole experience felt like committing suicide. But once safely down, he felt drunk on adrenalin. He had been conscious of his fear of heights, but with his new attitude from recruit training, 'P' Company and RAF pre-jump training, he found he could control it. It was a fantastic feeling knowing he had conquered his fear. He agreed with a member of his stick who went around telling all and sundry, 'I feel nine foot tall and covered in hair.'

The first balloon jumps were enough for two trainees from other sticks, much to the wrath of the instructors, who had a pool going to see which instructor would come through the course with his stick intact and collect the winnings. *Another two for Siberia,* Travis thought.

The next big step for him and his fellow trainees would be their first jump from a military aircraft which, for most of them, would be the first time they had ever flown. So on a bright and early Monday morning, hot for the time of the year, the various sticks were in the sweat room or waiting area nervously standing by for a Valletta aircraft of RAF Transport Command to perform its flight checks prior to take off. Travis sat sweating buckets, with rivers of perspiration running down his back and between the cheeks of his backside. His tummy had a platoon, if not a company, of butterflies fluttering around it and he had no control over them.

'Outside you lucky people, shut up and chute up!' the senior PJI bellowed. Suitably attired they clumped and waddled along the tarmac like a clutch of pregnant king penguins towards the aircraft. The aircraft, its engines running up and prop blasts trying to bowl them over, made it a difficult operation to board, imprisoned in their parachute harnesses, to which the main chutes and reserves were attached.

The aeroplane stank of aviation fuel and sweat. Travis sat down in the 'stick order' in which he would exit the craft. He tried, unsuccessfully, to calm his nerves and allay his worst fears, which all seemed to centre on the exit door. He was trying to psych himself up and admitting, *God, I'm shit scared of the bloody door. If I can get through the feckin thing I'll be OK.*

The deafening noise of the aircraft engines built up to a terrifying roar, which entered Travis' guts and chased his butterflies away. As the plane lumbered down the runway to take off, his stomach was in trouble again as it was pushed down towards his boots. As the aircraft climbed and levelled out, Travis thought, *Wow! I like this, it's magic, or it would be if I didn't have to bloody well jump out.*

There followed an enjoyable flight over Oxford towards the DZ (Dropping Zone) at RAF Weston on the Green. Then the command came, 'First stick stand up and hook up,' the Dispatcher shouting to make himself heard against the sound of the engines. He confirmed his verbal order with both hands, palms up, waving up and down.

Travis hauled himself up with difficulty and attached his webbing strop clip from the back of his chute to the static line, a cable which ran the length of the aircraft. From his balloon jumps, he felt confident this dodgy-looking system worked and would automatically open his chute for him. Then it was down to checking his kit and the chute and kit of the guy in front of him.

The Dispatcher shouted again, at the top of his voice, 'Stick, tail off for equipment check.' The jumper behind Travis slapped him on the shoulder and shouted, 'Four OK'. Travis carried on in the same way until the front man shouted, 'Number One OK, starboard stick OK.'

Then came the waiting as the aircraft started its run-in to the DZ, the weight of the main and reserve chutes pulling at Travis' upper body as he tried to steady himself in the swaying aircraft. All this was set against an atmosphere of apprehension, exhilaration and suppressed fear.

The engine noise changed as the pilot throttled back to slow the plane down for the jumpers. *God, let me get out before I fill my boots*, Travis silently implored. The red warning light over the door flickered on, followed by the command, 'Action stations, stand in the door.' The stick shuffled forward and the green light flicked on. The Dispatcher roared, 'GO One, GO Two, Go Two!' But number two was going nowhere. He was paralysed with fear and holding on to the sides of the door with an iron grip, leaving Travis and jumper number four stranded behind him. It took two RAF PJIs what seemed like a lifetime to prise his fingers off the door frame.

The aircraft overflew the DZ and Travis, along with his fellow jumper, were ordered to stand fast while the plane circled around for another run-in and the PJIs struggled to unglue number two. The Dispatcher had given the reluctant trainee two commands to jump and he had ignored them both, or hadn't heard them in his state of shock. Travis, also in a state of shock, was nearly wetting himself as he waited to be called forward again, this time as number one, first man out. His mind filled with all sorts of doom-laden thoughts, such as *Can't do it, no way I'm going to jump out that feckin' door. I desperately need to pee. I've got a terrible pain in my guts, I need the toilet so badly. When the PJI comes to me, I'll tell him I'm too ill to jump today. My knees are knocking together and seem to be playing some bloody tune of their own, I'm sure everyone can hear them.*

The Dispatcher leaned over Travis, shouting to be heard over the roar of the engines, 'You blokes are now number one and number two of the second stick, and as you are now six jumpers you'll have to exit the door like shit off a shovel. Do you hear me?'

'Yes Flight Sergeant,' they shouted in unison.

To make matters worse, Travis had to stand there and watch as the Dispatchers carried number two from the door, still in shock, as stiff as a shop window dummy. They strapped him into a seat at the far end of the aircraft away from the other jumpers. Then it was that time again.

'Stand in the door!' *God, that has come around fast*, Travis thought, as he tried to get his jangled nerves to settle. *Come on Travis, are you a man or a mouse? What did the officer on the passing out parade say: Never give in-never, never in anything great or small. Come on Travis you can do it.*

Then he heard the dreaded command, 'Go One!' The Dispatcher slapped him on the left shoulder, and eyes tight shut, Travis fell rather then jumped out of the door. His eyelids snapped open as his body hit the slipstream and he was whisked away like spit from an express train. One minute he was looking at the aircraft, the next the sky and then the ground. Following a tug on his shoulders, his chute opened. Once again, he wondered at the thrill of it as he drifted down from 1,000 feet to complete his first descent from an aircraft.

"Beautiful flight and landing Travis, you came down as light as a fairy's fart' was his greeting from Flight Sergeant Ellison, waiting on the DZ. *High praise indeed*, thought Travis, as he fought to get his stomach out of his mouth.

Despite the elation of his first jump from an aircraft, he couldn't help but feel sorry for the boy who had refused. Travis thought he knew the anguish the lad must be going through at having to leave the Paras.

Kitted up for his second and last jump, Travis' stick was the only remaining one with a full complement of trainees. All the other sticks had lost people to injuries and refusals. As Ellison still had a full stick he was in pole position to win the pool money. All went well with the penultimate flight, and Travis felt he had made a good exit from the aircraft, but when his chute deployed, he found his rigging lines had twisted so much they looked like a ship's hawser. The twists forced his head downwards, forcing his chin to dig painfully into his chest. He started to spin his body in the opposite direction to the twists to unravel the rigging lines, as per standard procedure. But as the ground came rushing up he had to stop twisting and prepare for landing. Looking at the marker smoke on the DZ, he judged he was coming in on his left side, so with feet together and pointed forward he waited the impact and ready to execute a parachute roll. Unfortunately, as he was about to land, the twists forced his body into a spin which ended with his landing in the forward position. His feet and toes, which should have been pointed away for a forward landing, hit the ground first, curling back. As he crumpled to the ground he screamed out, the pain unbearable. Unable to collapse his chute, he was dragged over the DZ like a unhorsed rider with his foot caught in a stirrup.

It was a very angry Ellison who finally deflated Travis' chute and bore down on the crying youngster. He started to kick and shake him, shouting, 'You bloody stupid bloody Irishman, you didn't listen to a word I said about getting out of twists during the training sessions, or you wouldn't be in this state now and I would have won the money in the pool. You can get yourself off the bloody DZ on your bloody own and I don't want to see your stupid face ever again.'

Not satisfied with that bollocking, the PJI visited him in the medical room to yell at him once more. But as luck would have it, bad weather closed in and the final descent was put on hold until it blew over.

The x-rays on Travis' feet showed he was just suffering from strain. Nothing was broken and suitable treatment was applied. When the weather cleared he was passed as being fit to jump and returned to his barrack room to be with his mates.

The last jump went like a dream, and Travis had his parachute wings, a cloth badge with a khaki background, blue wings and a white parachute-canopy embroidered on them, presented to him on parade. He had become a member of the Parachute Regiment and the Airborne Brotherhood, a graduate. From now on, if he refused to jump he would be subject to a court-martial, the sentence eighty four days' detention in a military prison, with a dishonourable discharge at the end of it. Having invested a considerable amount of money in his training, the Army wanted payback.

Travis and his fellow graduates were given the rest of the day off, which they spent in Oxford on a monumental booze-up. They were in the company of the now friendly Flight Sergeant Ellison, who was celebrating, having won the money in the instructor's pool. Generous with his winnings, he turned out to be human after all as he got well and truly drunk. He was drinking copious amounts of gin and tonic and Travis and his mates kept asking him to order his own drink just to hear him say, 'A gim and tomic preeese,' which reduced the new Paras to drink-fuelled fits of laughter.

The following day the much-depleted group of Paras were trucked back to Aldershot and installed in the transit block. There they waited for a posting to a battalion as one of the Paras ready to go to any trouble spot in the world. At that time most, if not all, of the trouble came from the Middle East.

Travis hated being stuck there. It meant having to hang around all day like a bad smell, doing all sorts of boring jobs like delivering coal to the married quarters, while wishing he was the hell out of there and with a battalion. But the coal run had its compensations for some of the transit boys. Lonely housewives whose husbands were away from home for months at time sometimes offered favours. It was a dangerous game to play, and Travis stayed well clear of it.

Finally the big day arrived and he was assigned to one of the three regular battalions that made up the Independent Parachute Brigade. It was a mobile unit employed in various parts of the world protecting the colonies and territories of the shrinking British Empire, suppressing dissidents whose aims were to bring about a bloody and speedy end to British domination and rule. This was what he had signed up for. The fact that his best mate had ended in a different battalion hacked him off no end, but that's life. In compensation, he had foreign climes, adventure and danger to look forward to. Another step in proving himself as a man and a good soldier.

CHAPTER FOUR

MIDDLE EAST

A long-haul military flight to the Middle East, and joy of joys, he didn't have to jump out of this aircraft. It landed in the early hours of the morning at Nicosia Airport, Cyprus. As the doors opened, hot air exploded into the cabin, drowning Travis in sweat. The passengers were ordered to remain seated until an officer came on board to lecture them on security in the event that they were attacked. It was designed to scare the living shit out of the passengers before disembarkation.

An RAF bus picked up the passengers, dropping them off at their respective units. Travis and his three mates were dressed in British Army battledress, a rough, thick, hairy khaki uniform. The dress was unsuitable for normal British summer wear and utter hell in a semi-tropical climate. Soaked in perspiration and already experiencing sweat rash, they were dumped from the bus on a dusty road leading to their battalion camp.

To Travis it looked like a scene from the film *Beau Geste* about the Foreign Legion. It was a large area of barren land covered in dust and housing near on 750 Paratroopers, all living in five-man tents laid out in straight lines, a line for each company of about 120 soldiers. In a tour of the camp, he found that the officers and senior NCOs' tents were sited at the top, just above the company lines, with the ammo dump, cookhouse, dining areas, medical facilities and motor pool, along with some mess tents for refreshments and relaxation. The parade ground was a dustbowl at the bottom and the camp was surrounded by barbed-wire entanglements, floodlights and lighting to show up any attackers at night. In fact the lighting made marked men of the patrolling sentries.

One other facility Travis got to know and love was the DTL (deep trench latrine). This, an oblong trench with a wooden box with round holes built over it, served as a latrine. This contraption seated about twenty-four men, sitting back-to-back and side-by-side, all crapping and farting to their hearts' content. The smell was appalling, but, when you have to go, you have to go.

Despite the conditions, the DTL was almost the social centre of the camp. There, one could read the British newspapers and catch up on all the news and gossip. With the waves of dysentery sweeping the camp from time to time, it was the most popular place after the canteen.

It was a godsend for Travis to get out of camp, but unfortunately, the usual ways out were on counter-insurgency operations, injury or death. Duties were made up of patrolling the city, towns and villages, the plains and the mountains, dealing with dissidents and hunting terrorists.

He noticed an article in the newspaper stating that French troops in North Africa had killed 350 Algerian rebels in heavy fighting and that they had 200,000 soldiers hunting some 15,000 rebels. In contrast Britain had some 14,000 doing the same role in Cyprus, hunting some 300-plus hardcore mountain-based Greek-Cypriot and Turkish terrorists and gunmen in the towns and villages. In the conflict, Travis and his mates were up against Greek Cypriots who wanted union with Greece, Turkish Cypriots who opposed the Greeks, left-wing Greeks, right-wing Turks and communists. Initially, all these groups were anti-British. Their main opponents however were the Greek Cypriot extremists belonging to an organisation called EOKA (Ethniki Organosis Kyprion Agoniston, or National Organisation of Cypriot Fighters). General George Grivas, an ex-regular Greek Army officer who had trained at the Royal Military Academy, Sandhurst, headed up EOKA and signed his terror directives 'Deghenis' (the leader). He directed operations, such as ambushes and assassinations, with each group trying to outdo the other in horrific murders. Like killing a man whom they shot while he was in bed with his wife, murdering another while he was singing in church and an abbot in his monastery, plus a mother of three young children sleeping in a deckchair.

Travis' duties varied from dealing with riots in the capital, Nicosia, during which shops were wrecked and burnt out, cars overturned and burned and people killed and injured. In some cases schoolgirls started the trouble, by boxing the Paras up in small back streets for terrorists to drop home-made bombs and Molotov cocktails on them from the rooftops, causing death and injury.

In one such riot, a soldier from another regiment was killed and five others hurt before the rioters were driven back. Following this, fourteen secondary schools closed, affecting 8,000 pupils, an action that exacerbated the situation. The army was forced to construct a series of barbed-wire barricades, which was known as the Mason Dixon Line (taken from the 1763 line which symbolised the cultural boundary between the North-Eastern US and the South-Eastern US) to separate the Greeks from the Turks. In one month, eleven people were killed and seventy-seven injured in Famagusta, where Travis and his company operated. Eventually the company was sent on village patrols, search and destroy missions and the really tough work up in the Kyrenia and Troodos Mountains hunting guerrilla groups.

On Travis' first big operation in the mountains, the Paras, along with troops from other regiments, had a gang surrounded. To escape the ever-tightening ring of soldiers, the group set fire to the forest to create a diversion. The ensuing fierce blaze roared through the mountainside, trapping twenty-one soldiers, including two Para officers and a private soldier, with sixteen others injured. The gang was captured, but Grivas got away by posing as an old man collecting firewood who slipped through the cordon. The Paras were incensed at losing some of their own. It was a tough and upsetting introduction to this type of warfare for Travis.

From then on battalion casualties started to increase, with some lads never to see home again. Those that didn't make it lay in Wayne's Keep Cemetery just next to the Para encampment on the outskirts of Nicosia.

The majority of the soldiers in the battalion had been together for the best part of three years and had formed close friendships. When Travis moved into a five-man tent to replace one of its number who had gone home on demob, it was difficult to fit in and be accepted. He always felt like an outsider. It wasn't that the occupants were intentionally unkind, it was just the way they had bonded with each other. But as long as he performed well in the field, he continued to have a peaceful home with them.

He gained in pride and respect as a member of his section when they found a terrorist hide in the forest. It happened on his first patrol with his new eight-man section. They had spent the best part of that day patrolling through the forest when they came across a shepherd's hut, a simple affair, cut back into the hillside with the roof and front wall made out of split logs. The door was old sacking held down by two heavy rocks. The flat area in front of the hovel was covered in goat droppings, some fairly fresh, indicating it was well used. It showed there had been a lot of recent human activity there. Imprints left in the droppings showed numerous stud marks, the sign of EOKA terrorists, as the army wore rubber-soled boots.

The section commander, using hand signals, spread his unit out and around the hut in a wide circle, but still in sight of each other. As Travis was the newbie, the NCO kept him by his side. Together they entered the shelter, giving each other cover with their weapons. It was empty except for on old camp bed and a pot-bellied stove. The stove looked suspiciously out of place in such a setting and the section commander enlisted Travis' help in moving it, to reveal an escape tunnel. Without further ado, the senior rank dropped a hand grenade down the shaft and waited for results.

The resulting explosion was followed by a shout from a member of the cordon. Leaving Travis on guard over the tunnel, the NCO sprinted around to his rearguard to see two terrorists face down on the ground, their guard standing on their weapons with his rifle covering them. They had been caught trying to get away through their escape tunnel.

In attempts to escape, EOKA men sometimes fought to the death, but not in this case. The mountain guerrillas had a fearsome reputation, but these two had given up without a fight. They were escorted around to the front of the shelter, and Travis noticed how miserable, cold and hungry they looked.

Blindfolded, with their hands tied behind their backs, the captives were hustled downhill, encouraged by the butts of their captor's rifles. Travis almost felt sorry for them, but quickly remembered that they were killers of the worst kind, shooting, burning and maiming not only the security forces, but their own people. The captives were later hanged for their crimes.

Travis found himself admiring and envying his new comrades. They were burnt to a mahogany colour by the Mediterranean sun, their red berets faded pink and sweat-stained. They looked lean and mean, and he wondered if he could ever live up to the standards of such a tough and aggressive-looking bunch. They took no shit from anybody, especially when they were told their demob dates had been postponed due to a looming war against Egypt. The rumour machine in the DTL had informed all its visitors that the Middle East was about to erupt again.

Britain and America had decided not to finance the Aswan Dam project in Egypt, and this had upset the Egyptian President, General Gamal Abdel Nasser. He promptly seized control of the Suez Canal and nationalised it to use the taxes from international shipping passing through the waterway to pay for the building of the dam. Prior to that, the British Government had come to an agreement with Egypt to withdraw their forces and leave protection of the Anglo-French canal in their hands. When talks to defuse the situation proved fruitless, and the British, French and Israelis decided to act against Nasser, Travis found himself on standby to invade Egypt, along with French and Israeli troops, to wrest control of the canal. To his delight, he was detailed in the role of batman/bodyguard to see to the needs of an officer from his battalion. The officer was assigned as an observer on this first combat jump into action since World War Two.

Travis' new orders brought some sleepless nights as he worried and wondered if he were up to the job. He was very aware that he was just out of recruit training and classed as a 'cherry' or 'chalky' because of his pale skin and lack of time served. He also thought he had got the job because he was expendable.

Pre-jump nerves kicked in when he was informed that the attacking force of British Paras would not be issued with reserve chutes. It meant that if anything went wrong with the main chute his part in the invasion would be over before it started.

On the day planned for the attack, Travis was fully kitted up and weighed down with numerous pieces of baggage, his personal kit, ammo, grenades, food and weapon, along with spare batteries for the radio, motor bombs and rockets for the rocket launcher. As he waddled out to the plane he wondered how the hell he was going to get on board the plane carrying this bloody lot. He needn't have worried. The RAF dispatchers hauled him into the tiny Valetta aircraft, where he was crushed between two hulking mortar men from Support Company.

Early morning on the 5th November 1956, Operation Musketeer got under way. Travis could feel the pent-up nervous energy in the plane as it winged its way towards the Egyptian Coast and Port Said. At this stage all he wanted was to pee. He wasn't flying with a commercial airline, so he just had to hold it. It was only nerves anyway.

The coast appeared as a smudge on the skyline as the odd assortment of Vallettas, Vikings and Hastings aircraft carrying the battalion levelled out for the run-in.

'Stand up for equipment check,' came the command. Training kicked in and the Paras stood up and began checking kit and chutes. 'Number One tail off for equipment check.' 'Number One OK Starboard Stick OK.'

Travis felt sorry for the poor buggers behind him, as they would have to step over a boxed obstacle (wings) which created a low barrier to the door. Loaded down with kit, it was an awkward manoeuvre. They had to move very quickly as the jumpers in front were leaving the plane at some speed. It was catch-up with a vengeance.

'Action Stations, Stand in the Door.' 'Green On, Go.' Travis got more than a helping hand from the Dispatcher as he exited and hit the slipstream still running, with his legs flaying like some comic book character.

Chute open, thank God. Got to get rid of this sodding container, can't land with that bloody thing still attached. Shit, what's that? My God, the bastards are shooting at me. Please God, get me down safe!

'Here sir, Yes, I'm OK sir. '

Then, into the battle for the airport. Soaked in sweat, breath coming in rasping gasps from lungs sucking in searing hot air, he stumbled after his officer towards the control tower. An Egyptian soldier appeared around the corner, aimed and fired at the officer. Missed. Travis swung his Sten gun up to his shoulder and fired off a short burst. The enemy soldier dropped his rifle, hands clutching his neck, blood spurting out through his fingers as he fell back around the corner. The soldier was dead. Travis had killed a man, and he knew he would have to kill again.

If I'm going to become a professional soldier, I'll have to get used to killing, otherwise I'm a dead man walking, he thought. The ghastly sight of the dead enemy soldier had a calming effect on him. Travis felt nothing could touch him now; nothing could stop him. He was here to win, the Paras were here to win, and they would, of that he had no doubt.

The fight for control of the airfield was short and sweet for the Paras, but bloody for the Egyptians. The next objective was to clear an adjoining cemetery of the enemy. Another bloody battle and they had control of their objective. It was time to dig-in and protect the western approaches from any enemy reinforcement. With time on their hands, Travis and the rest of the attacking force cleared the scattered oil drums that had been placed on the runway to stop planes landing and then settled down in all-round defensive positions. Waiting for any further enemy action, Travis struggled with his beliefs and emotions over the fact that he had killed a man, probably a young man like himself with his whole life before him. He had taken that life away. However, later, looking at the bodies of his dead comrades as they lay side by side on the airport runway covered by groundsheets, he revised his thoughts.

It saddened him that the successful action had been achieved only with the loss of four dead and thirty-six wounded. All good lads, brothers in arms who had gone through the 'Maroon Machine' like him, showing the courage and skill honed during and after selection to the regiment.

There was more scattered action for the battalion over the next few days, but then, much to the chagrin of Travis and the rest of the attacking force, pressure having been brought to bear by America, the invasion was halted. All fired up and ready for more action, Travis wanted to go on, as did all soldiers in his battalion, but it was not to be.

Eventually, the invasion force pulled back and returned to their respective countries and duties. In Travis' case, it was back to Cyprus and Internal Security duties. He was now well and truly blooded, with all the hallmarks of a good infantry soldier.

He didn't get much time to practise his new-found skills back in the bleak and cold Troodos Mountains on EOKA hunting duties. Rumours, later confirmed, came down the line that the battalion was to be pulled out of operations preparatory to return to UK. Travis was in high spirits on hearing the good news. He wouldn't have been so happy if he had known that EOKA was organising a farewell hit to send the Paras on their way.

He was detailed for escort duty, ferrying the battalion intelligence officer to a staff meeting in Nicosia. With two Champ drivers, an eight-man section and the officer, four to a vehicle, they set off for the city. The little convoy bristled with weapons, mainly sub-machine guns. The drive down was uneventful. However, on the way back, as they were in the middle of a long, open stretch of the main road, a four-man EOKA gang set off an IED, an improvised explosive device, electrically detonated. It was hidden in a culvert under the road.

As the convoy drove into the killing ground, there was a violent explosion. Luckily for the Paras, the terrorists got the timing wrong and the landmine exploded between the first and second vehicle. The drivers of the Champs, though deafened and shocked, were able to veer off the road in their damaged vehicles in a controlled manner before the enemy opened up on the convoy from a high embankment on the far side of the road. It was a poorly-placed ambush in that there was a drainage ditch on the Paras' side of the road. The grateful and uninjured soldiers quickly scrambled into it and started to return fire.

After the initial shock, Travis became icy calm and went about the business of winning the fire-fight. The sub-machine guns of the Paras kept up a sustained rate of fire to keep the enemy heads down. The high rate of fire forced the EOKA men to break off the action, leaving one of their number dead on the ground.

The ambush brought the curtain down on internal security duties for the battalion, and before long it was back home to England. With two weeks' leave, Travis travelled to Ireland to spend his time with his girlfriend Melissa. He was confident that he could now start a new and happy phase in his life with her.

After three years of courtship, albeit for the most part long distance, Travis was quite clear as the mail boat moved closer to home and Melissa that he wanted to spend the rest of his life with her. She was everything he wanted in a woman. She had a dark Italian beauty, thanks to her father's blood, and she aroused him, delighted him and thrilled him. She could also hold her own in mixed company. But most of all, she was his best friend. He recalled how she had comforted and supported him during his trials and tribulations with his father and stepmother. She kept him sane and anchored. Not only did he want her, but he also knew that he needed her in his life. He wanted this very special young woman to be his wife and spend the rest of his life loving her and being loved by her.

He remembered the first time they had met, at the Scouts Hall Saturday night dance. He had got his chance to talk to her at the soft drinks counter. 'Let me carry your drinks for you, where are you sitting?' he had said.

'Thanks, I'm with friends at the table next to the exit, it's much cooler there.'

'Thanks again, that was good of you,' she said as he laid the drinks on her table.

'No problem lady, do I get a reward, like a dance maybe?'

'OK, just one.'

That was the beginning. They made a date for the movies on the following Saturday. It was a beautiful summer's day, and they arranged to meet at Cleary's store in O'Connell Street in Dublin city centre. She was early. As he approached her he appraised her, taking note of her off-the-shoulder, flower patterned summer dress. Her bare arms and shoulders were lightly tanned, complementing her auburn hair. Her full lips were fixed in a slight smile, and his heart melted at the sight of her. *If this is love, then I want it more and more.*

That was two years ago. Now, as he made his way up the front garden of her house to knock on the door, all he wanted was to be with her forever. From the moment she opened the front door of her parents' house the magic started. It was all he had hoped for. His two weeks' leave went by in a blur of excitement and happiness. Very apprehensive how his proposal would be received, he left it to the last night of his leave. It was a lovely, bitter-sweet night, filled with every emotion from happiness to love and sadness as another goodbye loomed. It had been a wonderful two weeks with, as a friend put it, 'Travis and Melissa joined at the hip.'

They were walking together hand in hand up a quiet, tree-lined road to Melissa's home with the sea at their backs, a full moon and the heavens alive with twinkling stars. *Perfect*, thought Travis, *here goes*.

'Melissa, darling, how's about we get engaged on my next trip home?'

Melissa had stopped dead in her tracks, a look of shock on her pretty face, to be quickly replaced by anger.

'Are you asking me to marry you Patrick Travis?' She always gave him his full name when she was annoyed about something or other.

'Yes, my darling.'

'Well, if you want an answer, you will have to ask me in the proper manner.'

Caught in the act and red-faced with embarrassment, he went down on one knee and there and then, under a weeping willow tree that hung over a high stone wall, he took both Melissa's small hands in his and looking up into her sweet face he said: 'I love you Melissa Brandini, and I want to spend the rest of my life loving and making you happy. Will you be my wife, will you marry me?'

'Yes, yes, yes, a million times yes' was the breathless reply.

It was a moment of pure magic for both of them. Travis was wishing he had a camera to capture the look of love and happiness on the face of the woman he loved. For Melissa, who had loved Travis from the moment they met, looking down at the eager face of her lover, the man who was now to be her husband, she knew that all her romantic dreams had come true.

A long, lingering goodnight kiss at Melissa's front door sent Travis floating home, his feet barely touching the pavement, or so it seemed. His departure on the Sunday evening was not so upsetting, as the young lovers were full of plans for their future together, with wedding dates, talk of married quarters and how quickly they could be together as man and wife.

CHAPTER FIVE

RECALL TO THE MIDDLE EAST

Soldiering in the UK was at times a very boring business, broken up by military exercises, parachuting, and lots of route marches in full kit, as well as parades in dress uniform when the regiment received the Freedom of Aldershot, or on the Queen's Birthday Parade. On occasion high-profile parades were tinged with light relief as when the Regimental Mascot, a miniature Shetland pony who had been fed all kinds of garbage by patrolling sentries, built a pyramid of shit on the parade ground in front of all the dignitaries. On a hot summer's day the smell was atrocious. Subsequently the pony, which carried the rank and pay of a sergeant, was marched in before the Colonel of the Battalion. The Regimental Sergeant Major read out the charge against the poor animal, to the effect that Sergeant Ballerophon had defecated on the parade ground at the Queen's Birthday Parade to the detriment of the Queen and the Regiment. The said pony was then reduced in rank to Corporal. It could only happen in the British Army. Travis, who loved eccentrics in any walk of life, felt that this had to be the high point in eccentricity.

About this time there was a great deal of coming and going of soldiers to and from the Battalion, and Travis' Company had a major change in personnel, with new soldiers coming in to take over from the old sweats. Travis could now build up some new and lasting friendships of his own. Apart from that, his only relief from the grinding routine of soldiering in the UK was his leave periods and extended 72-hour passes home to Dublin and Melissa.

All this was about to end with 'the shooting season in the Middle East' as the newspapers called it. It appeared that an Arab country had suffered a coup d'etat, its King and Prime Minister murdered in the process. An army general seized power who was more than unfriendly towards Britain. His first act was to threaten British workers resident in the country. In a hostile act he had his Arab army surround a large oil complex occupied by British technicians and their families, threatening them with annihilation.

The British Government had to act fast. On Friday 13th, Travis had just arrived at Melissa's home from the Holyhead to Dublin mail boat. After a fierce hug and a welcoming kiss Melissa handed him a telegram from his regiment recalling him back to duty. The couple were left with only a few hours together before Travis caught the night boat back to England and the long train journey back to camp.

Sunday found him crammed inside the belly of a Shackleton bomber on his way back to the Middle East, pumped full of injections for every disease under the sun and spaced out with the pain and tiredness.

In the early hours of the morning he found himself, with his battalion, on Cypriot soil once again. The Paras trained like dogs in the merciless heat for a special operation to release the trapped oil workers and their families. They were on the go both day and night. They tramped around, up and over the Kyrenia and Troodos mountains on a regular basis, and at the hottest time of the day. In between, they managed to fit in company and section attacks, ambush drills, live firing on the Goshi ranges and parachuting. This programme also included 24-hour guards on the Airport, Governor's mansion and the home of the General Commanding the Cyprus Garrison, Major General Kenneth Darling, an ex-Para. All this with never a day off to rest and recuperate.

In the end the British workers and their families were released unharmed and the Special Mission cancelled, much to the disgust of the Paras, who wanted to have a go at the defiant Arabs. This gung-ho attitude was the result of the subtle brainwashing techniques of recruit training. The cancellation left a frustrated Travis, who would have loved to do another combat jump into hostile enemy territory.

Following 'Stand Down' the battalion was reassigned to internal security duties again. Their new role was fuelled by the comment of their Major General, 'The only terrorists I'm interested in are dead terrorists.'

EOKA reacted quickly in attacking the Paras. It all kicked off when a Para vehicle was blown up and the driver and escort were very seriously injured. This type of attack became a daily occurrence. The battalion fought back with much success. The Paras moved into the Kyrenia Mountains on a big operation to once more clear the mountains and valleys of guerrilla groups and village terrorists, this time for good. Working in threes and fours, they concealed themselves during daylight hours, watching and reporting every movement in their area of responsibility. At dusk, they slipped noiselessly into the night to set up and man selected ambush positions during the hours of darkness. By now they were so accustomed to the essential drills of alertness, duty roster, concealment, silence and the like that it all fell naturally into place.

At first light, they turned their ambush position into a covert observation post reporting in by radio on a timed sequence. They stayed in situ for up to three or four days at a time, with covert resupply from a given map reference. The hours and days on operations were tense and tiring. Their reports, for the most part, were of normal village life, dogs barking at night but no signs of enemy movement. The going was very debilitating on the soldiers, but they lapped it up. This was what Travis and his mates had joined the army for, not to paint coal white for some arsehole of an officer's inspection back in the UK.

Like the Paras, the terrorists operated in twos and fours, joining up into larger groups for specific raids. They lived in special hides dug underneath the floors of village houses or olive groves. There they would spend their time constructing IEDs and other nasties. When a good target presented itself, on a word from their village, they would emerge, link up with other groups and go on the rampage, whenever or wherever the intelligence or notion took them.

Some of the less disciplined ones used their quiet time to settle old private scores with their fellow Greeks. On one particularly dark, moonless night, Travis, recently promoted to the rank of Corporal and in command of a four-man ambush group, lay silent and alert in their position. They heard firing off to their right, indicating possible enemy contact. This was followed by an all stations report on their radio from company HQ confirming that one of their ambush positions had had a brush with an enemy group. The message warned all positions to be on the lookout for any of the enemy who might have evaded the ambush and were now trying to make it back to their hides before daylight. Travis found the anticipation of action at night to be particularly unnerving, as he couldn't see if there were two or twenty terrorists lurking out there in the darkness. He would soon find out.

It was about three in the morning and still pitch black when the fugitives came into view. They were so close to the ambush position that they almost stumbled on the waiting Paras. Travis held his fire until the entire length of the designated killing ground contained the enemy, then he fired at the man to his immediate front, springing the ambush. The noise was deafening as the Paras emptied their weapons into the dark shapes in front of them. Travis yelled out an order, 'Cease fire, cease fire!'

The silence that followed was almost as palpable as the noise from the fire-fight had been. As per SOPs (Standard Operating Procedure), Travis' section fitted new mags to their weapons and applied safety catches, but they didn't go out to inspect the bodies and check the area until first light as Travis ordered them to stand down.

They lay there too hyped up to relax. For the next couple of hours, they had to endure the unearthly screams of a dying terrorist who had been shot in the stomach. Travis lay there numb, praying that the man would die sooner rather than later. If only he could take the dying man out of his misery and stop the dreadful noise shredding his nerves. The wounded guy kept screaming until he eventually died from his wound.

During the action only a few scattered rounds were fired off at the Paras, one of which had slightly wounded one of the ambush team. A field dressing applied to the flesh wound made the soldier comfortable and able to take part in any further action. Travis was totally shattered, amazed at the exhausting effect the short burst of action had on him. He was glad he had the ability to cope with it and that he belonged to this highly trained tight-knit group. They were not just his section, they were his friends. He knew that, if needs be, he would give his life for them and they for him.

At first light two of the ambush party moved out under cover of the rest of the section, to inspect the area, check and search for bodies. Three terrorists had been killed and one seriously wounded. He walked among the enemy dead. *I don't feel anything. I don't feel elation that we won the fight. I don't feel pity or remorse, but I do feel for the wounded man. Is it because I can hear and see his pain? With the dead, I feel nothing. Maybe it's because they look non-human in death, in fact, they look just like manikins. I may not have killed them. We all fired together, in the dark, at a group of shadowy figures. I might not have hit a single one. This night's work may come back to haunt my dreams, and disturb my sleep. But I sure as hell hope not. The only problem with these dead terrorists is that we collect no information or intelligence from them. Bit of a waste of really.*

Travis and his ambush party found out later that the terrorists had also lost two men in the first ambush. It was an exciting and very productive night for the Paras.

In the main, the Turkish community bore the brunt of the atrocities meted out by EOKA. However, the Turks were not 'behind the door' in their reactions to the bombing and shooting of their fellow citizens. This was borne out when Travis, as part of a QRF (Quick Reaction Force), was called out to a cornfield near a Greek village where eight villagers had been massacred and their mutilated bodies set on fire. Travis could still smell the burning flesh days after the event.

The hideous scenes of death and destruction were to get worse as the campaign wore on, but by now Travis was wired, with a feeling that he could handle anything the army or the enemy could throw at him. His reactions and movements were fast, and he was known in the Company as a racing snake. He never accepted compromises in his efforts to be a better soldier. In his relationships with others he was testing all the time, thinking, *Do they share my value system of duty, reliability and trust?*

Those values were soon put to the test. One peaceful Sunday morning Travis was in command of a VCP (Vehicle Check Point) on a remote mountain pass. He was accompanied by three other soldiers. They were in radio contact with their Company HQ. The duty was a relief from the hot and tedious hours lying in observation post and ambush sites. Unknown to him and his half section and by sheer bad luck, terrorists had laid a mine in the road, just around a blind bend from their VCP. It was triggered by a wire leading to a torch battery. As a means of a safe getaway the terrorists laid a booby-trap at the trigger site. They were now hidden and waiting for an appropriate victim.

The first vehicle to approach the VCP was a low-slung Austin Healey Sprite sports car. It contained an elderly British couple who had worked for the British Government on the island, but were now retired and living in the coastal area. They were on their way to the capital to visit their son, daughter-in-law and grandchildren. They were a jolly couple, and they spent some time chatting and reminiscing with the young Paras about England. The car finally pulled away and with much hand-waving and horn blowing disappeared around the bend. There followed a very loud explosion, then a numbing silence. The soldiers ran around the corner to find the old lady dragging herself along the road on what was left of her legs. Of her husband and the car there was no sign.

Travis was stunned, and fighting with his emotions and his breakfast he sent a soldier back to the radio to get medical help and back-up. Borrowing two wound dressings from two of his men, he sent the same two to trace the visible command wire connection, to try to capture or deal with the terrorists. As he knelt down to treat the dying woman, he shouted after them, 'Mind how you go lads, there could be a very nasty surprise at the end of the wire.'

'My husband, look after my husband!' the old lady cried. 'Don't worry Mam, we'll look after him for you' he replied. As the death rattle sounded in her throat, Travis heard an explosion from further up the mountain and his blood ran cold. He shouted up to his two soldiers, 'Are you guys OK? Receiving no response, he knew that they had been either killed or severely wounded. It ended as a bad day for all concerned, with the only relief that the two Paras sent to get the mine-layers, although badly injured, as Travis guessed, would live to fight another day.

Cordon and search was another tactic designed to net EOKA men hiding enemy, and was based on intelligence gleaned from informers. An operational platoon was used to search the suspect house or area and the other two platoons in the Company were used to act as cordon and containment. The plan worked out by command was to get a convey of four-ton trucks carrying the search and cordon platoons through the suspect village just before first light. But instead of stopping outside the village to unload the troops, the vehicles slowed down to let the soldiers drop off and take up position. This tactic would be repeated at the far side of the village, with wagons carrying on as if heading for another destination. On operations this ruse worked to the extent that the first the villagers knew of the presence of the Paras was when they were kicking open their doors. When the initial search proved fruitless, the Paras retraced their steps, only this time they were carrying buckets of water which they poured over the flagged floors of the houses.

During a particular search Travis and three men entered a large dwelling on the outskirts of the village, which another section had searched in the first sweep. They poured the water from buckets onto the floor and watched as the water disappeared around the sides of a large floor tile.

'OK guys let's see what we've got. Get your bayonets out and let's have that big flag in the corner up. Mind how you go, there could be somebody down there ready to blow you away given half the chance. I'll give covering fire if needs be.'

Using their bayonets the soldiers started to lift up a section of the flooring. As the big flag was raised up, a burst of automatic fire erupted from below, hitting one of the Paras. Taking 9mm rounds to his face and upper body, the young Para was blasted back across the room by the force of the bullets hitting his body. The flag was also broken into little pieces, leaving a gaping black hole in the floor.

Without a second thought, Travis dropped a Mills grenade, followed by a phosphorous grenade, into the hide below. The three terrorists manning the hide didn't stand a chance. Travis rushed to the aid of his wounded rifleman and started working on him using battlefield first aid. The wounded soldier would survive, but never fight again.

When the back-up troops raised all the flags and exposed the room-like hide, they puked on the acrid smoke of the grenades drifting up from the horror below. Travis was sick to his stomach at the whole incident, wondering if he could have done things differently. The terrorists held all the intelligence cards on troop movements and tactics, being informed by a cooperative and supportive population. Raiding villages on an ad-hoc basis and doing snap searches was the only way of fighting back.

When the Paras hit a village in broad daylight, they would round up all the villagers, place the females in the local church and cage the males in a compound surrounded by barbed-wire entanglements. Then an unmarked van would reverse into the village square with an informer in the back. Bulrushes were placed on the ground at the rear of the van, to alert the informant of an approaching villager. A male would be brought forward for identification by the informer, who was hooded and looking through a spy hole in the rear window of the van. This proved to be a lucrative way to capture EOKA men and their sympathisers, although there were times when the informant would pick out an innocent man, to revenge some minor insult in the past.

At other times, a wanted person would not wait to be identified and would make a break for freedom over the wire. The Para snipers would make short work of the potential escapee.

If they were lucky, the Paras would uncover a hide with its haul of weapons, ammo, grenades, home-made pipe bombs and supplies. Such a rare occasion would send the troops back to camp in high spirits.

Their actions were hated by the civilian population, who despised the British soldiers, looking on them as an occupation force. They had a particular hatred for the Paras, whose actions could be pretty brutal at times of immense stress, like the loss of a comrade to a bullet or an IED.

Travis and his mates were becoming dehumanised and uncompromising to some extent in their dealings with the local population in their areas of responsibility. They seemed to be always bone tired and hungry, which did nothing for their temper. 'Fed up and far from home.' as one soldier put it. This attitude led to some rough handling during search missions.

By this time Travis cared for nothing or no one other than his fellow soldiers in his section, company and battalion. Certainly he did not care for the cause, however noble.

Towards the end of the operation in the mountains and the defeat of the enemy groups operating there, Travis came down with dysentery and was in a very bad way. The medics moved him to an old seaside hotel which had been taken over by his battalion as a Regimental Aid Station. He was given a bag of pills and instructed to take a set amount every hour, on the hour, but as he could hold nothing down in his stomach, he spewed the first dose all over himself and the patio. There he rested on hard ground in a space allotted to him, with only a thin lightweight blanket to cover him and a groundsheet to lie on. The patio looked like the railway scene in *Gone with the Wind*, full of wounded and dying soldiers. In this case bodies were lying all over the place, with the badly injured and the seriously ill waiting to be casevaced back to the British Military Hospital.

Travis spent four days lying there, vomiting up pills, not eating and defecating in his pants. He slept fitfully in between, never speaking to or seeing another medic again. On the fourth day of his ordeal he felt a little better and seeing a driver from his own company he asked to be taken back to his unit. As he was a corporal and outranked the private driving the Champ vehicle, he got his way, but not before the driver had hosed him down to dispel the excreta clinging to him and the God-awful smell. Travis firmly believed that if he had stayed in the Aid Station for a few more days, he would have died. He had felt abandoned and extremely depressed on top of his debilitating illness.

Within days of his return to his unit and active duty, his battalion was on the move again. From the intense heat of the operational area at summer's end, they moved up into the Troodos Mountains for the winter. Their mission and orders were the same as for the Kyrenia Range - to come to grips with the heavily-armed bands roaming around the mountains creating havoc and dealing out death. Even in summer you could get snow in the Troodos, so winter months made for some real hard soldiering. Ambush parties had to be dug out of the snow and trucked back to base camp like frozen seals, unable to stand or walk unaided.

The company lost some good men, mainly through ambushes and booby traps. But as far as Travis was concerned the cold, fresh mountain air and snowy weather had a good effect after his recent illness, and he started to pick up in health. It amused him that nobody seemed to care or notice that he had discharged himself from the Aid Station.

About this time he was appointed Company Intelligence Officer, a job he came to enjoy. His main task was collating, evaluating and processing the scraps of information coming in from observation posts, along with IEDs that had failed to detonate, which in turn were passed on to the Para Engineers, who had the unenviable task of bomb disposal. He collated diverse morsels of fact and semi-fact which could then be assembled and moulded into a piece of firm intelligence. With good 'intel' he could help in placing ambushes, or even save lives on convoy runs.

His first call-out in his new role was to the remains of a farmhouse, where bomb makers had been working around a stout, wooden kitchen table. However the explosives they were handling had gone off, and all Travis and his patrol found was four pairs of mountain boots with the men's feet and ankles still inside. Of the bodies of the bomb makers there was no sign. He chalked that one up as an 'own goal' by the baddies. Better them than us, Travis thought.

The pattern of violence was to continue for some time, until peace talks were held between the British Government, the Greek Cypriots and the Turkish Cypriots and an agreement was ironed out. With peace about to return to the island the Paras flew home. Travis, now coming to the end of his three years of service in the army, had every intention of signing on again for the full twenty-two years. He had made up his mind that soldiering was what he wanted to do with his life, to achieve his old aim to be a professional soldier. With this thought in mind, he journeyed home to Ireland and Melissa, where he was in for a rude awakening. Melissa met him off the mail boat with the news that her family were emigrating to Canada, and she was going with them.

'What about us?' Travis cried in alarm.

'It's not about you and me,' Melissa cried, 'I must go and support my family, they are depending on me, that's the way it is.'

'We're engaged to be married for God's sake, doesn't it mean anything to you Melissa?'

'Of course it does, but you don't seem to understand.'

'What I understand is that you are leaving me. Don't you love me any more, is that it?'

'Of course I love you, but I love my family too.'

'There is only one thing for you to do, and that is to keep your promise to me, to be my wife.

'It's not as simple as that, and you know it.'

'That's, the problem Melissa, it is as simple as that, for me.'

'You're just being pigheaded and stupid Patrick, I never thought you could be like this.'

The long and bitter quarrel carried on until Travis, consumed by anger and despair, walked away from Melissa, she in the middle of a hissy fit, having thrown her engagement ring over the sea wall. Travis was so distressed that he cut his leave short and returned to England. He spent the last of his leave back in camp in a drunken stupor. Some weeks later he was pulled aside by his platoon sergeant.

'You're fast becoming a drunken pain in the arse, Corporal Travis, and as of now you are barred from drinking in the Mess' he announced. 'You've always been a steady lad, but now you seem to have gone to hell in a handbasket. Take my advice mate, buck yourself up and sort yourself out or you will lose your rank and spend your last days in the army in nick. That's it, don't let me catch you in here again.'

Travis spent the last few days of his time in the army in anger. He had tried to find solace in the booze in the local pubs, but to no avail. In the end, he took his discharge from the British Army and found himself out in civvy street once again. He checked into a small cheap hotel in the Kings Cross area of London and tried to enjoy his first few days of freedom from army bullshit and discipline. But it was not for him; he just couldn't hack it. He felt like a fish out of water and still full of pain from his break-up with Melissa. He didn't feel he could go back to the Paras, but he needed to punish his body to distract his mind. He searched for a way to do it, trawling the clubs and pubs of the West End of London.

One night he got talking to an old fellow countryman in the Leinster Bar in an Irish pub in Piccadilly. A great character, the man had served a full five years in the French Foreign Legion, leaving with a good conduct discharge and a French passport. He had some grim tales to tell, but he told them with pride and a keen sense of belonging to a very special family. When Travis woke up the next morning, with one hell of a hangover, he knew what he wanted to do.

CHAPTER SIX

ALGERIA: THE FOREIGN LEGION

Having spent his last day in London taking a trip down to the East End to get rid of most of his possessions in the first pawn shop he came to, Travis took a short ride on the Underground to Victoria Station, where he caught a train to the Port of Dover and a ferry to France. Landing at Calais, he travelled by train to Paris and checked into the first small hotel he could find.

He had never been to France before and had no idea of the language. He had bought a little phrase book on the ferry, in which the pronunciations of the words were given phonetically. With its help and much use of the pointed finger, he bumbled his way around Paris and in doing so, he fell in love with this beautiful city, its sights and sounds.

When he had blown most of his money on lodgings, food, drink and sightseeing, he approached an elderly gendarme, or *flic* as the Paris police are called. He was a kindly man with more English than Travis had French. He directed him to the Fort de Nogent, a Foreign Legion recruiting office, and wished him *bonne chance*.

With his mangled French and much waving of arms and hands to the sentry on duty at the entrance, Travis conveyed his wish to join the Legion and was ushered into the recruiting office by a duty Legionnaire. There, he was interviewed by the Adjutant on duty (a Warrant Officer) who spoke good English. His first question was, 'Why do you want to join the Legion, young man?'

'I want to be a professional soldier and get as much experience as I can. I have served in the British Army, and I think the Legion can help me further my career.'

The officer seemed satisfied with Travis' explanation and sent him through to another room for a medical examination, which he appeared to pass. He was informed that he would be accepted into the Legion and was advised, in English, of his commitment to the Legion and France. Following this he signed five years of his life away to whatever the future would bring. After taking the oath of allegiance, he was now a member of the French Foreign Legion.

Travis and some other potential Legionnaires were quartered in the fort overnight. The next morning they were on the move, by train, to the Port of Marseilles, part of the shipment of new recruits from all over the continent and even further afield. He arrived in Marseilles on a cold, wet night, with his morale at a very low ebb. He and his fellow recruits were quartered in Bas-Fort St. Nicolas, along with the arrivals from the other recruiting centres.

It was then that he had his brightest moment since leaving the sights and sounds of Paris behind. Believing he was among men who didn't have a word of English between them, he was surprised and thrilled to hear a rich Scottish voice sounding off across the barrack room. The voice belonged to a Hamish Grant, who, like himself, turned out to be an erstwhile member of the Independent Para Brigade. Hamish was tall, at least six foot, and had workable, schoolboy French, a hearty laugh and an open honest face. Well educated, he still had his soft Scottish accent, which had mellowed during his three years in the Paras.

To Travis he was like a lifebelt to a drowning man. He approached the blond, rangy young Scotsman with hand outstretched.

'Hello Jock, my name is Patrick Travis, my friends call me Travis, and I'm very glad to meet you.'

'I'm Hamish Grant, and the feeling is mutual.'

'You're a godsend Hamish, being able to speak French.'

'It's Mickey Mouse French, Travis, but I seem to get by with it.'

'I speak Irish and a fat lot of good that's going to do me in this mob.'

'Well I speak a bit of Scots Gaelic if you ever get homesick. So, apart from your French, what brings you to the Legion?' asked Hamish.

'I suppose you could say I was sowing my wild oats, but that would be a lie, as I well and truly sowed them in the ranks of the Parachute Regiment this past three years. My God! When were you demobbed, Hamish?

'About a month ago. I went back to Scotland and was bored to hell after a couple of weeks.'

'We must have similar army numbers because I have just finished three years with the Regiment' Travis replied.

A broad smile lit up the Scotsman's face as he exclaimed, 'Bloody Hell!' They hugged each other. It was the beginning of a lifelong friendship.

Little did the newcomers know as they went through the formalities and rigours that this was the beginning of a momentous time for the Legion. The troubles now raging in Algeria would almost lead to the end of the famous fighting force. The 'Algerie Française' situation had been ongoing for some years and was now approaching boiling point. With all this to come, Travis was about to embark on his second boat trip, this time to Oran in Algeria. Prior to that, he was re-interviewed, questioned and quizzed again about his past and reasons for joining the Legion. He felt he gave a good account of himself to the Deuxième Bureau, the military intelligence branch.

The inquisition over, the next stop was Oran. The sea voyage wasn't unpleasant as the weather picked up again, with sunshine, clear skies, the sea a mirror-like calm. On arrival in Oran the recruits were billeted overnight in Fort St. Thérèse. The next day they were trucked on to Sidi bel Abbes. They entered through the vast main entrance and assigned to quarters in the four-storey buildings at each side of a tree-lined avenue. At the end of the avenue and to the right of the headquarters building stood the Salle d'Honneur, the museum and archive centre of the Legion. After a visit there, Travis reflected that the Legion had been created by Louis Philippe, King of France in 1831 to support his campaign in Algeria. Now, over a hundred years later, the legion was still fighting in Algeria and he was going to be part of it. He was to find that since its early days the Legion had quickly developed an incredibly austere and rigid code of discipline, far exceeding other contemporary forces. It was called the *base de la discipline*. He practised remembering the code until he had it off by heart: '*Discipline being the principle strength of the Legion, it is essential that all superiors receive from their subordinates absolute obedience and submission on all occasions. Orders must be executed instantly without hesitation or complaint. The authorities who give them are responsible for them and an inferior is only permitted to make an objection after he has obeyed*'.

The *base de la discipline* had proved to be a most effective way of keeping a tight rein on the beggars, cut-throats and runaways who flocked to the force, and not a lot had changed in discipline since it was drafted. Arrival and settling in was followed by another round of questions, quizzes and tests. Then Travis, accompanied by his now inseparable companion Hamish, was on the move to an instruction battalion, Compagnie de Passage, the Foreign Legion training company for their basic training. This was another chance to test his limits, both mentally and physically.

If he thought recruit training in the British Paras was hard, then he was in for quite a shock. This was no walk in the sun. Early reveille was followed by muster parade and inspection, then a five-mile run, then on to regular ten-mile route marches in full kit. Following the run, it was into a punishing series of drill, weapons training and language classes for recruits like Travis who had no French. The afternoons were given over to various forms of very arduous physical training. It seemed unending.

Whilst Hamish and Travis were trained soldiers, they had long forgotten the rigours of recruit training and were, to some degree, not as fit as they should have been from service in the Para battalions. But then, you tend to relax when on home service duty and get a little soft.

The Legion training was backed up by harsh punishment and cold-blooded brutality. Both Hamish and Travis collected some heavy bruising around the stomach and kidneys from being kicked and punched by corporals and sergeants alike. During the long months of basic training, they were brainwashed in the history and traditions of the Legion. They had to learn all the marching songs by heart and the traditional marching. In this, it was just like the British Paras. By the end of their training they lived, breathed and shat the French Foreign Legion, and felt part of the greatest family in the world, certainly the strongest. This fact they were to test and find not wanting in the years to come.

Finally, after days, weeks and months of harsh treatment and intensive training, Travis, along with the other recruits, paraded before the Chef de Bataillon and was presented with the coveted White Képi, the famous headdress of the Legion. They had made it - they were Legionnaires.

The new Legionnaires were posted for further training in various specialist skills. Travis asked Hamish what specialist role he fancied, and the response was crude but to the point: 'I'd like to get some more slipstream up my arse'. So they both volunteered for parachute training and hopefully, eventual posting to the *Regiment Estranger de Parachutistes* or REP, an all-volunteer regiment. Its men, the cream of the Legion, were hand-picked and hard. Hamish and Travis were honoured to be chosen for Para training. The fact that they had served as Paratroopers in the British Para Brigade no doubt helped them, but it cut no ice with their trainers. If they both thought they had left the rigours of basic training behind, then they were made to think again. Pre-Para training was a damn sight worse than all the brutality and shit they had taken in the recruit training battalion. They seemed to spend hours and days naked from the waist up, carrying sacks of stones with wire straps on their shoulders, which seemed to cut through to their very bones as they humped their heavy loads on ten-mile route marches, which gave way to twenty-five milers. The Legion, like the British Paras, also put considerable stock in long-distance marches. In fact, their ethos was 'marche ou crève' (march or croak). It was little wonder that many Legionnaires wore the medal of, and prayed to, Saint Michel, the patron saint of Paratroopers. All this was interspersed with a modicum of parachute training, where the equipment was very sparse compared to the British Parachute School at Abingdon in the UK.

About two months later came another move, this time to the

parachute training centre where, just like Travis' move from the pre-Para course with the British Army to the RAF, life started to pick up big time. After the horrors of basic and pre-Para, their new home was the lap of luxury.

On completion of their parachute course, and at a very special ceremony, they were awarded the parachute insignia of stylized wings with central parachute to be worn on the right breast; they were now fully-fledged Legion Paratroopers.

By the time Travis and Hamish were ready to join their REP The 2eme Regiment Etranger des Parachutistes or the Deuxième REP, their regiment was constantly on the move as they searched for, chased and killed those in armed resistance to 127 years of French rule in Algeria. The rebellion was in full swing and soon they were in the thick of it, fighting against the dissidents in the native population.

At this stage of the campaign, the well-organised and equipped guerrilla force the Front de Libération Nationale, FLN/ALN or the Fellagha, Fell for short, were heavily involved throughout the country. They were a ruthless outfit which was very efficient on hit and run missions in the mountains. There they operated from mountain caves and *mechatas*, small and isolated farms, the desert, hills and countryside as well as in city and coastal towns. In the cities and towns, their use of explosives in public places brought death and carnage on a random basis. It was bloody and indiscriminate. The Arabs, knowing their towns like the backs of their hands, always had the advantage. They could ambush the French forces in dark alleyways and make good their escape. It was the avowed aim of the Fell to conduct military strikes to disrupt the economy, to expand the conflict from the cities to include the regions of the Sahara and to divide and harass the French military, conducting guerrilla strikes where and when they would be most effective.

Travis and Hamish were sent, with their company, to patrol the Aures mountains and the mountain *dours*, Arab villages, where they entered every *mechata*, Arab dwelling, they came across, on search and destroy missions. The Paras worked in small sections, scouring the countryside by day and setting ambushes by night. Shades of Cyprus, Travis thought. Sometimes, it was the Paras who were ambushed and into such a situation one day he and his patrol stumbled. It was a perfect ambush site, a narrow track through boulders and rock-strewn rubble. Apart from the sharp crack of a sniper rifle, the first Para to be hit died in silence, and then all hell broke loose. The Paras scattered into the nearest cover to return fire and try to overcome the hostiles, but to no avail. Under heavy enemy fire and outnumbered two to one, the Paras started a fighting retreat, moving back in textbook manner, always with covering fire. In the final manoeuvre, the last two to drop back were the gun group with their machine gun. The weapon was manned by a massive Russian gunner and assisted by a small but tough little Spaniard. Both were hit at the same time. As the gun fell silent, Travis looked out from behind his cover and saw that both men were still alive but unable to move unaided.

As it was instilled in every Legionnaire that you never leave a comrade, alive or dead, Travis, without a second thought, raced out and pulled the little Spaniard and the gun back into cover. He raced out again to bring back the big Russian. By this time, every Fell weapon seemed to be aimed at him, with bullets thwacking and whining around the two Legionnaires. Their comrades upped their rate of fire as cover and somehow Travis and his very heavy burden made their way safely back to the shelter of the boulders.

That was when his action hit home. Prior to that, he had acted without thought or feeling, acting almost like a trained animal, which in a sense he was. But now, under cover, the full magnitude of his rashness washed over him and he started to shake so much that his teeth rattled. The sobs of pain coming from the poor little Spaniard brought him out of it, and he turned his attention to trying to help the wounded men, applying field dressings to their wounds and giving them morphine to ease their pain.

The shooting was slackening off by now as the Fell slipped away. This was their custom in ambushes, hit and run and live to fight another day. The big Russian, although badly wounded, sat propped up against a boulder. He didn't make a sound, which was normal for him as he never seemed to speak to anybody, except his Spanish number two on the machine gun and then only when he had to. He was a massive man, brooding and menacing. Members of his company gave him a wide berth. Right now, he just surveyed the scene with pain-dulled eyes.

The Spaniard, who was hit in the stomach, was in desperate pain and Travis did all he could to help him, cradling him in his arms and telling him in broken Spanish that he would be all right, that help was on the way. To Travis, still in a daze, it seemed an age before the situation was sorted out and the dead and wounded flown back to the base hospital.

A few days after the ambush the squad was called back to base, to serve as Guard of Honour at the funeral of the Spanish Legionnaire, who had died from his wounds. During the church service for their dead comrade, Travis noticed that along with the dead Legionnaire's white képi, his green beret and his medals, someone had placed a chalice on the coffin. Puzzled at this he asked the Army Padre about it when the burial was over. The priest told him a truly sad and strange story.

'Did you know that Legionnaire Sanchez was, in fact, the late Father Pedro Lazarus, an ex-Roman Catholic priest?' the Padre asked.

'We had no idea' Travis replied.

'He started life as an orphan, without the benefit of a typical, long-tailed Spanish family to give him love and support. He led a pass-the-parcel type of existence, moving between foster homes and orphanages. Soon he became a street urchin, living on his wits in and around the Ramblas in Barcelona, begging from tourists, stealing anything of value which he could sell and make some money to survive on. He would have graduated to more serious crimes and in the long run, ended up in prison or the grave. But a kindly priest took him off the streets and into the children's home he ran up in the hills outside the city. Pedro loved it up there, in the clean and bracing air, with good wholesome food and clean clothes to wear. He settled down to become a model student and grew into a fine young man. To crown the joy of the staff, who had looked after him as if he were their own with much with love and devotion, young Pedro found God, truly and with great fervour. So much so that from then on he devoted his life to love and worship of Jesus Christ.

'He was found a place in a seminary and took to the arduous task of studying for the priesthood. After seven long, hard but enjoyable years, he was ordained as a Catholic priest in the beautiful cathedral of Barcelona. He was then posted to his first parish, a dirt-poor collection of villages in the mountains above Lourdes and Tarbes. It's wild country, from which his parishioners scratched a precarious living. On top of all their misery and poverty, the area was plagued by bandits.'

The Padre took a sip of altar wine to clear his throat and continued with the story: 'Father Pedro, as he liked to be called, threw himself into the work of his parish, giving it his all, even down to the shirt off his back. He begged, borrowed and oft times had to fight off the old urge to steal, to help the people he loved and served. Despite the hard and lonely life, he thrived on his ministry, and the only situation that stuck in his craw was the way the local bandits treated his flock. They raided the villages on a regular basis, taking the villagers' meagre stocks of animals, food and goods, using whatever force necessary. They raped the young village girls and enticed, sometimes blackmailed, the young men of the villages to join them in their life of crime, to support them and replace gang members jailed or cut down in police raids and ambushes.'

The Padre's eyes lit up with pride as he recounted the young priest's reaction to this very grave situation. 'It all became too much for Father Pedro. So he took it upon himself to find out where the forbidden and hidden lair of the outlaw gang was situated. He then boldly entered the camp to confront the bandit leader El Corazon Nero (Black Heart) in his den.'

It has never been revealed what was discussed or argued that day in the mountain cave. Some say that Pedro sold his soul to the Devil, for the sake of his flock. Nonsense, of course. But whatever the truth of the matter, things got better for parishioners and money started to flow back into the villages through the young priest, by way of some levy on the bandit's illegal gains. The young priest believed that true holiness was in right action. Although the mountain people were very close and secretive, word of their priest's generosity and where the money came from filtered back to the police and the church authorities. The word was that Father Pedro Lazarus was laundering money for the bandits, among other things. The police, with the backing of the Church Authorities, laid some sort of trap for him and this simple man fell right into it. What followed was not only a tragedy for his parishioners, but the end of the priesthood for Pedro. Excommunicated from the church he loved and three years' hard labour in a very tough Spanish prison, poor Sanches, as he now called himself, walked out of the prison gates at the end of his sentence a tormented soul, wishing only to die. But unable to take his own life and condemn his immortal soul to hell, he reasoned that the quickest way to get the job done, was to join the French Foreign Legion. He believed that he could lose himself in the Legion and, if luck would have it, his life as well. God help him, he got his wish. I placed the chalice on his coffin to show that, at one time, he had been a priest in Holy Orders.

'You know son, they say it's easy to die, but hard to live. Well, poor Sanches put the lie to that saying, for as well as living hard, he died hard.'

'He was a brave and courageous man, Padre,' Travis remarked.

'Always remember soldier, that bravery and courage are only fear that has said its prayers' the Priest answered. Travis, taking the Padre's advice to heart, consigned it to the notebook of his mind. The Army Chaplain crossed himself, blessed Travis, shook hands and wished him every grace and blessing of the Lord God.

As Travis walked out of the garrison church, he hoped he could show the same kind of courage and commitment Sanches had shown in his short but eventful life and match the stoicism shown by the little Spaniard. Travis knew that his action in the recent ambush could never be compared to the actions of Sanches.

In its almost 200 years of existence, the Legion had been home for many strange bedfellows, many with even stranger stories to tell, and he was soon to stumble on another such story. After the funeral, he paid a visit to the base hospital to check up on Legionnaire Alexchenko, the giant Russian wounded in the ambush. He found him to be quite comfortable and recovering from his wound. Much to Travis' embarrassment, Alexchenko greeted him like a long-lost brother.

'Tell me' he said, 'You hardly know me, so, why come for me when I was all but a dead man?'

With no immediate words to mind, Travis mumbled, 'It just seemed like a good idea at the time.' '

Well from where I'm sitting, it's the best idea you've ever had, and I thank you from the very bottom of my heart. I owe you my life, and I will never forget it. Any problems you have with anybody or anything, just let me know and I'll be there for you, as long as you are in the Legion.'

Alex, as Travis called him for short, was a White Russian from Tashkent. His grandfather had fought against the Bolshevik Red Army during the Russian Civil War from 1918 to 1921. During the war his family, who were landowners, had had their estates seized by the Reds, plunging them into poverty. After the war had ended, his grandfather continued to harass their communist masters by joining a guerrilla band known as the Bismachi. During World War 2, Alex's father had joined the German Army to fight against the hated Reds. Finally, when young Alex was conscripted into the Soviet Army, he deserted and joined the French Foreign Legion. Despite his unfortunate background, Alex was well educated and spoke good English and fluent French. Dark featured, with a permanent angry scowl, and six foot six inches tall, with biceps and thighs like tree trunks, he looked like a dullard. This was a misconception, as he was a remarkably shrewd and switched-on man. Travis was glad to have him on his side.

At a later date, Travis was decorated with the Médaille Militaire for his bravery in the ambush, along with many other Legionnaires who had distinguished themselves in action. He looked on the decoration as tangible proof that he had the courage to react in dangerous situations despite the odds. He had proved once again that he was unlike his lily-livered father.

The patrols, sweeps and searches in the mountains continued, with monotonous regularity. Despite some success, Travis and the

Legion lost some good comrades in booby-trapped mechatas and caves, more than in actual fire fights.

Just as during Travis' service in Cyprus with the British Paras, the locals in the hill towns and villages fixed the drinks of the Legionnaires by putting piss or spit in each bottle or glass. At least that was what the post doctor put Travis' malaise down to, riddled as he was with the most appalling stomach pains and the hot streaming squitters, as the British Paras called galloping diarrhoea, where, more by luck than good judgement, he made it to the lavatory without shitting himself on the way. His illness led to him being laid up in hospital, while his body tried to fight off whatever hit him.

One evening as he started to recover, he ventured out of camp to the town area that had grown up around the Legion base and was dependent on the camp and the Legionnaires for its living. It was the only place a Legionnaire could go without being armed with a sidearm or such. He didn't enjoy it one bit, as he knew no one in the bars and cafés and wasn't interested in female company as he didn't want to spend any more time in the base hospital, this time nursing his private parts. Lonely and a little down, he started to walk slowly towards the camp. It was getting dark as he made his way back, and as he passed by one of many alleyways in the town, he heard the Legion cry for help, 'A moi la Legion!' (To me the Legion). A Legionnaire is honour bound to answer such a call, so he started to make his way quietly and slowly down the by now dark alley where the cry had come from.

He soon came across five extremely rough-looking Arabs with their backs to him. They were in a semi-circle around a Legion sergeant whom they had backed up against the end wall of a cul-de-sac. Travis moved further into the alleyway, quietly getting closer to the scene. The Arabs were armed with knives and chains and two of them had pieces of timber, picked up from the alley floor. The Legion NCO was unarmed. The five would-be assailants moved forward, with menace in their every step. The only plus the Legion Sergeant had was that a group of attackers can have a hard time fighting against just one person, as they can get in each other's way and can injure each other by mistake. But that was slim comfort for the sergeant.

Unseen, Travis picked up a length of stout timber from the ground and crept silently towards the unsuspecting Arabs. When he felt he was close enough, he charged forward, screaming the battle cry of the Legion. Twirling his wooden baton over his head like a Scottish warrior with a claymore sword, he tore into the Arab rank, almost beheading the first one he hit. At that moment, the sergeant swung into action too and with remarkable unarmed combat skills, he killed three of his attackers in a matter of seconds.

Travis, after his wild charge, was suddenly exhausted, his energy leaving him like air from a collapsed balloon, his illness catching up with him. Now confronted by a knife-wielding attacker, he was feebly trying to fend him off. The sergeant stepped up behind the Arab and grasped him by the head. Giving it a quick twist, he snapped his neck and spine, killing him instantly. The NCO checked that the attacker Travis had felled was dead, then grabbed Travis by the arm and hurried him up and out of the alley.

Back on the street they slowed down so as not to attract attention and started to walk in a normal manner back to camp. Travis didn't make it all the way, collapsing from exhaustion, brought on by his debilitating illness. The sergeant had to carry him the rest of the way back to the camp hospital over his shoulder in a fireman's lift.

It was the next day before Travis woke up in his hospital bed. There followed a telling-off by the medical officer about taking things easy before he lapsed back into a deep sleep again. When he woke the second time, the sergeant from the night before was sitting by his bed watching him. When he was fully awake and sitting up, the NCO, a medium-sized, thickset man with oriental features, introduced himself as Sergeant Nanak and thanked Travis for his help. Nanak, who said he worked with the Quartermaster, offered Travis kit replacement or any other favour he could in gratitude for his action against the Arab attackers.

'Thanks for the offer Sergeant, I'm sure there is something missing from my kit list' said Travis. 'Apart from that, I am most interested in your unarmed combat skills. Where did you learn to fight like that? It was amazing how you tore into the Arabs in the alleyway. Maybe you could give me a few tips in your off duty time.'

The sergeant's explanation revealed another strange story leading to his enlistment in the Legion.

'Nanak is the name I adopted when I joined up' he said. 'Before that, I had spent my life as a Buddhist monk, in a monastery, in the mountains of Tibet. I entered the monastery as a very young boy, and it was there that I learned my fighting skills. After many years of study, I rose from being a novice to full priesthood. In the years following my ordination, I became a senior member of the governing body.

'It was about this time that the Chinese started to take an unhealthy interest in Tibet and soon after invaded my country. In an effort to keep the population in order, the Chinese tried to get the High Lama and High Priests to submit to them. In answer, the clergy started quietly leaving the country to set up opposition in exile. One by one, with the Dalai Lama the first to escape, our religious leaders were spirited out of Tibet. In the midst of all this, I was tasked with the escort of a very holy man from his monastery home to safety outside of Tibet. I set off with a small band of brother monks and some bearers through the rugged mountain passes, on the wild and dangerous journey. In the middle of our trek, we were attacked by a warlord and his gang of cutthroats. While we were taught to defend ourselves if attacked, we were not allowed to take a human life, under pain of excommunication. The taking of any life would see the killer cast out from the priesthood and unable to practise his faith as a monk, for a long as they lived.' *Shades of poor little Legionnaire Sanchez*, Travis thought.

'I really had no choice, it was a case of kill or be killed, and I had taken a sacred oath to get my charge to safety. Following the principle that attack is the best form of defence, I led a charge on the bandits which killed or routed them. In doing so, I gave up my calling as a priest. Forced to leave the holy life, I became a seaman, roaming around the world and finally ending up in Marseilles docks. There I was drugged, robbed and beaten half to death. When I recovered, I found that my ship had sailed without me. So, penniless and without a job and no chance of one, I signed on for the Legion, where I found another type of monastic life.'

Once Travis was fit and well, he started to spend most of his off-duty time working out with Nanak, learning the Tibetan art of self-defence and being introduced to Buddhist beliefs and way of life. This brought more changes for the better in him, in every aspect of his life, both mental and physical. One of the things he enjoyed most was working military radio equipment, having eventually become a company radio operator in the British Paras. His enthusiasm stemmed from the fact that an army radio operator always has a good handle on what's going on in the big picture, as opposed to the ordinary soldier who gets blindly on with doing what he is told by his section, platoon or company commander in the main, never knowing what's going on outside his own little world.

Wanting to be a signaller again, Travis now did everything he could think of to get on a Legion signals course, but because of his very poor French the Legion wouldn't accept him for training. This did not deter him and he pestered all the radiomen he knew with bribery and corruption to teach him the French military radio voice procedure. His best teacher was his mate Hamish, who was already a company radioman. With persistence and regular coaching, Travis started to come on in leaps and bounds, so much so that his Chief Corporal would let him relieve his section radio operator so the signaller could get some rest.

Early in the New Year, Travis and his comrades were on the city streets of Algiers fighting in built-up areas. It was a far cry from mountain warfare. The FLN terrorists in the city ran riot, with bombings, shootings and general mayhem. A favourite tactic was to lure the Army into blind alleyways and ambush them - again shades of Cyprus, Travis thought. With nowhere to go and scant cover for the soldiers, the guerrillas sometimes took a dreadful toll. Their favourite targets were the officer or NCO leading the unit, or the radioman with his waving aerial and headset.

As the radio operator was so easy to spot, the rebels had considerable success in disrupting communications in this manner, to such an extent that calls went out on a regular basis for replacement radiomen to cover for those killed or wounded in action. Thus it was that Travis, without having taken a radio course, took over his squad's radio when their operator was wounded.

On a particularly bad day in the city, a call went our for the nearest radioman to report to the Company Commander as a replacement for his operator, who had just been killed by a sniper. As Travis was the nearest, he got the job. He loved being in the thick of things and with his radio to see to, he never had time to be afraid or uncertain.

A couple of weeks into his new but temporary job, the small headquarters group, comprising the Commanding Officer, his bodyguard and Travis, were visiting a squad on stand-down in a quiet street sector. Suddenly they were attacked by a force of about six terrorists. After a brief firefight, the Fell cut and ran with the Legionnaires in hot pursuit. The Arabs ran down a cul-de-sac and into a high tenement house at the bottom, followed by the Paras, with Travis as tail-end Charlie watching the rear. The CO was in front of him with his bodyguard, leading the small HQ group. As the last of the soldiers before the CO's bodyguard entered the doorway of the house to start up the stairs, the whole house blew up and started to settle down in a great pile of rubble. The blast killed the Legionnaires already in the house and blew the bodyguard back into the CO, thus saving the officer's life and in death doing the job the bodyguard had been detailed for. The officer was in turn blown on top of Travis. Whilst the CO was severely injured by flying glass and brickwork, Travis escaped with minor injuries.

As soon as the dust settled, he started to attend to the officer's wounds. It was then that the mopping-up trap was sprung, with shooters firing down into the alleyway from the rooftops. The only cover for the two soldiers was an oblong steel refuse container, and Travis started to drag his CO towards it. He had just made it into cover when he was hit in the thigh. He didn't feel much pain at first, but his leg went stiff and lifeless. From his new position, he returned fire as best he could and managed to take out at least two of his attackers. The remaining FLN poured fire and lobbed grenades down on them, most of which went into the container, doing very little harm. Meanwhile, between firing his weapon and shielding his officer with his body, Travis sent frantic messages down his radio for help. His calls were answered just as he had used up the last of his and the CO's ammunition.

Alexchenko was in the van of his rescuers and ignoring the unconscious officer, he picked Travis up in his arms and ran all the way to the nearest aid post for treatment for his friend. After a spell in hospital, Travis was back in action again, but the CO's recovery took a while longer. After his release from hospital, the officer sought out Travis and thanked him for saving his life, then like Nanak, asked him if there were any favours he could do for him in return. Travis just asked for a radio/signals course and the officer promised to look into it for him. The CO put him forward for one of the highest bravery awards and once again Travis stood in line on the parade square to receive the Croix de Valeur Militaire from the General.

He never felt quite right about this type of decoration. Campaign medals, yes, he believed he had earned them, but not medals for bravery, as he was only doing his job, as he saw it. His second reward from his erstwhile CO was a place at Corporal School, which was a back-handed compliment, as the four-month course was the toughest in the Legion, mentally and physically, even worse than recruit training. Travis certainly earned his promotion from *Soldat 2e classe* (Private) to *Caporal*, as did all Legion NCOs.

The long hard slog of attrition went on as the war escalated, with dead and injured on both sides mounting daily. Travis was saddened at the loss of comrades he had been close to. He looked on his fellow soldiers with high regard and grew very close to them as time went on. It didn't matter that the soldier beside you in a fire fight had been a habitual criminal in civilian life. Here he was just another soldier giving one hundred per cent for his Legion family. He worried about Hamish, Nanak and Alexchenko, as he was so close to them, but luckily they appeared to lead charmed lives.

The only respite, or change of scene, was to be sent to the

Moroccan or the Tunisian borders to police the electric fences the French had erected to prevent Arab FLN from crossing the borders from their training camps in the surrounding countries of Libya, Morocco and Tunisia. In this, the FLN was supported by the Egyptian President, General Gamal Abdul-Nasser, who provided funds, training and the Voice of the Arabs radio station. Travis felt it was a shame the Yanks had stopped the British Para Regiment, the Marines and their allies at Suez. If they had been given their head, they could have toppled Nasser from the world stage and saved Algeria a load of grief.

So it was that one day on border duty, he almost died in a savage battle with well-armed and well-trained Arabs who had cut a path through the strung wire marking the border using old Bangalore explosives charges. He was as close to an exploding grenade as one can get and live to tell the tale. But this time there was no speedy recovery and return to active duty, which in a way, shielded him from the events that almost saw the disbandment and end of the Legion. General Charles De Gaulle was elected as Premier of France, a situation that cheered the French settlers in Algeria. They believed him to be their champion, in that he would keep Algeria French. However, De Gaulle upset the settlers and also his own army chiefs by siding with the rebels and promising them freedom from France and French rule.

Following De Gaulle's announcement that he would set Algeria free, a secret army known as the OAS (*Organization de l'Armée Secrete*) came into existence. Its backbone was deserters from the Legion and dissident French Army and Legion officers, who mounted a killing and bombing campaign in an effort to change the French Government's stance on the future of Algeria. The Legionnaires could not ignore the sacrifices their comrades had made in the years they had fought to keep Algeria for the French.

They even planned the assassination of De Gaulle and the invasion of Paris and other strategic areas of France.

Finally his top generals in Algeria, Generals Raoul Salan and Maurice Challe, plotted and led a *putsch* or *coup d'état* by pulling a major Legion unit into the fray, against the orders of the French Government. The 1ˢᵗ Legion Para Regiment under the command of Major Helie Deniox de Saint-Marc, who loathed De Gaulle's acceptance of Algerian independence, moved into Algiers, occupying all key points in the city. Declaring 'Algérie Française' they were backed by the 1ˢᵗ and 2ⁿᵈ Legion Cavalry Regiments and various other units. Swift action and condemnation of this move by the President and fading support for the generals broke the resistance. The main Legion formations involved returned to their bases without a shot being fired, being immediately disbanded. Generals Salan and Challe tried to escape the clutches of the French Government, but were eventually captured.

When order was finally restored on this piece of bloody history, and Algeria had achieved its independence, the wrath of the French Government and the French people descended on the Legion. A putsch started that almost tore the heart from this proud and great fighting force. Many good men and true fell by the wayside, some dying for their cause, others shot as deserters. Many more were driven into obscurity as punishment for having chosen the wrong side or the wrong set of ideals.

On top of this, the Legion eventually lost its ancestral home in North Africa, Sidi bel Abbes. The remaining Legionnaires were heartbroken as they marched out, for the last time, from the great Fort of Sidi bel Abbes. Algeria was lost, and the Legion was in disgrace for its part in the mutiny and rebellion against de Gaulle and the French Government. The First REP was disbanded, and it seemed to be only a matter of time before the entire Legion itself was disbanded.

Travis, who was still on the sick list, moved with the rest of the Legion Paras to a new home in Corsica where he settled down in good Legion fashion. As he grew in fitness and strength, he wondered what France had in store for the Legion and him in particular. He didn't have to wait long to find out.

CHAPTER SEVEN

FRANCE

Near the end of the Algerian conflict, recruiting into the Legion was suspended and with the loss of many good NCOs, both as battle casualties and during the clear-out of suspected sympathisers to the OAS cause, there was an acute shortage of senior NCOs. As soon as the Legion got the news that it was to be retained as a fighting force as part of the French Army, Travis, fit again, was surprised to be offered a five-month sergeant's cadre. This was followed by an all-arms signals course. It emerged that his old CO from the battle-torn streets of the Algerian capital had kept his promise and landed him a prime posting, to a top French Army signals school and regiment in the heart of rural France. He couldn't believe his luck as it was rare indeed at that time for the Legion to grant such freedom to a Legionnaire, with the possible opportunity to desert.

From the start, Travis loved his new posting and his signals course, where he would be reminded again of the need for fast and reliable communications, how each type of equipment functioned, how it was used and how to get the best out of the equipment, so it could fulfil its task of speeding information to its destination, often many miles from its source of origin, as the success of any operation depends on the rapid spread of orders down the chain of command. Any failure in the line of communications could jeopardise not only a battle but the lives of men involved in the operation. It was a serious business, not to be taken lightly. With his active service experience in two armies, Travis needed no reminding of that.

The area in which the signals camp was situated reminded him a little of rural Ireland, and once again he settled into his new, if temporary, home with customary Legion ease. On his first Sunday in camp, he got up at the crack of dawn, meditated for the first half hour, as per his good friend Nanak the ex-Buddhist monk, and then had his morning jog.

It was a beautiful summer morning. During his run, he made up his mind to go out and about and recce his new home. Returning to camp, he showered and shaved, put on his best uniform and donned his green beret. He exited the main gate of the camp, where some other soldiers were waiting for buses at the two stops. Travis just wanted to walk, so he flipped a coin for which way to go, right or left. He turned left and in doing so, made a turn that was about to change his life.

He walked until he encountered a quaint and typically French village called Chalonne. As he started up the main street, the Market Street, he came to the church on the edge of the market square. Villagers were going in for morning Mass. He followed them in, sitting at the back of the church. He didn't take communion as it had been a long time since he been to confession.

The service was enjoyable and the atmosphere was warm and friendly, and he vowed to try to attend Sunday Mass in this church whenever he could make it. At the end of Mass, he remained seated, as a mark of respect, until most of the parishioners had left. Picking up his beret he walked slowly out into the sunshine to encounter a barrage of abuse from the old men of the parish. They spoke so fast and with such strong accents that Travis couldn't understand what they were saying, but he knew by their tone that they were not a welcoming committee.

As he struggled to understand and respond to them, two young ladies came out of the church, one of whom was devastatingly beautiful. They both stopped to listen to the tirade for a minute or two and quickly summed up the situation the sergeant was in. The young beauty stepped forward and asked if she could help, to which Travis replied, 'Yes, if you can understand and speak English.'

'Yes I can' came the reply in perfect English, spoken with that sexy French accent that always sent a tingle up his spine.

'Thank God. Would you please translate?'

'But of course' the girl replied. 'They say you are not welcome in their church, now or ever. They say, that the criminals and murderers of the Legion of the damned should never be allowed into any church, or mix with good living decent people.'

After her translation, the French girl rounded on the old men and gave them such a dressing down that they flinched at her words, most of which went over Travis' head. She then grabbed Travis by the arm and half dragged him around to the back of the church to see the Parish Priest, Padre Lefèvre, who greeted the young woman warmly and listened to what she had to say with great attention. When she had finished her explanation, the Priest sided with the protesters.

'Antoinette, I am sorry but I cannot go against the wishes of the majority and in fact, they are quite right in their disgust of the Legion, the ungodly men it employs, and all the ungodly things it has done.'

Travis thought that the beautiful one was going to have a fit. Instead, she just stamped her pretty little foot on the ground, snorted her disgust and, still clinging to Travis' arm, dragged him away from the unrepentant priest. With her friend clinging to his other arm, they frogmarched him off up the village. The dark-eyed beauty was still prattling on in the local dialect.

Suddenly, Travis stopped dead in his tracks. The girls tried to walk on a few steps more, but only succeeded in bumping into each other. The stop had the desired effect. The verbal abuse ceased, and the girls looked enquiringly at Travis, who promptly thanked them for their support in the fracas and invited them for coffee and croissants. So, seated in the local café, they finally got to know each other.

The walking, talking, living doll was Antoinette and her friend was called Chantelle. When Antoinette excused herself and went behind the counter into the back of the café to talk to the lady who owned it, Travis started to quiz Chantelle about her friend.

'So Chantelle, tell me about you and Antoinette' he said.

'Well, we grew up together and were best friends at school. She's not married or engaged and she has no current boyfriend,' Chantelle replied with a coy smile.

'I guessed that for myself, I noticed that she has no rings on her left hand' replied Travis. 'So tell me something about her that I don't know?'

'Well, she's the daughter of the mayor of our village. Her family are quite well off. They own a small chemical plant in the main town in the region, which she runs with her brother Raymond. Both she and her brother are chemists, but Antoinette runs the administration side of the business. They live with their parents in an old house on the south side of the village. The family have large holdings in land for agriculture, animal stock and a medium sized vineyard. For myself, I am a hairdresser, with a small shop in the market square. You can't miss it. It's called Chantelle's. I am an only child and live with my widowed mother not far from Antoinette.'

Before Travis could question her further, Antoinette came back to the table to captivate him once again, and he lost himself in her liquid brown eyes. When she sat down again, Antoinette asked him what his plans for the day were.

'I'm going to get a Sunday paper and read it on a bench in the village square, in the lovely sunshine' he said. 'That is, if the men of the village don't run me out of town.' He grinned. 'After that, a pleasant stroll back to camp and catch up on some sleep in the late afternoon. Then after lunch, a visit to the camp cinema. Not terribly exciting, but a lovely relaxed day after the weeks of hard training.'

'How would you like to come to Sunday dinner in my home?' she asked him. He didn't need another episode on the demerits of the Legion and declined with a 'No, thank you very much.'

'Oh, but you must come. I have just spoken to my parents on the phone and they are looking forward to meeting you.'

'In that case, how can I refuse? Thank you.'

Leaving the café, with thanks to the kind lady proprietor, they linked arms again and strolled off down the village, past the church where they had met to the crossroads which led to his camp on the left and to where Chantelle lived on the right. Both girls said their goodbyes there, kissing each other on both cheeks. Very French, thought Travis. The couple carried on down a leafy country road and around a bend, just out of sight of the village, where the Leclerc family home stood. It was a big old rambling, three-storey French-style farmhouse, showing eight windows, two of them over an old oak door. The house was covered in ivy, a feature Travis loved from his childhood in Ireland. It always appeared to him to make a home more comfortable and warm. The gardens were well kept and the whole scene had a feeling of friendly opulence to it, which tended to put him at his ease and make him feel welcome.

As they entered through the front door into the large hallway, a tall handsome lady with dark hair with silver streaks in it was coming down the broad staircase. She was the image of Antoinette, except that she was taller and older. It was obviously Madame Leclerc. He fell under her spell straight away, as, just like her daughter, she gave him her undivided attention.

'I am so pleased to meet a member of our great Armed Forces' she greeted him.

'Thank you Madame, for your kind invitation to dinner.'

'You are most welcome young man, it's the least we can do for one of our fighting soldiers,' she said, her voice soft. Added to this was the warmth emanating from the friendly brown eyes her daughter had inherited from her.

Sending Antoinette upstairs to change, Madame Leclerc ushered Travis into a drawing room off the hall, where a man was sitting reading the Sunday paper and drinking coffee. As he stood up to greet him, Travis noticed that he was smaller than his wife, about Travis' height of five foot eight inches. This was where Antoinette got her petite figure from. Anton Leclerc was looking at Travis with a kindly smile on his face, but Travis could see at a glance that it wouldn't do to mess with this man. Someone had once told him that you could see how a man lived his life by his face, and this was never more true than with this man, the Mayor of Chalonne. Monsieur Leclerc held out his hand and said, 'You are most welcome to our home, Sergeant.'

'Thank you sir, I am honoured.'

Before they could say much more, the cook/housekeeper came into the room to announce that dinner was ready and they all trooped across the hall into a imposing oak-panelled dining room, where Antoinette joined them. Travis could feel and smell the past happy history of this room and again felt very much at ease and at home there.

As they were sitting down, a tall, good-looking young man pushing six foot tall entered the room, obviously Antoinette's elder brother Raymond. He was the image of his father. Introduced by Antoinette, he grasped Travis' hand in a warm handshake and in that moment both young men seemed to click together. Somehow Travis knew that this man could be a friend for life.

Business talk kicked off as the soup was served and Madame brought that to a swift halt by reminding everyone that they had a guest. A short period of silence followed, and Monsieur Leclerc started to question Travis about his army service. Travis skipped lightly over his years with the British Paras and his time in the Legion. The older man smiled at his son, who winked back at some shared secret.

'You don't get the medal ribbons you are wearing by marching about in the sunshine, and your two medals for bravery were not won on cookhouse duty', Anton said. 'You can't fool an old soldier like me or an ex-conscript like my son. We both know that you are a good and brave soldier, and we are honoured to share our table with you. Raymond served his National Service as an infantry officer and saw some action in Africa. Madame and I were involved in the Resistance during World War Two, so you can't pull the wool over our eyes.'

Everyone, including Travis, laughed at that, and the rest of the meal was a relaxed happy affair, with tall tales and funny stories about army life. Travis pitched in with the story about the pony mascot of the British Paras, the animal relieving itself on the Queen's Birthday Parade and the pony's demotion to Corporal on Battalion Orders, all of which had the Leclercs in fits of laughter.

Anton recalled how he and his comrades in the resistance had blown up a sewage farm next to a large German Army base. The Germans and every item of their kit and vehicles were well and truly covered in prime French excreta. Madame Leclerc tut-tutted, but with a broad smile on her face.

The meal over, Antoinette took Travis on a stroll around the farm and out-buildings, ending up at the stables, where she showed him the family horses. She appeared to be quite a horsewoman, having ridden since she was a tiny tot, winning cups and rosettes which were displayed in the tack room. He guessed that she was in her mid-twenties. He had already seen her strong personality in action and knew she was nor fragile flower. She was in fact all woman.

Travis was in his element. He loved horses, having ridden ponies and exercised racehorses on the plains of the Curragh in Kildare, Southern Ireland, home of the famous Curragh Races. Antoinette suggested that he might like to take a horse out the next time he made a visit and his heart jumped at the thought of seeing this gorgeous girl once again.

All too soon, the day was over and he had to go back to camp. In fact, when he took notice again, he was shocked to see how late it actually was, and he made haste to take his leave of the family. Antoinette was missing as he said his goodbyes, having gone to bring the car round to take him back to camp.

'Would you like to spend a weekend with us sometime in the near future, Patrice?' asked M Leclerc.

'I'd love to, sir. It can't be next weekend as I am on duty as Sergeant of the guard. But I could come along the following weekend, if that would be all right?'

The parents agreed and so it was arranged. Antoinette drove him to the camp gate in a beautiful old Citroen open-top sports car. With the breeze blowing in her hair, she looked like a Greek goddess. At the gates to the camp they shook hands and he kissed the back of her tiny hand, but as he made to get out of the car, she grabbed his head in both hands and dragged him towards her, kissing him full on the lips. He would carry the memory of that kiss for the rest of that week.

To whistles and catcalls from the camp guard, he waved Antoinette goodbye and with a happy smile and a wink at the guard he made his way to his quarters a very happy man.

The following Saturday, an hour before the evening meal was due to be delivered to the guardhouse, Travis was called to the main gate by the sentry. There he found Antoinette, looking more beautiful than ever, with a bright scarf holding her hair in place, sitting in the Citroen with the engine ticking over.

'What? Why?' Travis stuttered, to the amusement of the sentry, who could hear everything.

'I've brought you dinner,' said Antoinette. 'May I come in?'

He nodded to the sentry, who lifted the barrier, and she drove the car into the parking space in front of the guardhouse. She slid lightly out of the car and bent over the back seat, to the very obvious delight of the entire guard. She picked up a large wicker hamper and strode straight into the guardroom with the guard scattering before her, then following her like lovesick calves. The astonished and delighted Travis decided to bask in all the attention. The food was delicious and enough to feed a section, let alone one person. It also contained some bottles of excellent red and white wine. The only downside was that as he was on duty, she could only stay for a couple of minutes, and when she had gone, this time with a long lingering kiss, he felt that the sun had just gone in.

The next week just dragged on; it was the longest week he could remember. Friday found him with his small overnight bag, waiting for Antoinette at the main gate. She was bang on time at five o'clock, and his heart leapt to see her. She looked with some surprise at his small bag and asked him where his civilian clothes where, to which he replied that a Legionnaire did not possess civilian clothes. Without further comment, she planted a kiss full on his lips, much to the delight and envy of the guard, and then gunned the old car down the narrow country road to Chalonne.

His bedroom at the Leclercs' house was everything he had expected, with a large, soft, four-poster bed and all the trimmings. He came down to dinner without his tunic, just wearing a shirt and tie with his summer dress trousers.

'Why are you still in uniform, young man?' asked M Leclerc. 'We don't stand on ceremony here you know. It's quite OK to wear a pair of slacks, shirt and jumper.'

Antoinette spoke up for him, explaining the situation. Her father promptly offered Travis his wardrobe, as they were both about the same size. Next day, after an early morning jog and dressed in jodhpurs and riding boots, items he could never afford in Ireland and had always wanted to wear, he and Antoinette exercised the horses. They took a ride around the boundaries of the homestead, which had everything, included a large wooded area and an enchanting lake where they tethered their horses. Holding hands, they walked to the water's edge. There he took this beautiful young woman into his arms, caressing her lustrous black hair and the soft tanned skin of her arms. They kissed, and he wanted the kiss to last a lifetime.

When they got back for breakfast, everyone started to get ready for church. Travis took Antoinette aside and said, 'Is there another church nearby, other than the one in Chalonne? I don't want to go back there again after all the upset'.

'Yes Patrice' she said - she had taken to using the French form of his name - 'there is a small church in the village of Foy just five kilometres away, and if you're going to go there I will go with you.'

Her decision to accompany him to Foy caused all consternation in the house as the Leclercs were leading lights in the village and had had their own family pew in the Chalonne church for generations, but Antoinette would have none of it and they both set off for the village of Foy. They arrived in good time for the service and were welcomed by the Padre and greeted by some of the congregation. The fact that Travis was in full Legion uniform did not matter a jot to any of the members of the little church, young or old, and he was overjoyed at this display of Christian fellowship.

Foy became a regular Mass stop and a watering hole for the couple from that day on. Their weekly trips there become a regular part of their weekends together. When he was on week-long signal exercises in the countryside, Travis always managed to camp out in the woods on the Leclerc farm. Much to the delight of the other three members of his team in the radio vehicle, who were mostly privates or corporals, the four soldiers never had to dip into their army rations packs, as they were fed like fighting cocks by Antoinette and her mother.

By now, Travis and Antoinette were head over heels in love with each other. It all came to a head one late afternoon when they were alone in the house, except for the housekeeper, who was buried in the basement kitchen preparing dinner. Anton and Madame were visiting relations until late evening. Raymond was off playing rugby. The couple had been out for a long walk together, and as it was an extremely hot day they arrived back sweaty and tired. They decided to take a shower and have long, cool drinks on the back porch in the rocking chairs while they waited for dinner.

Travis was drying himself in his room when the door opened

and in walked Antoinette. She shut the door with a wiggle of her cute backside and then just stood there with a cheeky grin on her face. She was wearing a white towel on her head, turban style, and a large fluffy white towelling robe. She looked so desirable that he wanted to grab her. With a dramatic gesture she whipped the towel off her head and ran her fingers through her hair, then shook her head like a gundog emerging from a duck pond, her hair falling around her shoulders, framing her beauty. Then, very slowly, she opened her robe and slid it off her shoulders onto the floor. He was mesmerised at the sight of her supple body, with her ample breasts, enough to fill an honest man's hands and then some.

She sauntered over to him, flaunting her hips, and when she reached Travis, she snatched his towel out of his hands. Taking his hand in hers, she led him to the bed. She lay down and pulled him down on top of her and with a whispered 'Please, be gentle with me darling,' she gave herself to him.

Travis, who had been to hell and back once or twice in recent years, finally found his heaven. When it was over, they lay together in blissful and loving comfort until the bell rang for dinner. It was the most romantic evening of his life, and he made the most of it.

It was motherly, loving Madame Leclerc who brought him down to earth. The next weekend, she found him on his own for a moment in the drawing room. She sat down beside him on the couch and took his hand in hers, saying, 'Patrice, everyone except my husband know that you and Antoinette are in love, and it's lovely to see. But please tell me what your plans are for the future as far as my daughter is concerned.'

To Travis, the future was next weekend, but he could hardly say that. He mumbled something about sitting down with Antoinette in the near future and sorting it out.

'I'm glad to hear that Patrice, and I look forward very much to hearing of your future plans' said Madame Leclerc.

The brief conversation brought Travis up with a jolt and during the following week he thought long and hard about the future. In the end he realised that in fact, there could be no future for him and Antoinette while he was in the Legion, nor if he was out of it. Soldiering was all he knew or ever wanted to do. He decided to break it off with Antoinette for her sake, but before he did so, he would talk it through with her mother.

The next weekend, Travis drew Madame Leclerc aside and clearing this throat said, 'Madame, you know I love your daughter with all my heart. But I cannot offer her marriage while I am in the Legion, or offer her a decent living anywhere else. It's my intention to stop seeing her because I love her so much. I only want the very best in life for her and I can't give her that.'

Madame Leclerc, very troubled by this confession, replied, 'Patrice, please think this through a little bit longer. I'm sure that love will find a way. It found a way for my husband and me. I loved Anton so much that I joined him in the French Resistance during the war, just to be near him. I felt that, if Anton should die, then I would die with him. He was my first love and France my second.' Travis remembered Anton's words at the dinner table that first day, when he had said, 'Madame and I saw some action during the war.' So this fine, lovely, country girl had learned how to kill Nazis with various weapons, including the garrotte and even her bare hands. She told him that she had been an expert in demolition and could handle a Sten gun or a German Schmeisser sub-machine gun with the best of them. She and Anton had been married in a little out-of-the-way church at the height of the war while on the run, to avoid capture by the Germans, with just their two best friends as witnesses. Days later their four-man team had been ambushed in a country lane, on their way to mount an ambush of their own. The group made a fighting retreat in which their friends, their bridesmaid and best man, died in a hail of machine-gun fire. It was a miracle that the newly-wed Valerie and Anton had escaped. The experience had left them in no doubt that it was the power of God that spared them both and they finally had their big, white wedding on Liberation Day.

Despite everything Antoinette's mother said, Travis decided to go ahead with his plan. He could not put off his announcement any longer.

He finally got his chance on Sunday night. Antoinette was a little off colour, and Raymond offered to take Travis back to camp. Before they left, he drew her out onto the back porch, which held such happy memories for them.

'Antoinette, darling, this is the hardest thing I have ever had to do in my life' he said. 'But I must be straight with you as you have been so good and loving with me. I am about to go on the final test weeks of my course and then it's back to the Legion. I won't be coming back again. I'm so sorry to say that this is goodbye for ever.'

At first, she seemed to be struck dumb, and then as if a dam had burst in her heart, her grief at his words flooded out. She was in despair, and he could not placate her. In the end, he kissed her lightly on a tear-stained cheek and quietly took his leave.

The following Monday morning, with kit packed and vehicles loaded, the Signals Regiment set off on its two-week exercise into the Loire Valley. This was to be the conclusion to his signals course. Within a week or two after this exercise, he would be on his way back to Aubagne and the Legion and far away from his beloved Antoinette. It would all be for the best, thought Travis. Antoinette would come to understand that, and perhaps forgive him. But he would never forget her, and she would always have a place in his heart.

On the Friday after his return to camp from the signals exercise he was supervising the dismantling of the last vehicle-mounted radios when a corporal from HQ came running up to him with the message that he was to report to the Colonel's office.

'What's it about, Corporal?' asked Travis.

'I was just told to tell you to get over to HQ and report to the Adjutant' the corporal replied. Travis went at a jog to the HQ building, where he barely had time to catch his breath before Sergeant Major Belaire had him lined up outside the CO's office. The Adjutant knocked, opened the door and marched him in at the double. When the order to halt was given, he found himself looking down at the fatherly but stern features of his silver-haired Commanding Officer.

'That will be all, Mr Belaire, thank you' the Colonel said, and the door closed, leaving Travis alone with the CO.

'I have a favour to ask of you, Sergeant Travis,' requested the CO.

'Yes sir' he replied, astonished.

'I want you to see an old and close friend of mine and listen to what he has to say to you.'

Again, 'Yes sir' from a puzzled Travis.

'He is waiting for you next door. Carry on.'

Travis saluted and fell out in the correct drill manner. Then, opening the door, indicated by the Colonel, he stepped through, to find himself in a large room which was furnished like a cross between a boardroom and a dining room, with antique mahogany chairs and a very large old oak table with a silver candelabra at the centre. Paintings of famous battles adorned the walls, along with the requisite French flag.

The room appeared to be empty and silent as the door closed gently behind him, leaving him alone and confused.

Travis was facing the back of a big, high-backed chair at the end of the table. He took this to be the CO's chair, as it was larger than the rest. He walked slowly past it, admiring the paintings of death and glory of days gone by.

Suddenly a voice spoke softly from the depths of the big chair. 'Hello Patrice.' It was Anton Leclerc.

'Sit down please, next to me' said the older man. Travis slumped into a chair in deep shock, but he remembered his Colonel's words, 'Listen to what he has to say.' So this was the CO's friend.

'I am sorry to have you called to see me in this way' said Anton. 'As you know, I was a leader in the Resistance during World War Two. I followed this with service in the Free French Army until the end of the War. I resigned with the rank of Colonel to run my home, my business and my village. So I couldn't have you called to the guardroom to speak with me in front of the camp guard. I have my pride and my position to think of, and I knew that you wouldn't come to the house to see me.'

Travis was silent.

'As you can guess, I am here for my little girl. She has been hurt very badly and is desperately unhappy.' Travis made to speak, but the Mayor hurried on, 'No need to say a word Patrice, I know the whole story from my wife. Let me say that you must love my daughter very much to make the decision to end your relationship with her, for the sake of her future.'

There was a lump growing in Travis' throat and his eyes were growing moist as he remembered Antoinette's tragic face.

'We should try and resolve this sad situation, you and I, as best we can' Anton said, still in a soft voice. 'My beloved wife tells me that you would not be allowed to marry during your last two years in the Legion, in fact, until your first five years are up. If you took your discharge from the Legion after five years, you would have little or no prospects, which would stop you from offering my daughter a life with you.' A nod from Travis. 'However,' Anton carried on, 'I believe that if you were a part of the French Regular Army, with prospects of betterment, say, a commissioned rank, that the situation could change for the better.'

If pigs could fly, thought Travis.

Anton, noticing the look of doubt on Travis' face, continued, 'Let's suppose that after you finish your course here, which is in a few weeks' time, you were to go back to the Legion for an immediate transfer to the French Army and a return to this signals regiment to pursue your career under my friend the Commanding Officer. Then, within the year, you were allotted a place in a military academy, to study for a commission in the French Army as a base for a lifelong career and possible further promotion in the years ahead. What then would be your message to my daughter?'

Travis' mind was racing. Could this be true?

The older man was silent for a moment and then, taking a deep breath, he said, 'Look my son, I could not stand idly by and watch my only daughter in such anguish. I have been extremely busy on your behalf during the last two weeks. I am not without influence in this man's army, or in government circles for that matter. I fought alongside most of the fellows running the country and the army. I got on the old boy net and pulled a few strings. You can have your transfer from the Legion and your opportunity at Officer School.

'I don't know what to say' said Travis lamely, still in shock.

'I don't want you to say anything right now' said Anton. 'I want you to leave by the side door, go away and think about my offer and the future happiness of a very warm and loving young woman. I would be grateful if you would telephone me, say on Sunday evening, with your answer. If the answer is no, then the subject will be closed between us. Antoinette will never know about this conversation, and her mother, her brother and I will do our best to help her put this behind her and get on with her life.'

The Maquis leader had never looked so old as he did at that moment. He stood up slowly and held out his hand. Travis sat there quite still for a few moments. Then he stood up and gripped the older man's hand in both of his.

'You don't have to wait for my answer, sir' he said. 'I can give it to you right now. First of all I thank you from the bottom of my heart for the trouble you have gone to on behalf of your beloved daughter and myself. I love your daughter with all my heart and every fibre of my being and I gladly accept your offer. In the fullness of time, should I be accepted into Officer Training School and graduate with a commission, when the time comes for me to ask you for your daughter's hand in marriage, I will remember, with deep admiration and heartfelt thanks, a man's great love for his only daughter.'

At this the tears started to run unchecked down Anton's aristocratic face, and then Travis lost control too. Both men embraced. The old man whispered 'Thank you son.'

'Thank you, Papa' murmured Travis. Both men slumped back into their chairs.

'Now, why don't you come home with me now and give Antoinette the good news' said Anton. 'Maybe I could persuade you to stay for the weekend?'

'There is nothing more I could wish for right now,' replied Travis. 'But I would rather you dropped me off in the village to make my own way, so as not to alert Antoinette to this arrangement just yet.'

'Good thinking' the old man said. 'You slip away through the side door and get ready, I will square things with my friend the Colonel. I will be in the officers' mess having a cognac and a coffee until you are ready, just ask for me there.'

They both stood up and embraced again, briefly. Then Travis, putting on his beret, moved to the door. As he opened the door, turning to look back at his future father-in-law, and coming smartly to attention, he gave a very correct military salute to which the old man gravely responded.

Anton dropped Travis off just outside the village on the main camp road, with a weekend pass in his pocket. He walked into the village and up the main street, where he bought a bouquet of flowers and a box of Antoinette's favourite chocolates. He walked back down the village and over the crossroads, then started down the Foy road to the Leclerc house.

The road was quiet and peaceful and the tall hedges were a riot of wild flowers. He hadn't gone far when a familiar figure appeared around the bend, heading for the village. It was Antoinette. She looked drawn and haggard, her eyes cast to the ground as if searching for something she had lost. She had an old cardigan thrown over her shoulders and a scarf knotted around her head. She looked much older than her years.

When she finally looked up and saw Travis, she stopped dead in her tracks. He stopped too, choking up with love and pity at the sight of her. She lost her grip on the basket she was carrying, and it fell to the ground and bounced to the far side of the road. She cried out, putting a hand to her mouth, and then she was running, sobbing, into his waiting arms. She covered him in wet, tear-stained kisses, clinging to him fiercely.

There was no need for words as they stood there at the side of the road, holding each other. Then, with his arm about her and her head on his shoulder, they walked slowly towards the house, the basket lying forgotten on the road.

Dinner that evening was a joyful affair, and it marked the start of a very happy weekend for the young lovers. Later that day, Travis took Antoinette aside and held her hands, looking into her beautiful eyes.

'Darling, I have been given the opportunity to transfer to the French Army as a regular soldier, and if I get it, there is a fair chance that I will be posted back here to the signals regiment' he said. At that, she hugged and kissed him in delight. He decided to leave it at that as he didn't want to have her upset again, if it didn't come off as her father had planned. In his heart of hearts, he didn't really believe it himself.

A few weeks later, the signals course came to an end. Finally, the passing-out parade was followed by the conventional celebrations and one more night in the Leclerc house. Then, after tearful goodbyes, Travis set off for Corsica and the Legion, in great trepidation.

He need not have worried. By the time he arrived the transfer had been arranged. All he had to do was sign on the dotted line. The strange thing was, now that he was leaving the Legion, one half of him wanted to stay. He felt deeply sad about leaving his friends and comrades.

Nanak checked in his kit and let him keep his beloved képi and beret as souvenirs. He had a night out on the town with his platoon, then a private dinner party with Hamish, Nanak and big Alex, followed by a special mess night in the NCOs' mess. Then with a handshake and a 'bonne chance' from the Colonel, he left the Legion forever.

Some months after his return to the signals regiment, he received notification of his acceptance for the next officer training course, due to start in six months' time. That was when he started to panic. He should not have worried, because everyone pitched in to help. First it was Raymond, helping him with his French and digging out his old books from his officer cadet days. Then it was the young officers in the regiment, some fresh out of college, passing on their books and offering to tutor him in their spare time. The CO gave him a leave of absence from duties so that he could study. Study he did, all the hours that God sent him.

His departure date for officer training arrived all too soon and there were more tears from Antoinette at parting. She gave him a packed lunch with wine for the long train journey. Anton wanted to drive him to the station, but he would have died of embarrassment and shame if they had. As he leaned out of the carriage window at the start of his long train journey, Antoinette whispered, 'You are a good person Patrice Travis, you are my man and, I love you. I have faith in your abilities, and I know that you carry my love in your heart. You can succeed, my love, and you will.'

CHAPTER EIGHT

MILITARY ACADEMY, FRANCE

The military college was awesome and very intimidating with its rules and traditions. However, it didn't faze Travis. After the British Para, Legion recruit training and NCO cadres, he took this new challenge in his stride. His fellow potential officers, for the most part, were all young men fresh from college or university. They were well switched on when it came to theory but all fingers, thumbs and two left feet when it came to the practical and physical aspects of soldiering.

Travis quickly found he was a saleable commodity and traded his hard-earned military knowledge and skills on the parade square, with kit, weapons, fieldcraft, map-reading and all the other major skills that make a good infantry soldier, for further tuition on the subjects he struggled with.

The study and work were hard and unrelenting and the going was extremely tough, more mental than physical as far as Travis was concerned, but somehow he coped. He was a mascot and father figure to the other cadets, because of his age, experience and nationality, as well as his French/Irish accent, which the cadets loved to listen to. He kept his past service history a closed book from the rest of the course members.

His room-mate Gerrard was a great help to him, they shared their various skills. Weekend passes were few and far between and even at home with the family, there was no letting up on the study. If it wasn't Raymond or Antoinette helping and pushing him, it was Anton, and sometimes it was Madame Leclerc, where she thought she could help. He had a big team on his side, but even so he doubted his ability to 'do the business' and obtain a commission.

Part of the weekends were put aside for discussion of wedding plans. The lovers settled for the weekend after passing-out parade to get married - if he passed - and they were working towards that end. One Sunday morning, Madame hurried out onto the porch, where the young couple were having coffee on returning from Sunday Mass at Foy.

'You have a visitor waiting for you in the drawing room,' she informed them. 'It's Padre Lefèvre, and he wishes to speak to you both.' She said this with a knowing smile. When she had gone, Travis said: 'You know darling, it's high time the Padre apologised for his unchristian behaviour towards me and helped bury the hatchet. So, let's hear what he has to say. After all, if he and his parishioners hadn't had a go at me that first day in Chalonne, we might never have met.'

Padre Lefèvre was waiting for them, sipping a glass of wine and looking full of himself. Travis hadn't seen him since that fateful day when he had first met Antoinette, but the priest hadn't changed a bit. He was an austere, miserable-looking man with a long beak of a nose which had a permanent drip on the end of it. He smelt of cheap cigarettes and stale wine, and Travis was glad that he never had to go and confess to him, as his confession box must stink to high heaven.

'Your parents have informed me of your impending wedding' Lefèvre began, speaking directly to Antoinette and ignoring Travis. 'I've come to discuss it with you as I need to have some dates, to see if I can fit you into the church calendar. I am surprised that you haven't made an appointment to see me before now, as much has to be done, and there is so little time to do it.'

Travis looked at Antoinette, who was blazing and looked ready to explode. No apology, no attempt to make the peace. The man was totally insensitive.

'You surprise me, Padre,' replied Travis. 'As you know, I am a military man, and as such would want a military wedding, so we are arranging to be married in the garrison church by the Army Chaplain, with full military honours. But, thank you for your implied dispensation for a heathen Legionnaire, to be allowed to enter your church to be married. It's good to know that Christianity is not dead and buried.'

With that, Travis bid the cleric 'au revoir' and with Antoinette in dutiful tow, stalked out of the room with head held high.

Outside, Antoinette, who couldn't contain herself any longer, burst into raucous laughter. 'When did you decide that we were going to be married in the garrison church?' she asked Travis.

'Just a few minutes ago,' he replied. This drew another gale of laughter from Antoinette. 'You have made my day, darling,' she cried, 'and maybe my weekend, certainly our wedding.' She gave him a big hug and sealed it with a long, passionate kiss.

Travis' officer training squad had just started their last term leading to final exams, with midnight oil being used by the bucketful. Almost before they knew it, final exams were upon them. Then in the blink of an eye it was all over. They could do no more, except reflect on what they could have done better. They questioned each other about the possible answers, each fearing that the other person had answered correctly and they hadn't. This all led to an air of nervous anticipation and dread. You could almost feel and touch the tension in the dorms and rest areas. Appetites were lost overnight.

Travis, despite his hard upbringing and tough army background, was in a state of total funk, just like the rest of the course members. Sleep was impossible during pre-results night.

First light revealed a bunch of haggard and drawn students. They reluctantly crawled out of bed feeling like condemned men, but unlike the condemned, they were unable to eat a hearty breakfast.

Then it was time. They all grouped together like a herd of cows in the assembly hall, waiting for the results to be posted on the notice board. Finally, the senior admin officer strode into the hall without a glance at the waiting cadets. He pinned up the results list, slowly and methodically. Then, without a by your leave, he swept out again.

There was a hushed silence, then the mad rush to see the results was on. The whole squad hit the notice board like the Charge of the Light Brigade at the battle of Balaclava, with the front runners crushed up against the board.

Travis lingered well behind the throng. At first he couldn't bring himself to look, but when he did it was with shock and joy. He had passed, and to crown it all, he was best student. He had not been awarded the sword of honour (they explained later that this was because of his years of army and military experience), but it did not matter – he had passed, and was soon to be proclaimed an officer and a gentleman by the French Government and Army.

Travis thought back to his humble beginnings and his lineage of good, brave and distinguished soldiers and felt proud for them, proud to carry the line onward and upwards. He could now marry his beloved Antoinette.

He was trembling with delight as he dialled the Leclerc number. Antoinette answered it after one ring - she must have been sitting by the phone, waiting for his call, for he could hear the tension in her voice as she answered.

'May I speak to the future wife of Lieutenant Patrice Travis of the French Army, please?' said Travis. Squeals of delight from Antoinette. 'Mama, Papa, Raymond, it's Patrice, he's passed!' Her shouts reverberated around the old house and down the phone so loudly, that it deafened him for a moment.

'Ask me who got best Cadet' he said.

'Your room-mate Gerrard' replied Antoinette, a giggle in her voice.

'Oh you woman of little faith,' he replied, 'only your husband to be'. This brought another bout of excited shouting around the house. Then with a quick, 'I love you darling and I'm so very, very proud of you' from Antoinette, the entire household queued up to congratulate him. This was followed by a breathless Antoinette asking, 'When is your commissioning day and when are you coming home?'

This caught Travis on the hop, and he had to phone back with all the details. He need not have bothered, as an official invitation landed in the Leclerc post box the very next morning.

Commissioning day was a grand affair, with the entire population of cadets on parade. Travis, to his surprise and honour, was given command of his class, and as he marched out onto the parade square, he felt that only his wedding day could possibly surpass this great event in his life. Anton and Raymond, both still reserve officers, were in full uniform and decorations. They looked magnificent and Travis felt an immense pride in belonging to this noble family.

When the final dismissal was given he was almost bowled over by Antoinette as she ran to him, flinging herself into his waiting arms. A special lunch followed, with introductions being made to senior officers who could guide Travis in his future career. Then it was off back to Chalonne and a great party in the old house with friends and family in attendance, which included the couple's friend, the Padre from Foy, and in sufferance, Padre Lefèvre. Travis didn't mind, he was too happy.

A special mess dinner in the camp followed this, and then it was down to planning for the wedding. The ceremony took place on a beautiful, hazy, lazy summer's day. Both the village and the camp had been buzzing all week, getting ready for the social event of the year. Bunting in French national colours was hung across the main street of the village. There was great excitement in the air. All was now ready for a weekend of ceremony, pomp, singing and dancing, with good company, food and wine.

Approaching midday, the camp hustle and bustle had started to settle down. The parade and inspection of the guard of honour and dispatch rider escorts was over and the motorcyclists were on their way to Chalonne to escort the bridal party to the camp. The honour guard, in dress uniform, was posted to form an avenue of blue, red, and gold from the main gate to the garrison chapel door.

After a stiff cognac, Travis, accompanied by Hamish, Gerrard, his room-mate from officer training, Nanak and Alexchenko from the Legion, along with his boyhood friend John James, left the officers' mess for the garrison church. The three Legionnaires were in full dress uniforms, which Travis felt outshone his Regular Army dress uniform. As it was a military wedding, Travis had asked Hamish to be his best man. Commissioned in the Legion a month before Travis, he looked magnificent and Travis was proud of his Scots friend. Nanak, who was now an Adjutant, and the big Russian had just been promoted to Corporal-Chef.

As they entered the church they were astounded at the vast array of flowers. The altar was covered in blooms and blossoms in the colours of the French tricolour. Each bench had a red, white and blue posy tied to it. They composed themselves and marched down the rich red carpet to take their places, Travis and Hamish in the right front row and Gerrard, Nanak with Alexchenko seated behind them to give support. The groom's side of the church was filled by the garrison officers, in ceremonial dress and carrying swords. Beside Gerrard and the two Legionnaires sat Travis, Aunt Betty Brennan and his Uncle Jimmy Dillon from Ireland, who were there to represent his Irish family, along with the Padre and the Mayor of Foy. The left-hand side of the church was filling up with family and guests of the Leclercs, along with many high-ranking government ministers, military men and old Maquis friends of Anton.

Back at Château de Leclerc, Chantelle as bridesmaid was putting the last touches to Antoinette's wedding dress. Down in the foyer, a tiny pageboy dressed in a miniature army dress uniform and armed with a toy sword was teasing the small flower girl he was to escort. Madame looked very *chiche* in a cream two-piece suit and a wide-brimmed white hat with red and blue ribbons falling down to her neck. Both Anton and Raymond were again in full dress uniform.

With a roar of engines, the motorcycle escort arrived outside the house, frightening the two handsome white horses with their plaited mane full of little tricolour bows, harnessed to a shiny black landau, which looked as if it had been made out of shiny patent leather. Bang on time Antoinette, looking radiant, swept down the main staircase into the hall, reducing her mother to tears of pride and joy. Anton and Raymond were fighting with their emotions at the sight of the beautiful young bride. She emerged from the house on her father's arm, to the cheers of half the village. Then into the landau and away at a steady trot towards the camp, escorted by twelve army outriders.

The escort was followed by a convoy of vehicles of all kinds with Madame, Raymond, Chantelle and the two little children, pageboy and flower girl, the bride's cousins from Rouen. Arriving at the camp, the landau swept through the main gates, where the dispatch riders stopped. Thy passed a full turnout of the Guard, who presented arms, and on through the lines of soldiers of the guard of honour, who presented arms in twos as the landau approached them. A brief stop outside the church for photographs, and then down the aisle to the bridal march and a fanfare of trumpets from the corps of drums.

Travis was bowled over by his bride's beauty. She floated towards him in shimmering white that gave her a halo effect. Her jet-black hair was piled up on to her crown and topped off with a veil and tiara. The centuries-old traditional mass, with its smell of incense, candle grease and tinkling bells, went by all too quickly for Travis. Their vows were taken, each holding a lighted candle taken from a candle holder containing three lit candles. They exchanged rings, then, as they blew out their candles and only one lit candle remained, they became husband and wife.

The trumpets pealed out as Travis lifted Antoinette's veil. As he gazed into his new wife's serene face, her eyes shining and moist with tiny tears of happiness and love, he just couldn't believe how blessed and lucky he was, to be able to look forward to a lifetime of loving and sharing his life with this, his own special angel. Taking her in his arms, he kissed her softly and sweetly to seal their marriage vows. Then it was into the vestry for the signing of the register. Out again to the altar, this time facing the congregation.

Travis was awestruck by the guests, who appeared to be from every corner of France and of French high society. He wondered what he was getting into. He looked towards his family and his uncle, an old Irish soldier, who just rolled his eyes to heaven, winked and grinned.

By this time, the garrison officers were formed up outside with swords drawn and points touching, forming an arch through which the young officer and new wife walked, to great cheers and much throwing of confetti. Then on to the officers' mess for the formal wedding breakfast. The mess was unrecognisable with bunting, flowers, flags and dressed tables. Soldiers with dress trousers and white coats with regimental buttons and collar dogs, white shirts, white gloves and black bow ties were waiting to serve. It was a typical military operation, behind which Patrick could see the hand of the Adjutant.

Hamish did the honours in fine style, taking the mickey out of Travis in his speech and proposing to Antoinette, should she ever fall out with her husband. There was a nice speech from the Army Chaplain who conducted the service, commenting on the French and Irish Catholic family traditions. Then an emotional speech by Anton hardly left a dry eye in the place. He recalled his own love story and the trials and tribulations both he and Madame had suffered during WW2 to reach their happy ending, comparing it to the rocky road to love endured by the happy couple and its own happy ending.

Breakfast over, it was into the landau for Antoinette and Travis and through the honour guard again, this time waving their caps and cheering the couple. Travis was well liked by the men, and there was also a special lunch laid on for them with much wine, courtesy of Anton, as a thank you gesture, which the soldiers appreciated.

The outriders were waiting outside the camp gate and with much blowing of horns, a very much enlarged convoy rolled towards Chalonne. Up to the crossroads and a right turn up the main street of the village, past the church where they had first met and on to the Town Hall for the official civil ceremony, in which

Anton as the Mayor of Chalonne was the major player. The main street was crowded with villagers, and among them Travis could see the old men who had harangued him that first day in Chalonne. They were waving tricolours and cheering, showing toothless grins and tobacco-blackened teeth. Travis felt no animosity towards them. Why should he? Without them he would never have met his beautiful bride. There was a simple, short, ceremony in the main hall, followed by a massive buffet lunch, again with some of France's finest wines. A string quartet played classical music in the Town Hall. The local brass band played traditional French music and tunes in a large oblong marquee pitched on the lawn at the back of the building, which housed food-laden tables, jugs of wine and a medium-sized dance floor.

For the newly-weds, the afternoon and evening passed all too quickly, and it was soon time to go. They changed to light summer clothes in an annexe off the main hall and with lots of kisses and hugs they fought their way out to the old Citroen, which was decked out in ribbons and bows, with confetti everywhere. They jumped into the car, Travis took the wheel and with a roar of the vintage engine they started back down the main street.

Once again the cheers of the villagers lined the route, most of which was drowned out by an awful racket coming from the back of the car, where a collection of army mess tins, old boots and metal water bottles had been attached. Travis felt like a god with his goddess beside him, driving down beautiful country roads to link up with the Route National on their way down South to St Tropez.

They broke their journey in a lovely old château which was surrounded by a moat. Their bedroom was centuries old with a big double bed complete with canopy. There the new husband and wife made love as only honeymooners can.

St Tropez was everything Antoinette had said it would be, quaint and old-fashioned with a cosy harbour where they dined in the open-air bistros and watched expensive yachts come and go. There was a very trendy and chic side to Tropez, with France's latest screen beauty, Brigitte Bardot, leading the rich and fashion-conscious in wild parties and much frolicking on the now nudist beach of La Pampalone. The two sides of St Tropez only added to their excitement and pleasure, and again all too soon that time was over.

Half way through their journey back to Chalonne, they realised that they were truly starting the first day of the rest of their lives together, and it was a contented Antoinette who rested her head on her new husband's shoulder and dozed through the heat of the afternoon until they reached home. As for Travis, he believed that by marrying Antoinette he had found the loving family he had always longed for.

The newly-weds soon settled into garrison and village life as a married couple. Travis had been appointed to the post of Training Officer, which forced him to keep his nose to the grindstone in keeping up with his workload and the training needs of the regiment. He enjoyed his new role and rose to the challenge.

It wasn't all work and no play, as along with Antoinette, he became involved in the village life of Chalonne, both civic and social. Anton had always encouraged his wife and children to take an active part in village life, and he now steered Travis in the same direction. It was no hardship to him, as anything he did which involved Antoinette was a big bonus, and they were almost inseparable. In order to spend more time with her husband Antoinette even tried her hand at being a rugby football supporter, as Raymond had by now introduced her new husband to the game. In the end she backed out, leaving the Saturday afternoons to the men. The rowdy drinking sessions after the games may have had something to do with her decision, but she also noticed the strong bond and deep affection growing between her beloved brother and her husband and wanted to encourage it. Raymond looked on Travis as the big brother he had never had. It seemed strange, as Travis was of medium height, and Raymond towered over him. They were both about the same age, but Raymond deferred to his brother-in-law's tough upbringing and background. As he was often fond of saying to his friends and fellow villagers over his umpteenth cognac, 'You don't mess with the likes of my brother-in-law.'

Travis, for his part, looked up to Raymond, who had a smart business head. You couldn't help but like Raymond; he was so open, honest and outgoing. He was very sober-suited and businesslike during the week, as befitted a successful factory manager, then boisterous, happy and even a little reckless during the weekend, as he abandoned his yoke of respectability to take on the role of ardent football supporter. He was well liked by his contemporaries in the village and worshipped by the entire unmarried female population of Chalonne, which included Chantelle. But much to their chagrin, Raymond seemed not to notice. Except for his hard and diligent work in the factory, he could be something of a good-time Charlie.

Antoinette, always well involved in village life, now spread her wings and her energies to include the officers' wives group. Here she got involved in looking after the interests of the young wives and children of the garrison soldiers. The group worked closely with the camp welfare officer, who passed on various cases of social concern for them to look into and act on.

Sunday was a day for the family. The family had taken to riding out every Sunday afternoon, weather permitting. They would take a packed lunch and dismount in some peaceful valley to eat and take in the beauty of rural France, letting the cares of the week wash away as the horses munched the lush grass in the background.

Travis had never known such happiness, and in the dark, deep recesses of his mind, he worried that it might not last. He was waiting, as it were, for the boot to fall. But despite his foreboding, life carried on. The only blot on the copybook of their happiness was the fact that Antoinette seemed unable to conceive the child she so longed for.

Their first Christmas was magical, and the Leclerc house looking like a scene from an old-fashioned Christmas card. It was a wonderful Christmas, except for Antoinette breaking down in floods of tears when lighting a candle in the little church in Foy, after Midnight Mass and beseeching the Virgin Mary to bless her with a child in the New Year.

When the New Year came it was as full and exciting in love and happiness as the previous year had been. The couple were inseparable, except for Travis' army exercise away from home and his weekends as duty officer. Worst of all were the two fourteen-day camps, one near Easter and the other in the height of summer 'somewhere in France.'

Before Travis knew it, he was into his second Christmas as a married man. The Leclerc family had just returned from Midnight Mass in the village and were well settled down in the large and comfortable parlour, with its twinkling Christmas tree and decorations and tucking into rich Christmas cake and sipping glasses of hot mulled red wine. Soon it was time for the giving and opening of the presents. There was much crackling of festive wrapping paper, excited exclamations, quick kisses and hugs of thanks and the usual atmosphere of this type of celebration.

Halfway through this rumpus, Antoinette whispered in Travis' ear, 'I have a very special present for you this Christmas darling, upstairs in our room'. She was always buying him little surprise presents and he worried that he had nothing extra to give her in return. For a split second, his soldier's mind wondered if she wanted to make love to him, a feeling which he dismissed as quickly as it came, although he was not quick enough to stop his bodily reaction at the fleeting thought.

They slipped quietly out of the big room, and hand in hand they mounted the stairs, Antoinette leading him into their bedroom. Still holding his hand, she lay down on their big double bed. She looked so beautiful she reminded him of the Sleeping Beauty after the handsome Prince had kissed her awake. He was puzzled by her actions and his soldier mind clicked in again momentarily, but before he could expand on his imagination, Antoinette placed his hand palm down on her stomach and with eyes now full of tears of happiness and love said, 'Your special Christmas present is in here.' Stunned, Travis could only blurt out odd words: 'You're pregnant, A baby? You, we, are going to have a baby. When? Are you OK? Shouldn't you be in bed, or something?'

The torrent was cut short by his wife pulling his head down to her and giving him a long, lingering kiss. This had to be the best present of his life, thought Travis, as he lay beside his young wife with his head on her stomach and her fingers running through his close-cropped hair.

They were interrupted by a shout from Raymond downstairs. 'What are you two up to? Come down and join the party!' This brought them out of their reverie, and they climbed off the bed and walked slowly down stairs.

As they entered the room, Travis had his arm protectively around Antoinette's waist. The family knew in an instant that something wonderful had happened as they looked at the glowing young couple. Travis, as the husband, had the honour of announcing the pregnancy.

'Mama, Papa, brother Raymond, Antoinette and I have

something special to tell you. We are going to have a baby. Well, that is, Antoinette is.'

The room erupted at the news, with everyone hugging and kissing, many tears and much excited chatter. What a New Year it's going to be, thought Travis happily.

With Christmas and the New Year celebrations behind them, Travis and Antoinette settled down again to military and civilian life. While Antoinette appeared to handle her pregnancy well, she did seem to suffer from frequent headaches. As the days and weeks turned into months, Travis grew to be quite concerned by their increasing severity. Finally, after a particularly severe bout, he called in Dr Bonet, the family doctor, who diagnosed migraine and started treatment. However, the treatment didn't appear to have much effect on the frequency and extent of the attacks.

One evening, when Antoinette had gone to bed early nursing another attack, Chantelle paid a visit. When she had spent some time with Antoinette, she asked to see Travis alone. He steered her into to the study, where they could talk in private.

'I'm getting very worried about Antoinette, Patrice' began Chantelle.

'So are we all,' he replied.

'Please read this note she sent me about a council meeting,' Chantelle said, passing the note to Travis. He was quite shocked on reading it, or trying to, as it was all gobbledegook. The content started with a capital letter, and then continued with no more capitals, sentences or paragraphs, the words just running into each other. His wife seemed to have been writing nonsense.

Travis, now deeply worried, told Chantelle, 'Rest assured Chantelle, I will move heaven and earth to get to the bottom of this situation. Thank you for your love and concern for Antoinette, let me see you out and thanks again for bringing it to my attention.'

With that he escorted her down to the main gate and wished her *bonne nuit*.

Travis went immediately to speak to Raymond, who was relaxing in the lounge over a glass of brandy. 'Raymond, please read this note that Chantelle has just given me, it was written by Antoinette, what do you think?' he asked. Having read the note Raymond stood up and said, 'Follow me Patrice.' He led the way back into the study, where a further shock awaited Travis when Raymond produced the chemical company's account books. 'Take at look, Patrice' he said. Travis studied the books. They looked as if they had been scrawled upon by a young child trying to write for the first time.

'Why didn't you tell me about this?' Travis said, with annoyance in his voice.

'I have only just discovered it and wanted to show it to my sister first, to give her a chance to explain, and I didn't want to alarm you, or our parents at this stage.'

'That's it' said Travis. 'We must get a second opinion. What on earth is Dr Bonet thinking about?'

'Don't blame the old doc, Patrice' urged Raymond. 'He's a good man and he keeps up with new advances in medical science as they are published.'

'Well I still want a second opinion, just as soon as possible,' demanded Travis, in a determined voice. 'I want a head to toe examination with x-rays, the lot, like yesterday.'

After breaking the news to a shocked Anton and Madame, they all agreed to contact Dr Bonet the next day. So it was arranged. The family doctor promised to lay on a full examination and obtain a second opinion at the town's General Hospital. Much to Travis' chagrin, the hospital visit was set for the middle of his first week away with the Army, on the pre-Easter training camp, which was to take place about 200 kilometres from Chalonne. He approached his Commanding Officer to see if he could get compassionate leave, but as Training Officer, he was responsible for the smooth running of the exercise, and there was no chance that he could miss the camp.

Antoinette scolded him over trying to get time off to be with her and reminded him that now she was an Army wife, and had to make sacrifices like the rest of the married troops.

She was her usual bright, healthy self on that last Thursday night before he had to report to camp on the following day. The lovers booked a table in their favourite bistro, in Foy. They sat at their usual table next to the open fire, in the quaint dining room with its stained oak-panelled walls and brass bric-a-brac. They dined well and sipped their wines as they gazed lovingly into each other's eyes. Travis held her hand and kissed it from time to time throughout the meal. They fed each other with tasty morsels as lovers do, and talked dreamily of the baby. They decided that if they had a boy they would call him Anton after his grandpa, and if it were a girl it would be Antoinette.

That night, their lovemaking was without peer. They spent the dark hours awash in a sea of loving tranquillity, with peaks of intense passion and abandon. The dawn light found them still half awake in each other's arms. 'Such a night should be pencilled into Army Rules and Regulations as a must for all married soldiers on pre-deployment' commented Travis, as he struggled to free himself from Antoinette's embrace.

Later she drove him to the camp gates, where they held each other fiercely before tearing away. Then, with a mock salute from Travis and the wave of a tiny embroidered hanky from Antoinette, they parted. His last sight of her was her muffled figure in her Eskimo parka as she gunned the open-topped old Citroen back to Chalonne.

He was five days into the military exercise and based in a small camouflaged command post at the edge of a large wood when his radio operator handed him a message from the regimental Command Post, signed Sunray, Call Sign 'O'. It was from the Commanding Officer. 'Report to H.Q. Immediately,' was all it said.

Travis jumped into a scout car and raced to the command bunker. He rushed inside to be confronted by a grave-faced Colonel De'ath.

'It's Antoinette, Patrice,' said the CO, wasting not a second. 'She is desperately ill in hospital and your family have sent for you.'

An icy hand clutched at Travis' heart. He stopped breathing, and for a few moments he couldn't bring himself to say anything. The Colonel spoke kindly. 'Don't try to speak Travis, there's a chopper out on the helipad ready to take you to the General Hospital where your wife has been admitted' he said. 'Now go and God speed. Give Antoinette all our love.'

Travis didn't need to be told twice. Still in combats with a face full of camouflage paint and a pistol at his hip, he turned and sprinted out of the command post and threw himself into the helicopter, shouting, 'Go, go!' to the young pilot officer.

The journey to the hospital was taken with the engine on full revs and the aircraft at maximum speed, which was much too slow for Travis, who kept urging the pilot on with every second breath. They soon flew over the Garrison Camp and then Chalonne before starting their descent to the special emergency helicopter pad in the grounds of the General Hospital. Travis, well trained in helicopter assault tactics, hit the ground running as the machine dropped into the hover position. He rushed to the hospital doors, pushing at them and trying to hurry up the automatic system. Hospital visitors and staff looked on startled as this armed wild man ran down the corridor to the reception area.

'Madame Antoinette Travis?' he shouted before he reached the desk.

'Room 12A' was the instant reply. Antoinette was well known to the staff from her work at the chemical factory. Again, his Para boots pounding on the polished hospital floor, he sprinted all the way to Room 12A. There he stopped short, almost afraid to go in. Then, pushing the door slowly open, he walked into the room.

The group of people surrounding the bed looked around as he entered. At the foot of the bed were Anton and Raymond, and next to them Chantelle. Sitting beside the patient and holding her hand was her distraught mother. On the other side Padre Plessy from Foy was in the act of giving the patient the Last Rites of Mother Church.

The woman in the bed was Antoinette, yet surely it could not be his Antoinette. She had a turban of bandages around her head and wires coming from every part of her body, as well as a tube up her nostrils and an oxygen mask on her face. She was lying upright, naked but for a white sheet up to and covering her breasts. Her skin appeared to be translucent; he could almost see the light through it. Her face, what he could see of it, was like that of a china doll. *No, this is not my Antoinette*, thought Travis. *There is some ghastly mistake. Why don't the family do something about it? Tell someone that there is a dreadful mistake. Antoinette must be in another room. But what are the family doing here? Maybe there was a car crash, and this was one of the victims. It's not Antoinette!*

His mind raced, full of jumbled thoughts as he walked trance-like up to the side of the bed. His mother-in-law stood up and moved aside so Travis could be near. No words were spoken. He sat down and looked at the tiny, exquisite hand, with his engagement and wedding rings still in place. My God, it was Antoinette. The shock blew his mind and his world away.

He pressed her hand to his lips, and the flood waters of grief broke inside him. When finally his racking sobs started to subside, Raymond helped him from the chair, forcing him to let go of his unconscious wife's hand. He helped his stricken brother-in-law out of the room and seated him in a chair in the corridor. Sitting down beside him, he filled Travis in on the sequence of events.

'We all woke up in the early hours of the morning to screams coming from your bedroom' Raymond informed him. 'Papa and I raced in and found Antoinette writhing in agony in the bed, clutching her head. We got her to hospital in record time, and they found she had a massive brain tumour, it's terminal, there is no hope.' Each word was like a crucifixion nail in Travis' soul. 'They operated on her, to relieve the pressure' continued Raymond, 'but she lapsed into a coma and has been like this since the operation this morning. You have got to be strong Patrice, we have got to be strong. Mama and Papa are getting old now and are not able to cope as they used to. We have to be strong for them. After all, this is their beloved daughter, my beloved sister. Stay here Patrice and I will get you a hot drink and try to pull yourself together.'

How in the name of God was he ever going to pull himself together, he thought. His felt as if his life were over. Without his precious Antoinette, he could not go on.

Raymond came back with coffee and poured in a liberal amount of cognac from a hip flask.

'The baby?' was Travis' next question.

'It's too early in the pregnancy,' Raymond reported. 'When it's Antoinette's time, the baby will follow. They will be together for ever in heaven, try to think of it that way.' But right then, Travis just didn't have the faith. *Jesus, Mary and Joseph is this never going to end, is there no good news, is there nothing to hang on to?* He started to go into shock and Raymond summoned the medical staff to tend to him. Blackness engulfed him.

When Travis came round, he found himself in a small side ward lying on a hospital bed, fully clothed, with Raymond sitting patiently beside him.

'How long have I been out?' Travis asked.

'About a half an hour,' replied Raymond. 'The staff have given you a sedative, and they have said that you can stay here as long as you like, or until you feel up to dealing with things.'

Travis swung his legs over the bedside. 'I must get back to Antoinette, she needs me now,' he said. With that, he made his way to Room 12A with Raymond trailing in his wake. He hugged his in-laws and thanked Padre Plessy for his efforts and service. Then he sat down beside Antoinette once again, taking her hand in his.

There he stayed for the most part of the long days and nights to come. He prayed for and to her. He spoke to her as if things were normal between them. He talked about their life together, when their baby was born and their new life as a family. He slept and wept, still holding her hand, willing her to live, to fight this terror that had befallen her. He asked God and all the saints for a miracle.

It was early on Sunday morning when he suddenly felt her squeezing his hand. He had been dozing. He looked up to see his beautiful wife smiling serenely down at him.

'Hello my darling, aren't you supposed to be away playing soldiers? What are you doing here?' They were the first words she had spoken in days.

'You were very ill, sweetheart,' he replied, 'so they gave me special leave to be with you.'

'I'm sorry to spoil your fun, I know how you enjoy your war games,' said Antoinette.

It was an extraordinary recovery. She started to grow stronger, her good humour returned and she began to eat and drink. Travis was ecstatic. It seemed she had turned the corner and was going to pull through. Through the Sunday and into the Monday they talked and laughed and planned for the future. The family came and went in turn, uplifted by her recovery from the coma.

She was still seriously ill and tired easily, and between whispered discussions with Travis, there were long periods when she had to sleep and renew her energy.

Hope ended in the small hours of the following Tuesday morning. With Travis by her side, Antoinette was sleeping peacefully. He was holding her hand and admiring her peaceful beauty when he noticed a tiny trickle of bright red blood flow out of her left ear and begin to stain the white of the hospital pillow. Before he could react, the trickle became a flood, now running out of her nose in two streams, over her lips and down her chin and scattering in crazy patterns across her semi-naked breasts. Travis hit the panic button and ran screaming for help into the corridor. The medical crash team arrived on the run with the crash trolley and Travis was restrained from going back into the room.

There were no windows to the corridor, so he had no idea how things were going, but he could hear the sound of the electrodes as they tried to shock Antoinette's heart back to life. He could see in his mind's eye her rigid body and her arched back as the current tore through her.

Finally, all was quiet. The medical team, pushing the crash trolley in front of them, emerged from the room, their heads down. They did not look at Travis. The last member out was the medical team leader.

'She didn't suffer,' he said softly. 'She was gone before we arrived on the scene. I'm so very, very sorry.'

Travis couldn't speak. He was numb with shock, though this time, mercifully, the shock would help him cope.

From then on it was all a blur. After they had washed and cleaned Antoinette up, he was allowed to go back in and be with her. That afternoon they brought her home to Château Leclerc. They laid her out on the big bed in their bedroom, dressed in her white wedding gown. In the Irish tradition, Travis had six large, black candles in holders placed down each side of the bed. Antoinette had her hands clasped together, her rosary beads entwined in her fingers. Her body was rigid, and her skin had taken on a waxy tone. Her eyelids were partly open, and the beautiful, liquid brown eyes looked alive. She had a lovely, serene smile. Once more she looked like Sleeping Beauty, but this time there would be no awakening.

Relatives came and went, followed by all the chemical company staff and the villagers of Chalonne. Everyone spoke to or touched Travis, but he never heard or felt a thing. An old Irish priest had once told him, 'You never know death until it comes to your door.' Well, now he knew all right. What he knew was that nothing could ever be the same again. There would always be an empty place in his heart. He had seen death in three armies and learned to handle it, but this was personal and utterly desolate. Gone was the woman he loved, the person, the body, the hands and face he had known so well, but for such a short time. He was bitterly lonely. He wished he could have died, instead of her and the baby.

As Travis, with his Irish upbringing, believed it took some time for the soul to leave the body of a dead person, he made sure to be with her, without respite, until the funeral. He was still insulated by shock from the deathly and soulless ritual. The Army was protective and helpful. They laid on an honour guard for Antoinette, with the Corps of Drums beating out the slow march as the hearse with its skittish black horses headed slowly to the small cemetery on the outskirts of Chalonne.

In the dark recesses of his mind, Travis screamed out in horror as they lowered his beloved Antoinette into her grave. Outwardly, his body was rigid and his face set like granite.

When the Padre had finished the prayers, Travis stepped forward, holding a blood-red rose with a little bud shooting out of the long stem. He dropped it onto the coffin, along with a prayer of his undying love for his wife and unborn child.

In the two weeks following Antoinette's interment, Travis, now on compassionate leave from the Army, visited all the favourite places where he and Antoinette had been most happy. He was trying to hold on to his beloved wife; he could not let her go. But he found nothing but utter loneliness in the places he visited, and continued to retreat more and more into a protective shell. His whole demeanour was that of a zombie as he wandered through the village and the area like a ghost.

The locals were particularly supportive and would never pass by without commiserating with him. All they got for their trouble was a blank stare and some mumbled, incoherent words before Travis shuffled on, head down. It was heart-breaking to see.

Eventually his compassionate leave was up and with no tears left, he reported back to camp for duty. Back at work, he operated on remote control. There was no feeling in him. Yes, no, or a grunt were his only replies to any questions from the troops. He was spoken to numerous times by senior ranks, including the Colonel, and ordered to get a grip on himself, all to no avail.

In due course, his turn came up for Duty Officer. It was a weekend duty, and he was responsible for camp security and in charge of the camp guard.

In the small hours of the morning he visited the guardroom to check on the Guard; all was well. The sentries were out on patrol, while the remainder of the guard were trying to get some sleep in the empty cells. The Corporal of the Guard was asleep in his sleeping bag on a roll mat in the small kitchen area. The Sergeant of the Guard was at his desk writing up the Log.

As Travis entered the guardroom the Duty Sergeant leap to attention and made to call out the Guard. Travis said, 'As you were, Sergeant, no need to disturb the men.' They had a coffee together as Travis checked the log. Then Travis said, 'Why don't you go and get your head down, I'll cover for you. Things are quiet and I'm on top of everything.'

'Are you sure, sir?' was the reply.

'Yes of course Sergeant, off you go.'

The NCO hesitated, then with a shrug of his shoulders and a muttered 'Thank you sir,' he retired to the kitchen area where his sleeping bag was stashed.

Sitting at the desk with his head in his hands, Travis began to relive almost every scene from his life with Antoinette, steadily sinking deeper and deeper into depression and despair. He remembered their first meeting, and their first kiss in the old Citroen outside the camp gates. He remembered the happy time when she had brought lunch in a picnic hamper to the guardroom.

Almost without thinking, he removed his 9mm service pistol from its holster and started to strip and clean it. When he had finished, he reassembled it again and tested it, working the slide back and forth until he was sure it was operating smoothly. Then he picked up the loaded magazine and slipped it into the pistol. It made an audible click as it settled home into its housing. Then, without thought he cocked the weapon, sliding a round into the breech. Next, with another metallic click, he released the safety catch. The weapon was now ready to fire.

Slowly, still in dreamland, he raised the pistol to his head and pressed the cold muzzle into his right temple. In his mind's eye, he was jogging thorough the woods in the Leclerc estate; to his delight, he saw Antoinette walking up the path towards him. As their eyes met, she broke into a beautiful and loving smile and stopped, holding her arms out to him. He stopped jogging and walked slowly towards her, and as she whispered, 'Come to me Patrice', he took first pressure on the trigger of the pistol.

It was at that moment that the Corporal of the Guard woke to take his turn on duty and relieve his Guard Commander. Seeing his Sergeant lying beside him, he got up, puzzled, and went out to see who was looking after the shop. There was Travis sitting at the desk, his eyes closed, a strange smile on his lips, holding his pistol to his head.

The Corporal threw himself at the officer, wrestling the weapon from his hand. The pistol fired twice in the struggle, and the entire Guard stood to, tumbling out of the cells, weapons in hand. In a matter of minutes, the crisis was over, and the post doctor was called. Travis was removed to the camp dispensary and sedated. The camp settled down once more.

Next day, there was a full examination for Travis by the base medical team, followed by a visit by the Colonel, along with Anton and Raymond, as concerned family. The senior physician told them, 'We have made extensive tests, and there is no doubt that Lieutenant Travis has had a complete mental breakdown.'

'Please do your very best for my son,' pleaded Anton. The doctor assured him that everything possible would be done to return Travis to good mental health again. He was then sent, under escort, to the General Hospital, to be seen by a psychologist for screening. This was followed by a move to a special clinic, where he was to spend a few months undergoing treatment for severe depression.

It was some months later when Travis went before an Army medical board, where, with much string pulling from Anton, he was declared fit to return to duty. He resumed his military career, doing just enough to get by. His heart was no longer in it, or in anything else.

There was only one option for the future; to resign his commission from the Army and leave France, to get as far away as possible from the memories of his dead wife and unborn child and try to put his life together again. The Leclercs tried to talk him out of his decision, to no avail.

'Where on earth will you go, Patrice?' pleaded Madame. 'We love you so much, we are sure we can help you to recover and get back into life.'

'Thank you Mama,' was Travis' reply, 'but this is something I have to do alone. I will never forget you, you are my true family, and I love you. This will always be my home and I will always return.'

In the end, he decided to go back to Ireland to try and sort himself out. So it was that on a bright summer's morning, Travis bade farewell to his French family. Taking the train to Calais, he caught the boat to Dover and the boat train to Victoria Station in London, retracing the steps he had taken a lifetime ago, as it seemed now. It had been well over five years since he had left England for France and so much had happened during that time. He firmly believed that going back to his roots would give him the chance of a fresh start in life.

CHAPTER NINE

IRELAND

Travis caught the Tube to Euston Station and a boat train to Holyhead and shipped out to Dublin on the night ferry. He arrived in Dun Laoghaire in the early morning and another train ride brought him to the city centre, where he booked into a modest hotel. He had no inclination, or saw no reason, to contact his father and stepmother. Instead, he started to look up old friends and acquaint himself, once again, with his home town.

It was pushing midday as he strolled down O'Connell Street, the main street. He was just coming up to the General Post Office and his mind was flitting back to his first date with Melissa, outside Cleary's stores opposite the GPO, and the happy times when they queued for the Capitol Theatre and had supper in the Green Lounge after the show. The restaurant had long since gone and he wondered if the Rainbow Rooms, another old haunt, was still there.

A second later, he spied what he took to be Melissa herself, walking slowly towards him. He shook his head and then pinched himself. This couldn't be, he thought, she now lives in Canada. His doubts were swept away by a startled, 'Hello Patrick, is it really you?' from the girl.

'Hello Melissa' he said lamely. 'Are you home on holiday from Canada?'

'No,' replied Melissa, 'We never went.'

It was all too much for Travis, and he just stood and stared at his erstwhile fiancée. She brought him out of his trance by saying, 'Would you like to buy me a coffee, and we can tell each other all our news?' Not waiting for a reply, she linked her arm in his and guided him to one of the many espresso type coffee houses now springing up in the city centre. Over their drinks, Melissa told him, 'We were unable to get the Assisted Passage Scheme offered by the Canadian Government. The reason was my dad failed the medical. They found a spot on one of his lungs.'

Travis was dumbfounded to find that she had been here in Dublin all along. She had been unable to trace him, as he had never contacted any of his friends in Dublin while he was in the Legion. In turn, he told her about the Legion, the French Army and Antoinette. As he told her of his tragedy, her hand reached across the table to close on his, and she whispered her sympathy in a kindly and loving way. This was not lost on Travis, and he was grateful for her kind gesture and words, but then she had always been a kind person.

They talked for some time. Finally she asked, 'What are your plans now, Patrick?'

'I have no plans as yet, that's why I've come home. I'm going to go down to the country, to Kildare, to my mother's family and try to sort myself out in the peace and quiet of the countryside,' he replied.

'When are you leaving?'

'Not for a day or two.'

'Maybe we can get together again before you go,' suggested Melissa, more in hope than anything else. 'We've had a phone installed since you were last home. Here's my number, I'd love to meet with you again before you leave the city.'

Travis took the slip of paper and stood up to go. Melissa offered her hand to him, and he took it hesitantly. Then she leaned forward and kissed him lightly on the cheek. He did not feel repulsed by her kiss, or as if he was betraying Antoinette. In fact, it felt warm and good. It brought more memories of the good old times in Dublin which seemed so long ago.

They walked out into the bright sunshine together and went their separate ways. By the tenth day after his arrival in the Irish capital, Travis had made the rounds of his friends and reacquainted himself with the city. He spent some time with his childhood friend John and in his company visited all the places that had been so important to them during their growing-up, including Travis' former home, which he did not choose to enter. He still had no wish to make contact with his father and stepmother.

The friends also visited their former school and college. The whole area seemed much smaller than he remembered. His tour brought back the half-remembered lines from an old song: *Lonely I wander through scenes of my childhood, it calls back to memory those happy days of yore, gone are the young folk the town stands deserted, no more to their homes will those children return. Why stand I here now like a ghost and a shadow. It's time I was moving. It's time I passed on,* or words to that effect. It was indeed, time he moved on, in so many, many ways.

He phoned Melissa from a local call box and arranged to meet her at Clearys, their old meeting place and a favourite haunt for Dubliners. She was on time, and they decided to go to a show before eating. After the show, they had a late supper and talked until the restaurant was due to close. He drove her in his hire car to her home in Booterstown on the outskirts of Dublin. They sat in the car talking for some time until Melissa broke the spell by saying, 'I've got to go Patrick, it's a working day for me tomorrow, will I see you again?'

'I'm off to the country to my mother's people tomorrow', Travis replied. 'I have no plans, other than to drop out for a while for a bit of rest and recuperation. I'll give you a bell next time I'm in the city.'

Melissa stood up and Travis offered his hand. She squeezed it and reached forward to kiss him full on the lips, but instinctively he moved his head back. Melissa hesitated, then kissed him on the cheek, and with that she was gone.

The next day he arrived at his mother's family home, which lay between Kildare town and The Curragh Army Camp. He was welcomed like a long-lost soul, and plans were made for a welcome home party, to be attended by his long-tailed Irish family. He really wasn't in the mood for a party, but they were so generous and loving towards him that he couldn't upset their plans.

The whole family attended the 'hooley' and the 'craic' was great. He was glad he had been pushed into it. After a few glasses of poteen, the illicit and lethal brew made by the Irish from potatoes, he couldn't have cared less.

In the weeks that followed, he got into a routine of jogging in the early morning, followed by deep meditation, walks in the countryside and reading. One day, his walk took him to the army camp and he decided to take a short cut through it. As he was about to enter it from the eastern end, a platoon of young recruits in full battledress and steel helmets passed him in double time carrying their weapons. They were near to exhaustion, eyes bulging, lathered in sweat, breath rasping in their throats. As usual a scattered group of tail-end Charlies struggled behind, spurred on by NCOs shouting hell and damnation on them if they didn't catch up. Travis smiled grimly, remembering the British and French recruit training. This lot didn't know they were born.

He walked on down the military road towards the centre of the camp, passing the Recruit Training Depot and barracks. The main square was full of drill squads, some doing foot drill, others rifle drill. The scene was a mild re-enactment of the platoon which had passed him further back. Drill sergeants and corporals were screaming abuse at the poor squaddies and again he could see the pain and the strain on the young faces. Maybe this was just what he needed - the pain of recruit training, or as the British Paras called it 'a good beasting'. He could feel and smell the army again, and now he knew what he wanted; it was what he had always wanted, army life. Starting at the bottom again would be a cleansing for him, both in mind and in his body.

In the end, he decided he would try to join the American Airborne Forces. He travelled back to Dublin and visited the American Embassy in Ballsbridge, where he made enquiries about recruitment. While he was in the city, he opened a bank account with an Irish subsidiary of an American bank. When he had married Antoinette, she had had a sizeable sum of money in her name, from her directorship in her father's chemical company. During their marriage they had added to her savings, planning to buy their own home one day. Travis had offered the money back to the Leclercs, but they wouldn't hear of it, advising him that wherever he went, he would need liquid assets as backup. This had left him a very well-off young man.

He now decided to leave a third of his money in the chemical company's bank in France, transferring two thirds to the Irish Bank. He then drew out some travel money and started planning a move to the USA. Using his Irish passport, he obtained the necessary papers to allow him to gain entry into the United States. He decided to fly, as the sooner he got started the better. Any more hanging around and he would lose the incentive and maybe drift off into a deep depression again.

He bid his mother's family goodbye and thanked them for

looking after him so well. Driving back to Dublin, he remembered the days as a little lad, his journeys to and from the country and the city on his own, with a label tied to his coat collar, with his address in the country and the name of the person waiting to meet him, usually his beloved grandfather. On one such trip, he had got off the bus in Newbridge to visit the toilet and the bus had driven off without him. He was only five years old, and he remembered how terrified he had been. Despite the terrors of war in two armies, nothing could equate to the fear he had felt that day, so many years ago.

He saw Melissa and told her his plans. She asked him to write to her, to let her know how he was getting on, and he promised to do so.

Next morning he parked the hire car for the last time at Dublin Airport and caught the morning flight to New York. As the plane roared down the runway and lifted off into the bright blue yonder, he wondered where this next phase of his life would lead him.

CHAPTER TEN

AMERICA

The flight to New York was long and tiring. Travis was seated next to a middle-aged woman on her first flight. She asked him if he had flown before.

'Yes,' he replied, 'many times, but I've only landed a couple of times.'

The lady looked at him, puzzled. 'How come?' she asked.

'I was a Paratrooper,' he replied, and they both laughed. 'My brother-in-law was an ex-wartime Para with the American Forces in Europe. While on R & R after the invasion of Normandy he met my older sister and they married when the war was over and settled down in America. This will be my first visit. I'm excited and scared at the same time.'

'I know how you feel, lady,' he said. So, this woman's brother-in-law was a Para. This could be a good omen. It was the lady's first visit to the couple and while she was friendly and pleasant, she must have been inoculated with a gramophone needle, as she appeared to have verbal diarrhoea. Travis, who could talk the hind leg off a donkey given half a chance, couldn't get a word in edgeways and gradually started to lock off. Since becoming a soldier, he found that he could almost go to sleep on a bed of nails, and could drop off in an instant. The lady was still droning on as he slipped into oblivion.

Dublin Airport looked like a bus stop in comparison to New York. He got lost just looking for the exit, but he found people to be very helpful and soon he was out on the main concourse, looking at the cab rank full of yellow taxis. Yellow taxis - shades of the movies he used to queue for at the children's matinees on Saturday in the local flea pit. This was more like it, the America he had grown up with. But he was surprised to note that the Latino driver of his taxi had next to no English in his vocabulary. When Travis threw his basic Spanish into the fray, the cabby reverted to machine-gun Spanish in reply, leaving Travis at a loss. Having said all that, the driver knew his New York and soon deposited Travis at his hotel in central downtown Manhattan.

He couldn't wait to get out and about. A five-minute stroll brought him to Times Square. Every morning after that found him jogging through Central Park, followed by meditation in a secluded corner of the world-famous park. He saw Greenwich Village and the Empire State Building, again shades of the threepenny rush at his local childhood cinema. He was able to imagine King Kong hanging off the lightning conductor on the top of the building, roaring his anger at the tiny biplanes attacking him. He was a small child again, feeling all the emotions, hiding under his overcoat so that the great ape wouldn't get him, following every move through a buttonhole. Going back in memory again had a healing effect on him and he slept that night for the first time in weeks.

The next and last day saw him take a trip out to Ellis Island, where he climbed to the top of the Statue of Liberty. Later he roamed through the large building where in the old days the immigrants, newcomers to the New World, were processed, and which was now a museum. He finished his sightseeing just before the last ferry was about to depart for the mainland. Before leaving the building, he sat in the great reception hall, where many thousands of people had been processed, moving forward in lines, waiting their turn, to see if they would be admitted to the United States.

The great hall was all but empty as he sat on a bench to catch his breath. As the hall became silent, feelings of great sorrow descended on and around him. It was almost tangible, and it brought a lump to his throat and tears to his eyes. The feelings had nothing to do with his own deep sadness, but appeared to emanate from the great emotions of sorrow felt by the poor people who had passed through this hall on their way to what they hoped would be a better life, but at the cost of leaving all they held dear behind them. As in Dublin, when he had toured his own childhood home, the last verse of the old song came back to him, *It's time I was moving, it's time I passed on.*

Next morning found him at an Army recruiting office where, after much deliberating, he was informed that he would have to attend a Selective Service Board and if he passed that interview, his next port of call would be the Selective Service Office for his medical and to take the oath of allegiance. On the due date he checked out of his hotel and took a cab to the central bus station, where he relived another childhood dream by taking an overnight Greyhound bus, on the first leg towards his final destination. It was a hot, sticky summer's day, and the air conditioning in the centre was struggling to cope with the large intake of bodies, which made for a stressful day.

Finally, when every nook and cranny of his body had been inspected, prodded and poked and all his paperwork had been sorted out, Travis, along with his fellow volunteers and draftees, raised their right hands to swear to defend the Constitution of the

United States against all its enemies, both foreign and domestic, and to obey all orders of commissioned and non-commissioned officers appointed over him. Following this, they were shipped out to a recruit training camp, or boot camp as the Americans called it, where they would have to complete eight weeks of basic infantry training. Along with his fellow recruits he arrived at boot camp bright and early next morning, but completely shattered from the long overnight journey.

Their induction to their new home was accompanied by the screams and shouts of their appointed drill sergeant, who, with much pushing and shoving, formed the recruits into ragged ranks. That done, they were marched, or more like shambled, to the bedding store, then on to their barrack block. From there, they were hustled and bustled through the age-old routine of head shaving, uniform issue and being separated from their own clothing and all things civilian. The platoon he was assigned to started off with about sixty recruits, broken down into squads of twenty, with a drill sergeant in charge of each squad's training. As Travis' squad was again herded into some form of order, they looked a motley crew. Their squad Drill Sergeant was Kurt Bruhowser, a tough cookie of German extraction. He was over six feet tall, lean and mean, and to Travis' amusement he had a square head. When Travis was a young boy during World War Two, all Germans were called 'squareheads'. However Travis liked the cut of his jib and was further impressed by the Jump Master Para wings he wore over his left breast pocket.

The Sergeant sported a fair display of medal ribbons, but as yet, Travis had no idea what they referred to. Some could be 'I was there' medals or maybe, 'forgot to duck' wound medals. Because of his name and his tough, hard driving of the squad, the Drill Sergeant became known as The Brute. But it was when he spoke that he shook Travis, as he had a very thick German accent, on top of which his pronunciation of the words of command left all of the recruits looking at each other with raised eyebrows. They couldn't understand a single command uttered by the big non-com. 'Ten Hut' appeared to be 'Stand at Attention.' 'Hatch' appeared to mean march and right, left came out as Hi Het. However, as it turned out, all the other drill sergeants gave orders in many strange and varied ways. It reminded Travis of his first few days in the Legion, where he hadn't understood a word being spoken. He was to find out, later on, that the Brute had served with distinction in the Korean War, where he had been taken captive by the Communist Chinese and had had a very rough time as a prisoner-of-war.

Life became a whirl of perpetual motion, from morning to night, with jabs, paperwork, form filling, kit issue, kit cleaning and ironing sessions. Travis' joining orders stated that his combat boots must be highly shined but not spit polished. However, The Brute would have none of that, which resulted in tons of polish and buckets of spit being used by the Squad during the following nights to bring their boots up to scratch in the eyes of their Drill Sergeant.

It was during that first night's spit and polish session that Travis started to study his companions. By then, they had started to fall into protective groups. The black boys hung out together and spoke in a mixture of jive and street talk, which at times defied understanding, as it was supposed to do. Next came the French speakers from New Orleans and other French-speaking areas, along with two boys from Quebec in Canada. They seemed to struggle in understanding each other, as the French they spoke was a mixture of Old French and pidgin French. Travis, who by now was fluent in French, had a hard time following them.

The next big group were the Latinos, who spoke Spanish at 100 miles per hour. His Spanish was no match for theirs. That left four odd men out. One was a big Native American whom the Squad christened Chief, much to his annoyance. Then there was Travis, who was the oldest in the billet. The Squad were mostly teenagers, and Travis had at least five years on the eldest, so they called him Pop.

Last, but not least, were the Twins. They were massive Good Old Boys from the American South. The only problem was that they were not good, in fact, they were real nasty bastards and the rest of the Squad cottoned on to them pretty quickly and took to moving around them, as if walking on eggshells. On the second night of spit and polish, the Twins picked out two of the weediest kids in the billet and ordered them to work on their kit. The young guys never uttered a word of protest and got stuck into the extra kit. Flushed with success, the Twins started to enjoy their game and started picking a fresh couple to do their kit each night. Finally came the turn of the Chief, who was one big tough dude. He refused to knuckle under, so he was dragged into the latrine area by the Twins and given such a hiding that he ended up in the base medical centre.

Finally, it was Travis' turn. His bed space was opposite the Twins and when he came back early from the Mess Hall after dinner, he found all their kit on his bed. He promptly moved it back, all in one heap onto one of the Twins' beds, then lay down to wait.

The Twins also came back early from dinner, to see how Travis had reacted. They were furious and dragged him into the latrine. That was when he exploded. All his anger at Antoinette and the baby's deaths poured out, along with every attacking move and near death-dealing blow he had been taught by Nanak and other Legionnaires. He tore into the big boys, using their height and weight against them. It ended with both of them lying broken and unconscious on the floor, covered in their own blood.

Travis slipped unnoticed out of the back door of the billet, taking a change of uniform, boots and wash kit with him and dumping the leather gloves he had worn in the fight. He cleaned himself up and changed his kit in a central wash room, then rinsed and hid his soiled clothing for retrieval. He then went along to the Post Library and selected a book on military history. Taking his time, he strolled back to his billet to see the Twins carried out on stretchers to the Post Hospital and later, on to a General Hospital, as their injuries were so severe. A gaggle of Military Police were swarming all over the hut.

A cursory investigation was carried out, and all members of the squad questioned. Before a fuller inquiry, Travis had placed his bloodied uniform in the wash and spit polished his stained boots. In the end, it was concluded that the twins, for some strange reason or other, had fought each other almost to the death, and that was the end of the matter. Travis or the squad never heard of them again.

In a matter of days, the Chief returned to the group and settled back in. From then on the squad seemed to gel together and started working as a team. From the nods and winks of his companions, Travis accepted that they knew who was responsible for the exit of the Terrible Twins and friendships soon blossomed.

Sergeant Bruhowser's squad was now well into the Basic Training Course and learning to march with precision, with running, physical training in PT and tests every two weeks. There was weight-lifting in the Smoke Pit, a heavy sand-filled depression outside the barrack block which held a range of equipment to build upper body strength in the new recruits. Most of his companions needed to work on their upper body strength and, looking at the squad, Travis could see that a quarter of them would struggle when it came time to carry the weights an infantryman has to carry. He doubted if some of them would make it to graduation, let alone if any of them wanted to go for the Airborne. All of this training was conducted in around 100 to 120 degrees of heat and even learning to march produced sweat from every pore in the body. Some of the boys came from very poor backgrounds and suffered from lack of good food and in some cases hardly any food at all. There was no doubt that for some of them, it was going to be the longest and hardest eight weeks of their lives.

With the Twins out of the picture, Travis became unofficial squad leader. He pitched in to help at every opportunity in all aspects of training and he always had words of advice for the squad and in particular for the trainees who were struggling to master the physical, mental and in some cases, educational demands of a modern army. He was starting slowly to come out of his shell. His plan to let the physical and mental demands of Basic Training overcome his tortured mindset was starting to work.

He wrote to Melissa every week, outlining each phase of his training and how he was doing and letting her know about the other young men in his squad and life in the American Army. He settled for plain 'Dear Melissa' in his letters and, in her replies she addressed him as 'Dear Travis'. He also wrote to and telephoned the Leclercs in France once a month, without fail. When his first letter reached France, he had an impassioned letter back from Anton, begging him to return to Chalonne and offering him a directorship in the family business. This touched Travis deeply, but he wrote back turning down the generous offer, stating that, for his peace of mind, he needed to make his own way in the world.

The Chief was fast becoming attached to Travis. He was a fine figure of a man with the dark, chiselled features of the Native American, which at his age made him quite handsome and Travis wondered how the local females would react to him when he got leave. He was a well-educated high school graduate and very well read. He and Travis covered most subjects under the sun during the hours of spit and polish and weapon cleaning. Travis believed the Chief would make a top class non-commissioned officer, or even a commissioned officer if he put his mind to it. He was from the Sioux Nation and having an artistic bent, studied art and craft at college, with the emphasis on making jewellery, working with gold, silver, precious and semi-precious stones.

He set up an arts and crafts shop on his reservation, selling mainly to visiting tourists. During his holidays from college, he travelled the length and breadth of America and Canada, studying the craft work and jewellery making of the other Indian tribes and nations. He showed Travis some of his work, and Travis was amazed that the Chief, with hands as big a shovels, could do such delicate and intricate work. He looked more suited to athletics or football, where he could have been just as successful.

It appeared that he had built up a thriving business in a very short period of time. He employed a large number of Indian girls in the jewellery factory behind his shop and also had a small but regular export business on the go. His goal was to build a better life for his wife and child and his tribe. He told Travis that he hoped the business would continue, even if he didn't make it back home. He was, as far as Travis was concerned, a lovely bloke.

Doc, a fit-looking, good-natured African American recruit, had been so nicknamed because of his previous job as a nursing assistant in the casualty department of a general hospital, where his main job had been breaking up fighting drunks on weekend binges. He came from the Bronx in New York, where he had been a young tearaway, running with a gang and up to all sorts of mischief. He and his gang had running battles with the police on a regular basis. In a battle with a rival gang, the Doc's young brother had been knifed in the groin. The knife had cut through the kid's main artery.

Doc had had no idea how to treat him, and the young boy had bled to death in his big brother's arms. The boy's death had forced Doc to take a long hard look at his life and his lack of any qualifications or real education. He had decided there and then that he would become a nurse, and soon set out to achieve his goal. His starting place was as a nursing assistant in an accident and emergency hospital, hitting the books in his spare time to improve his education.

One evening Doc said to Travis, 'Hey Pop, how come you know all this Army stuff, have you been in the forces before?'

Travis had no intention of revealing his full military background; he would be in very serious trouble if he did so, as in order to start at the bottom he had only informed the recruiter of his service in the Irish and British Armies. He had made no mention of the Legion and the French Army, or his commission, on any of the forms he had filled in. He had covered the past five years by saying he had been doing farm work, giving the name and address of the family farm in the Irish Midlands. His cousins promised to cover for him, should the security services or police get in touch with them.

'Yes,' he told Doc, 'I served in the Irish Army.'

'Did you see any action?' asked Doc.

'No,' Travis replied, 'but I got top notch training from a very professional army. Since I left, they have fought with great distinction in the African Congo with the United Nations.'

This explanation seemed to satisfy Doc and the rest of the squad. From then on Doc started to hang around with Travis and the Chief and they soon became close friends. This tight-knit trio was soon to expand with the inclusion of Jean-Louis Clermont, a French Canadian from Quebec. Jean-Louis had served in an armoured unit in the Canadian Army. He was nicknamed 'Frenchi' by the squad. As they also called one of the other French recruits 'Frenchy' they changed the spelling. Frenchi enjoyed his nickname and always introduced himself by saying, 'Hi, I'm Frenchi with an 'i'. If the person he was talking to asked a silly question like: 'What's wrong with your eye?' Frenchi, who had nicked a glass eye from the medical centre, would place his hand over one eye and using his other hand, with much fumbling and grimacing, produce the glass eye from his pocket and drop it into the questioner's drink. This act always led to the victim of the prank losing his breakfast, lunch or dinner, plus a gut full of booze, down the nearest latrine.

The four friends soon became the backbone of the squad, becoming the engine room that propelled it onwards and upwards, to such an extent that they graduated in the number one spot, just ahead of a squad led by an ex-Canadian Army infantryman. Travis now became designated as a light weapons infantryman. It transpired that he and the ex-infantry soldier had tied for top recruit. However, they were taken aside by an officer who explained to them that because of their previous military training they were not eligible for honour recruit, as that would have to go to a recruit with no previous military training. But the officer assured them that it would be noted on their records. Travis was happy with that, as he remembered the same thing happening to him at the French Army Officer Training Academy.

Just prior to graduation, he signed on for the Airborne and was elated when Chief, Doc and Frenchi also signed on the dotted line. On graduation day they were given their orders for eight weeks' intensive Advanced Individual Training. This was to be followed by four weeks' Airborne or Jump School training. At all stages, the going was to get tougher and tougher, but Travis thanked his lucky stars that it wasn't on the same scale of brutality, harassment and extreme toughness he had had to endure in the Legion.

Finally, after much emphasis on weapons training and with Advanced Individual Training behind them, Travis and his mates moved on to Jump School, at Fort Benning outside Columbus, Georgia, Infantry Centre. There the new students were briefed on the course content and structure and advised that the aim was to develop a sense of leadership and self-confidence and an aggressive spirit through mental and tough physical conditioning.

The course didn't pull any punches in an effort to achieve its aims. The pain and abuse, which was designed to make a point, was not on a par with the out-and-out sadism of the Legion, so Travis was able to hack it, just. He was older and wiser now.

Week one was all ground work, which was conducted in parachute harness and the start of a continuing ball-breaking period. Week two was tower training, where the trainee was chucked out of a thirty-four foot tower, with harness of course. Then on to the 249-foot tower, where you were strapped into a parachute harness, hauled to the top of the tower and released in an already deployed parachute. Finally, week three was Jump Training, where at long last, he got to fly and jump out of an aircraft. All this was old hat to Travis, including his still-lingering fear of the door. Once he had exited the aircraft, he loved the flight and landing.

The fifth and final jump before graduation was just before lunch on the last day of the week and it brought family and friends and assorted girlfriends to the ceremony. After the final jump the new Paras went on parade with their trouser ends bloused into their Corcoran jump boots and were presented with the silver wings of a military parachutist. During the ceremony, Travis noticed a trio of Military Policemen giving him the hard stare and his mind raced over the possibilities for their interest. In the end, he decided they must have had information from France. Unfortunately, as it turned out, he was right.

With a shout from their Sergeant Instructor of 'Airborne!' and the reply of 'All the way!' the parade was over. The new Paras raced to meet their guests. As Travis, now re-designated Light Infantry Weapons (Airborne), started to walk slowly off the parade ground, he was intercepted by the police and handcuffed. His friends left their guests and rushed to his aid, to be told firmly by the MPs to 'butt out'. Travis ate lunch in a post cell, where he was held until the middle of the next week, when in mid-afternoon, he was marched before a Colonel in the Post Legal Section. The Colonel read the riot act to him regarding his sin of omission in leaving out his service with the French Army.

'Be informed that you are in very deep shit, soldier,' stated the Colonel. 'You have lied to the military authorities regarding your status and to the US Government. At worst you will spend a long time in a military stockade, and on your release, you will be served with a dishonourable discharge from the US Military and then handed over to Federal Marshals and officials from the emigration service. You may have to serve further time in a civilian prison. You will then be deported from the US with no chance of ever being allowed back again, not even on holiday. Do I make myself clear?'

'Yes sir' said Travis.

'Now, what in goddamn hell possessed you to do such a stupid thing? Not waiting for a reply, he went on, 'I have your jacket here with your full military record to date. You were a commissioned officer, for God's sake, and you are by no means stupid. Officers and gentlemen do not behave in this way. Have you anything to add to these proceedings before we go ahead with the case?'

Travis briefly explained his Legion career and his transfer and commissioning to the French Army, then related the harrowing story of his wife and unborn child. He ended by saying; 'Sir, I come from a long-tailed military family and my lifelong ambition has been to be a professional soldier, the very best I can be. I have trained with some of the best armies in the world and I have now chosen the greatest, the American Army, as my finishing school. My only wish is to spend the rest of my life in the service of your great country.' He noticed a flicker of the Colonel's eyes as he spoke. 'That's all I have to say in mitigation, sir' he finished.

'Lieutenant O'Brien', the Colonel called to a young officer in the far corner of the room who was sitting with an older man. 'In your professional opinion, is that what is called Irish blarney?'

O'Brien, his face softening into a half smile, replied, 'The best, sir, the very best.' Turning his attention back to the prisoner, the Colonel continued, 'Right, here's where it's at. I am assigning your case to Captain Ed Veeder and his assistant Lieutenant Dan O'Brien' he said, nodding towards the two officers sitting in the corner. 'You will be kept in the holding tank until this whole sorry mess is cleared up, one way or the other. These officers will be your only contact. Is that understood?'

'Yes, sir.' .

'Dismiss!' The two MPs flanking Travis about-turned with him and marched him out of the room and the building and back to his cell.

He found being locked up very hard to bear, mainly because it gave him too much time to think. He was locked up for most of the day, which as an outdoor person was a sentence in itself. The MP's treated him as a non-person. A dog in a home for strays would have had more humane treatment.

For the most part, the MPs were a dour lot. With a few exceptions the corps in any army he had served in attracted some people with the IQ of a doorknob, along with quite a few bullies and the odd sadist. In some ways, he was glad that they ignored him and left him alone.

After a couple of days of being locked up, he started to slide into depression again. He could feel the dark clouds starting to engulf him and once again stood on the edge of the bottomless pit of mental pain and blackness. The only thing that stopped him from losing his mind was his fitness regime and meditation. Any time he felt himself slipping he turned to meditation, thanking God he had met and made a friend of Nanak in the Legion.

Lieutenant O'Brien was his salvation. This young, bright Irish American, just fresh out of Yale University, was a godsend to the tormented soldier. O'Brien could trace his Irish family back to the Great Famine in Ireland, when in 1845 the potato crop, the staple diet of the Irish poor, was hit by a fungus disease, condemning thousands to starve to death. Survival for many meant leaving Ireland, with America being the chosen destination for the bulk of the immigrants. O'Brien's family had come a long way since then, and he was the proud product of their will to live and to progress. The young officer was a real tonic for Travis after the rough handling he had experienced from senior ranks since joining up.

In a full and frank interview, O'Brien delved into Travis' past, checking and double-checking every last detail of his story. In the meantime Travis, in the deepest of depression, had written two garbled letters, one to Melissa and the other to his brother-in-law Raymond in France, telling them of his plight, an action he later regretted. He thanked God that he had addressed his letter to Raymond and not his father-in-law, Anton, as he did not want to upset the elderly man.

After many weeks, his case came up for review. Once again he was taken, handcuffed and under escort, to face the army's legal system and learn his fate. As he was marched into the Colonel's office by his two-man MP escort, he noticed that both Captain Veeder and Lieutenant O'Brien were seated on either side of the senior officer's desk. They had their chairs turned towards the prisoner and escort. O'Brien gave him an encouraging smile, while Veeder looked expectant, the Colonel stern and non-committal.

The Colonel opened the proceedings by saying, 'Let me take you out of your misery straight away Trooper Travis, be advised that all potential charges against you have been dropped on the orders of the high command.'

Travis breathed a silent breath of relief and sent a mental prayer of thanks to the good God on high.

'Firstly, let me say that you owe a whole heap of gratitude to young Mr O'Brien here. He has put in hours of investigative work in an effort to defend you, and as it has turned out, to having your case dismissed. The telephones have been buzzing with his calls to all manner of people and ranks, both here in the USA and abroad in the UK and France. It appears that you have some very powerful friends in high places. I'm not sure I am happy with this type of diplomatic input, it's no way to run an army. On top of which, recommendations have been put forward as to your future status. Again, I am unhappy with what I believe is outside interference in army affairs.

'The recommendations are as follows. That Trooper Travis P. be released from custody, returned to duty, with all the rights and privileges of an enlisted soldier restored. It is further recommended that, subject to exemplary behaviour, this soldier be recommended for officer training school.'

At this Travis started to open his mouth in protest, but the Colonel cut him short with a curt 'Button your lip soldier, no one gave you permission to speak, just listen to what I have to say, and listen good. This is how it's going to be. You are going back to boot camp, but this time as a Drill Instructor with the rank of Acting Sergeant. You will stay in that post until such time as you have earned the right to be posted to one of the Airborne Divisions. Further to this, your jacket will contain the information you first supplied to the army, which will only show your service in the Irish and British Armies. Be advised that your case file will be placed on record, and should you step out of line in the future, it can and will be used against you.

'Sergeant of the escort, you will unshackle this soldier outside this room and discharge him from your care. You will hand this letter over to him on his discharge. The letter is addressed to the CO of Basic Training and covers his transfer to that unit. Carry on Sergeant.'

Travis wanted to shake every officer by the hand. As for Dan O'Brien, he just wanted to give him a big hug. But all he was allowed to do was about turn and march out. With his hands shackled he couldn't even salute and show his respect.

He left the room knowing that it would be a long time before the Colonel would feel anything but contempt for him. He was in no doubt that boot camp was the nearest the Colonel could get to a punishment detail without upsetting higher authority.

Cuffs off, he accompanied the MPs to his cell, where he collected his kit. He then signed for his valuables and with the jacket containing his documents and letter in hand, struggling with his kit, he made his way to the Admin Block to pick up travel documents to boot camp. After a long and tiring journey, he arrived back once again at boot camp, where he presented his credentials to the Orderly Sergeant. The Sergeant flicked through them, then whistled softly through his teeth, leaving Travis in no doubt what he thought of the newcomer.

'Wait here,' he instructed Travis, 'the CO is off base right now, so I'm taking your info to the Top Soldier'. So saying, he knocked on the door of an office on which gold lettering informed all and

149

sundry that its occupant was Command Sergeant Major Washington Huckle. Now, there's a name to conjure with, chuckled Travis to himself. A merciful few moments of silence; he assumed the Top Soldier was reading his file and orders. Then a loud string of profanities, followed by, 'Get this asshole in here on the double, front and centre,' boomed the Sergeant Major. The Sergeant stepped smartly out of the door, beckoning Travis with his head and rolling his eyes up to heaven.

Travis marched smartly into the office and stood to attention before the 'Big Man'. Big was the operative word in the case of Command Sergeant Major Huckle. This African American was built like a brick shithouse. His broad back almost blocked all the sunlight out of his office. The body was surmounted by an equally massive head, which God seemed to have plonked on his shoulders without adding a neck. The black face was handsome, with a greying moustache and a cropped head of receding silver hair. He was a newcomer to the post.

'What the fuck is going on in this man's army?' shouted the big fellow. 'This isn't a transfer, it's a load of horse shit. There is no way I want you on my team, and I'm going to move heaven and earth to make sure it doesn't happen. In the meantime, I'm assigning you to the replacement company until it's decided what to do with you. I will ensure that they run you ragged with every crap job they can come up with. You will not, I repeat, NOT' - this at the top of his voice - 'show any rank. You will carry the rank and status of Buck Private. You are confined to camp, and you are to sign in at the guardhouse three times a day. Is that understood?' the Top Soldier roared at him.

'Understood, sir,' Travis replied and then got the hell out of his office. The 'Top' was still ranting and raving as Travis hoisted his kit on his shoulder and beat a hasty retreat out into the bright sunlight, heading in the direction indicated by the Orderly Sergeant.

Time seemed to go slowly in the transit block, and Travis' envy grew and grew as he watched soldiers coming and going to new postings while his world seemed to have stopped dead. It was back to the tried and tested routine of jogging, gym, meditation and reading. He always made time for writing, with Melissa first, then the Leclercs and then his Legion buddies. With this regime, he remained fit and alert, ready for anything the Army might throw at him.

The call finally came to report to the command block. His first interview with the CO, confirming his posting to the Training Depot team, was very stiff and formal. The senior officer cautioned him to work hard and get the job done to produce as many graduate recruit passes as possible. His next stop was with the Command Sergeant Major, who didn't wrap his words up, advising Travis that he had done everything in his power to have his posting reversed to one in the Arctic Circle.

'Be advised, Acting Sergeant Asshole, that if you screw up just once, I will knock you down on the parade square and jump all over you until such time as your mangled body fits into a McDonalds burger box. Then I will post you back to England, Ireland or where ever the fuck you came from. Do we understand each other?'

'Yes sir' said Travis.

'Now get the hell out of my sight, I don't want to see or hear from you again. Report to the Orderly Sergeant for further orders.'

The Orderly Sergeant had now changed from interested civility to cold disdain, ignoring him and calling a corporal to show him the ropes. He spoke to his subordinate as if Travis were invisible. Here we go, he thought, the boot is starting to go in again.

The Corporal held open the exit door and he lugged his kit

outside once more. 'I'll take you to your squad block and tell you about new arrival times for tomorrow,' was the Corporal's input, with no acknowledgement of Travis' rank.

'Don't bother,' Travis retorted, 'just give me the block key and leave me to it.'

'On your head be it if you get it wrong,' the Corporal replied.

'Yeah, yeah, fecking yeah,' Travis replied in a fit of pique. He was sick to death of the whole business. OK, he had done wrong, he had bent the rules a bit, but he wasn't the first soldier to do it, and he wouldn't be the last, so why all the bloody fuss? He knew the answer - the Training Team didn't want some half-baked ex-Brit Tom being foisted on them when they were used to vetting, hiring and firing their own trained people.

He staggered down the company lines, found his billet and opened the front door. The main sleeping area smelled of spit and polish, rifle oil, sweat and a tinge of fear. The smells were ingrained in the woodwork, and no amount of cleaning could wipe them out.

He walked up through the rows of double bunks to the small room that was his home as Squad Sergeant. It contained a single bed and locker, with a writing table and chair and a small wash basin with a small square mirror tile stuck above the sink. Home sweet home, but at least it was his. He got stuck into the settling-in process, after which he threw himself down on his bunk wondering what the morrow would bring.

At breakfast next morning, Travis noticed that the Sergeant Major presided over a long table occupied by the headquarters staff and the Drill Instructors, the Top Soldier sitting midway down the table, which gave the scene a Last Supper look to it. God Almighty surrounded by his disciples.

Travis sat at one of the tables scattered around the NCOs' chow hall. He had just sat down when two new Drill Sergeants joined him. They smiled and asked, 'OK if we join you?' to which he replied, 'Glad of the company, guys'. They were both infantry soldiers, or as the British Paras would put it 'Wingless Wonders', but they were obviously good soldiers or they wouldn't be on the Training Team. Travis enjoyed their company, as it was the only normal conversation he'd had in the past month or so.

As he was leaving the dining hall, the Orderly Sergeant called to him. 'Sergeant Travis, wait up, just to let you know that there is no hurry for you to be down at arrivals as there is some delay with the coaches, could be up to an hour.'

'OK,' Travis answered, 'Thank you Sergeant.'

As he wandered back to his billet, he wondered if there might be a thaw in his relations with the Training Team personnel. He had spent a lot of his time in the transit block working on his kit and now, as he marched down to the arrivals point he looked and felt extra special with his brand new sergeant's stripes, his bloused, gleaming jump boots and shiny jump wings. He attracted some envious glances from passing soldiers. He had decided to make his way to arrivals fifteen minutes or so before the timetable timing as he always liked to be early on the job.

As he got near to the area he started to be passed by new arrivals, already squadded, on their way to induction, and he quickened his step. Something wrong here, he thought. He was right, he had been set up. As he approached the arrival point there was only one bunch of recruits standing in an unruly group, chattering nervously in loud voices with much shouting and hand gestures. The orderly room Corporal standing nearby handed him a nominal roll of the squad and with a smirk on his face, marched off back to HQ without a word.

Travis immediately got a grip on the squad and put them into some sort of order. That done, he stepped back and surveyed them.

They were without doubt the worst bunch of sad-sacks, losers, bums and ne'er-do-wells he had ever seen in one group. He realised that the coaches had arrived on time and prior to his arrival the new recruits had been combed for the least likely to succeed elements, who had then been assigned to him. Bloody bastards, thought Travis, as it dawned on him that the Training Team had screwed him big time.

Despite his disappointment at this setback, he got on with the day's work. He tried not to show his anger or take it out on his squad, but they were, collectively, so dumb and slow that he almost lost his cool once or twice during the day. Finally, by meal time his squad were starting to get things squared away and it was a blessing to be able to sit down to his evening meal. The grins and winks in his direction from the 'Last Supper' crew did nothing for his digestion, on top of which the two new sergeants walked passed him without a word or a glance to sit at a separate table. The screws were really starting to turn again.

That evening he gathered the squad together and got them, one by one, to introduce themselves to the rest of the group and give their reasons for joining the Army. Then he addressed them, saying, 'Listen lads, by and large you have all stated that you want to be fighting soldiers, which is good. However, if you haven't guessed by now, we are the odd squad. No need at this stage to go into details, but we, and I include me in that, have been put together to fail and fail fine style and every effort will be made to make sure that we do. I don't know about you guys, but it's like a red rag to a bull to me. I take it as a challenge, and I'd like to show the bastards what we are really made of. If you guys co-operate with me, even just meet me half way, I promise to turn you into decent soldiers in the short time we have together. Are you with me?' He pointed to the weakest-looking recruit. 'Yes sir,' was the reply. 'Thanks boy, but you call me Sergeant, not sir,' 'Yes Sergeant,' the lad replied.

Looking into each recruit's eyes and trying to access his soul, he asked the same question, always getting the same reply' 'Yes Sergeant,' with the tenor of the replies rising and rising until the last 'Yes Sergeant,' could almost be heard on the parade square. When all the affirmations were completed, Travis told them, 'For your information only, know that I am the product of three European armies and elite Forces. I know my trade. Draw strength from that, let's work together, work hard and where and when we can, let's kick arse. There is an old saying that goes, 'united we stand, divided we fall'. So from now on, our war cry will be 'UNITED'. Let's hear it.'

'United!' roared the squad in unison.

'Can't hear a bloody thing,' shouted Travis. The squad shouted, 'United!' some decibels higher.

'What did you say?' he shouted again, his right hand cupped around his ear. There followed a last roaring cry of, 'UNITED!' that nearly lifted the roof off the billet, bringing the meeting to an end.

As the weeks rolled by, Travis' boys showed a willingness and a fighting spirit that he had not believed possible. In return, he gave them his all. Night and day, time itself, meant nothing to Travis. His only breaks were to eat, write his letters, meditate and catch a few hours' sleep.

It was not long before the squad started to look good, feel good, and act well. They were soon making him proud. Yet the Training Team never stopped their efforts to defeat him and have him busted and posted. He still ate alone at his table, the two new Drill Sergeants having been invited to eat with the Command Sergeant Major and his Last Supper group.

Travis couldn't figure out if he was hated because they felt he hadn't earned his sergeant's stripes or because he was a Para among non-Paras. Especially when he found out that Huckle had weekly team training meetings where they discussed the training schedule and any new ideas that could be of help to the recruits and useful to the Team. Travis was never invited to attend. He gleaned any new information from the unit notice board.

One of the most annoying aspects of the harassment was when he and his squad arrived, on time, at a training area to find it already occupied by another squad who wouldn't move off. In the end, Travis and his squad took to arriving as early as possible at their next training area.

One afternoon, he had just taken over his allotted area and started the demonstration phase of his lesson when a squad arrived out of timing. The squad DI, who in Travis' estimation, was a brick shithouse on legs, was called Walchinsky.

'Get yourself and your bunch of wizened fucking goons off this stand, or I'll rip your fucking head off your shoulders and stuff it up your rear end,' growled the big DI.

'You're very welcome to try, shithead,' retorted Travis. The big Sergeant roared with laughter, breaking off in the middle and lunged at Travis, who swiftly side-stepped, leaving Walchinsky charging past. Infuriated, the big man, who was surprisingly light on his feet, turned quickly and caught Travis a blow above his left eyebrow which opened a very deep cut, drenching the side of his face in blood. Travis went down. Walchinsky's squad roared in delight. Walchinsky stood a moment to bask in his troop's cheers, then came at the run with the intention of kicking Travis' head in. The short pause had given Travis time to clear his head, and he quickly rolled away from danger, found his feet and went on the attack. His bitterness at this unjust treatment fuelled his will to fight and win. He tore into the big Sergeant, escaping from a neck hold by head-butting his opponent, breaking his nose, which brought blood gushing all over the man's face.

Stunned and blinded for a moment, the big man hesitated just long enough for Travis to launched a mighty karate kick to his private parts. His erstwhile attacker's eyes rolled up into his skull, leaving only the whites showing. A side kick to the solar plexus and another to the jaw brought the giant crashing to the ground. Stunned silence from the Walchinsky squad and roars of 'UNITED!' from Travis boys.

The duty medical wagon was quickly called forward to take the unconscious DI to the medical centre. That done, Travis detailed the squad leader of the downed Sergeant's group to march them back to barracks.

That evening, after a visit to the MI room and stitches to his eye, he sat with his back to the Training Team during dinner as a mark of his disgust. The next morning, as the squads were drilling on the parade square, the Command Sergeant Major strode majestically into view and started to wander around, casting a critical eye over the various squads under training. Finally, he approached Travis' squad. The DI had his squad at ease, giving them a breather. The Sergeant Major moved up behind him saying in a menacing whisper, 'Don't turn around Travis, just listen. Don't you ever sit with your back to me again in the chow hall or I'll stomp all over you, and the next time, if there is a next time, you put one of my Training Team into the sick bay, I will put you in the stockade, copy?'

'Copy, Top,' replied Travis, and the Sergeant Major moved silently away. Got your attention that time, you big gorilla, Travis thought.

As graduation day arrived, he found that his squad had secured third place in the final results, losing only two recruits from the squad due to medical problems picked up during training. He was well pleased with the results and in next to no time, he was at arrivals again to collect his new squad. By this time he had learned his lesson and was early on site, getting some good quality recruits along with the usual sprinkling of odds and sods. This time Travis pushed them into second place overall.

The day before his next batch of recruits were due to arrive, the Orderly Corporal knocked on his room door and informed him that he was to attend the Sergeant Majors' briefing in the mid-morning. This was a first, and Travis checked his dress, wanting to look his best for the meeting. With clipboard and pen in hand, he marched smartly to the HQ block. Half of the DIs were already there and seated when he entered the lecture room. The Command Sergeant Major was standing behind a table on a raised platform, shuffling some papers as Travis entered. Looking up, he nodded in recognition as Travis selected a seat at the back of the room.

The meeting that followed was lively and at times humorous, showing a different side to the Top Soldier. Finally, Huckle asked each DI in turn if he had anything further to say or contribute before he closed the meeting. When Travis' turn came, he offered a few pertinent points to the group, which were discussed with good grace.

That evening, as he started his main meal, the Sergeant Major shouted across to him, 'Hi, Sergeant Travis'. Travis looked up from the book he was reading. 'We're talking about one of the suggestions you made today, why not join us and put your oar in,' Huckle offered.

'Don't mind if I do,' replied Travis, transferring his plate to the big table, where room was made for him. Right enough, a lively discussion was in full swing, and before he knew it, he was well embroiled in it.

On the way back to his room, he realised that he had finally been accepted by the Training Team. Flushed with success, he decided to visit the NCOs' club for the first time and have a nightcap before turning in for another hard day on the morrow. As he pushed the door open, he found himself face to face with Sergeant Walchinsky.

One of them had to give way. The big sergeant's face broke into a smile. Then in a terrible mock Irish accent, Walchinsky said, 'Well if it isn't the bold Sergeant Travis himself.' Travis spread his hands out, shrugged his shoulders and returned the smile.

'Man, you're one hard little bastard, you really turned me over,' observed Walchinsky. 'But no hard feelings, buddy, let's shake'.

The big non-com held out a shovel-like hand, which Travis took. Then after a bone-crushing handshake, Walchinsky, grinning from ear to ear, stepped aside and let Travis move past him into the club.

Now he was back to enjoying his soldiering again. With all ill-feeling and tension gone, his third squad were a real pleasure to work with, which showed itself when his team won the top spot on graduation. He was elated, and there was even better news to come. Called first into the Sergeant Major's office, he was informed that he was to be transferred to an Airborne Division at Fort Campbell. There was a formal but cursory visit to the CO's office, where he was thanked for his services and wished 'Good Luck' in his new posting. Then he was on his way to what he hoped would be a better life with an active service unit.

Finally, Travis arrived at Fort Campbell, his new home. His pulse raced with excitement and anticipation as he made his way through the lines to the HQ block. As he began his processing, he once again felt the vibes of resentment coming from the NCOs as to his right to his sergeant's stripes. He just hoped it wouldn't rear its ugly head as it had back at boot camp with the Recruit Training Team.

Induction over, he was finally assigned as a squad leader, his rank being approved by his new commander and endorsed by the officer committee. To his amazement and delight he found that the Chief,

Doc and Frenchi were already members of his company, spread about different squads and platoons. With his full military history lodged in HQ and the words of praise and knowledge of his background by his friends from recruit training, the initial resentment he encountered was whittled away as his previous military experience was revealed. The Airborne Brotherhood is tangible and real, with Paras of whatever nation holding all other Paras in high esteem.

As time went by, rumours started to circulate that the Brigade could be on the move. Then training was stepped up as the rumours grew stronger, especially when they were sent to Fort Hood for extensive jungle training. On return to Fort Campbell, they were informed that the Brigade was due to ship out in the near future. Their destination was unknown at this stage, so the Troopers were given fourteen days' embarkation leave. This was his first real leave since enlistment, and he was determined to make the most of it. He immediately left for France to spend time with the Leclercs. It was to be a bittersweet homecoming.

FRANCE AND IRELAND

On the long flight home to France, Travis analysed his thoughts, his emotions and his feelings with regard to the greatest tragedy of his life, the deaths of his beloved Antoinette and their unborn child. He now believed that he had finally turned the corner with his feelings and painful memories. It had been the right decision to rejoin the Army with its intense physical commitment and his trials and tribulations. It had helped to cleanse his mind and his soul. He would never forget his beloved Antoinette as long as he lived and breathed, but now, she was in a treasured part of his mind where he could recall only the great love and happiness she gave him. He was slowly moving forward to a brighter future, near to closing the door on the darkness of the past.

This belief was to shine a bright light on his stay with his in-laws, who had their own personal struggles, fought their own demons and were slowly coming out the other side of their nightmare in finding a merciful closure to the early death of their beloved Antoinette and her baby.

Good, dependable Raymond met him at the station with a big hug. 'Hello tough guy' he said. As the car drove up to the Leclerc home in Chalonne, Anton and Madame Leclerc rushed to the door to greet him. His mother-in-law threw herself into his arms, weeping in happiness. 'Thank God you're safe, my son' she murmured in his ear. Then it was old Anton's turn to shake his hand and hold him close, 'As always son, you have made us proud.' There was no doubt that Travis' return had brightened their lives, as to them he was part of their beloved daughter Antoinette and they showered him with much love and affection.

During his leave with the family, Travis spent most of his time with his brother-in-law Raymond, renewing their closeness and friendship. As his second weekend approached, he caught a flight to the Legion Para base in Calvi in Corsica to meet up with Hamish, Nanak and Alexchenko. They had a great night out, with dinner and a booze-up to end all booze-ups. His friends filled him in on the latest exploits of the Legion and their venture into the Republic of Chad, a former French conquest. In Nanak's words, 'Chad was a whole new ball-game for us guys. We were supposed to act like bloody policemen and peace-makers between the Government troops and large groups of rag-tag and bobtail terrorists from the North, backed by that nutcase Gaddafi of Libya. Some of them were as young as twelve years of age. But in a kill or be killed situation, we had no choice but to take them out. It offended many of us, but where do you go in a situation like that?'

Hamish then took over with his summary of their next move to Djibouti, also a former French territory. 'Another shithole,' was his summing up. 'We lost a lot of good men to disease and suicide, that's how bad it was.'

In a daft way, Travis envied their active service exploits, as he hadn't fired a shot in anger since leaving the Legion. He felt he couldn't match their stories. However, his friends hung on his every word as he described his life and times as a Paratrooper in the American Army.

Back in Chalonne, nearing the end of his leave and all too soon for the Leclerc family, he bid them a fond farewell and made his way back to Ireland, to spend a little time with his mother's family. In his heart of hearts, he knew it was because he wanted to see and be with Melissa. During his troubled period while under close arrest at Jump School and the subsequent trying times as a member of the recruit training team, Melissa's letters of encouragement had helped him through some of his darkest hours. She had advised him to be strong, convincing him that he could hack anything the Army could throw at him, reminding him that he had survived and prospered in two of the toughest Armies in the world and most of all that she was with him every step of the way.

As time wore on, their letters to each other had become more intimate and sensitive. They had even spoken on the phone once or twice, and it had been great to hear her voice. Now, it was time to test those feelings face to face.

Although she knew he was coming to Dublin, he caught her by surprise by waiting for her outside the Irish Sweepstakes offices in Ballsbridge, where she worked. As she emerged, her day's work done, she stood stock still in happy shock to see Travis standing there with a big sloppy grin on his face and a large bunch of flowers in his hand. In an instant, she had recovered and ran to him, throwing herself into his arms and kissing him full on the lips. This time he didn't flinch or turn his face away, but responded warmly.

Melissa took some time off work and travelled down to Kildare with him to stay with his family. One evening during their stay, his beloved Granny Hewitt collared him and in a very gentle and sympathetic voice said, 'Don't you know that your Melissa is half crazy about you?'

'It's too soon Gran, to be thinking like that,' he replied. But he knew there was no need for the old lady to prompt him, he could see and feel Melissa's love for him. For his part, he knew that he was still in love with her, but he felt somewhat guilty and a sense of betrayal towards the memory of Antoinette. Hard as he tried, he just couldn't surrender his feelings or show his love for her in the way that she showed him.

Despite that, they had some wonderfully happy days together, and were much at ease in each other's company as they roamed the plains of the Curragh on long walks. They talked over their past, their happy times and especially their bad times.

'I'm sorry for the past, Melissa' said Travis. 'I was a right arsehole. Normally I'm the coolest dude on the planet, but when I go, I go, I just lose it completely. Do you forgive me?'

'There's nothing to forgive. I was just as bad, Patrick. I could have talked it through in a reasonable manner. We could have found a solution if we'd tried. Instead, I faced you with an ultimatum almost before you got off the boat for home. It was unforgivable, and I am truly sorry.'

'As you say, there is nothing to forgive. So just let's try and forget.'

All too soon his leave was over, and no matter how hard she tried to keep her emotions in check, it was a tearful Melissa who accompanied him to Dublin Airport, for the long flight back to the States and whatever lay ahead.

CHAPTER TWELVE

SOUTH VIETNAM

Arriving back at camp, Travis was soon up to his neck in brigade preparations for deployment and overseas movement, destination South Vietnam. Hardly anyone in the Battalion had ever heard of Vietnam or knew where it was, so that evening in the enlisted men's club, it was the sole topic of conversation among the drinkers.

When the subject was aired on Travis' table, he knew he could quote chapter and verse on it as it figured large in Legion history as a famous defeat, much like Arnhem in Holland during World War 2 for the British Airborne, where they had lost the best part of a division in their attack on the Arnhem Bridge over the Rhine.

'The French Foreign Legion lost some of it best men there in 1954,' said Travis.

'You know the place man?' questioned an interested trooper on the next table.

'No, I've never been there, but I know the background to the present conflict' he replied.

'Do tell man.'

'OK, well, at the end of World War 2, the Indochinese colony of Vietnam reverted to French control, and they formed a government headed by an Emperor called Bao Dai. But a Marxist called Ho Chi Minh set out to form a communist republic instead, and he got backing from Soviet Russia and Communist China. This move led to civil war. The French fought a hard and vicious war for seven years, making no headway against the Vietminh guerrilla forces, who received a great amount of help from the Chinese across the northern border. Then in 1954 the French military, in an attempt to lure the guerrillas into a major and decisive battle, decided to reoccupy a place called Dien Bien Phu to use as an air landing base in the North West, where they could regain control of the Tai country and protect Laos. They had a second objective, to pin down a maximum of Vietminh forces and relieve the pressure on the Red River Delta. Unfortunately, in doing so, they managed to get caught in a deadly trap. The French position was surrounded by 200 guns of the Communist artillery and 70,000 troops. The 13,000 French fought a heroic battle for 56 days, reinforcing their beleaguered troops with the cream of their airborne forces. They forgot the old military rule, 'never reinforce failure'. But despite their best efforts they were overrun.

'Their defeat spelt the end of French rule in Vietnam. It also cost the French Army and the Foreign Legion some of its finest infantry and airborne soldiers, as they lost over 2,000 dead and 5,000 wounded. In all, 10,000 ended up in captivity.

'One thing worth noting, the French Army are a highly-trained and equipped force and the Legion are among the toughest soldiers in the world. The Dien Bien Phu vets still in the Legion reckoned that the enemy soldiers they fought against had great courage and cunning. Which means that the Vietnamese commies must be very skilled and tough little bastards. We have a tough job on our hands.'

By this time, there wasn't a whisper or the clink of a glass as the packed club listened intently to Travis' tale. 'Then what happened, Sarge?' the same Trooper asked. Travis carried on with his story.

'Following a French withdrawal, the country was partitioned, with the north becoming a communist country and the south becoming the Republic of Vietnam. But the communist guerrillas were not satisfied with their lot, so they began a war with the South Vietnamese for control of the country. The US started to send aid and deploy some military personnel to help the Republic in their struggle with their northern enemies. Now it appears that, with the worsening situation, Uncle Sam is stepping up the supply of military aid and troops, and that's where we come in.

'Just one last point in all this. If any of you watched the President on CCN the other night, he was warning that if Vietnam falls to communism, the whole continent will fall, followed by the Philippines and possibly Australia and New Zealand. He said it was the mission of the good old US of A to stop the onward roll of communism, and the place to stop it is Vietnam. End of chat, guys.' Travis returned to his beer.

The massive logistics of a Brigade movement to a war zone was like a log race in a torrential river. This mighty river of war rolled out of its home base to the troopships moored at the docks, waiting to swallow whole battalions of men, like colonies of soldier ants entering their nests, followed by equipment and machines of war and supplies. There followed a long and often boring sea journey to the conflict, with stops from the history books of World War 2, like Midway and the Philippines, where the US Marines lost many good and brave men in fierce hand-to-hand struggles over tiny pieces of ground and small island strongholds.

The Troopers found reflections of the past to be particularly sobering, and it left some of the men more than anxious for their future. This was especially true for the married guys with young families.

Finally, by way of Quin Nhow and Vung Tau, the fleet of

transports arrived at Cam Ranh Bay, South Vietnam. From there they were trucked to the new home in Phan Rang. An all too brief period followed while the Troopers acclimatised themselves to the very humid conditions. Their time was filled with orientation, kit issues, and day and night training as units readied. Then on to their new home north east of An Khe. There the companies were used as general infantry in reconnaissance and intelligence patrols and sweeps through the countryside. They started to take casualties almost immediately from heavy enemy action. Travis and his squad were in the thick of it, and after their first major action, his assistant squad leader remarked, 'Pass the goddamned, freaking toilet roll Sarge.' He hadn't shat himself, but as he added later, 'It was a close run thing.' It was his first time in combat.

In fact, with the exception of Travis and a few others, they were all new to enemy action. From then on it was the dull, and at times hair-curling, seek and destroy patrols in triple canopy jungle, where the foliage seemed to close in on the Troopers as if it were a subhuman entity trying to suffocate and suck them down into the oily black bowels of the earth.

The Troopers' main tasks were to ambush and destroy enemy supply lines. They were also deployed in a variety of other roles, sometimes to assist, reinforce, or replace patrols already on seek and destroy missions. Patrolling could and did take many hours, moving at a rate of about a hundred metres per hour before contact was made. Then they would fight short, tough, hit-and-run fire fights with small enemy units, bugging out before enemy reinforcements could hit them. All the time they were tormented by blood-sucking leeches and half drowned by the sluice-like rainstorms. Then they had to try to sleep on stinking, buffalo dung-strewn ground.

The fighting at times was man to man and often hand to hand.

It was a case of spotting the enemy before he spotted you. A night never went by without a contact and an ensuing action. Command started to deliver recce patrols up country by helicopter. A patrol reported back that they were observing a large force of Viet Cong operating out of tunnels in their area. The patrol commander decided to withdraw, as he would have been heavily outnumbered if it came to a firefight. He asked for backup in case the worst happened.

As Travis was part of a quick reaction force, on standby for just such a situation, he was given orders to take his patrol out and back up the endangered Troopers. With a, 'Saddle up guys, it's airlift in ten' from Travis, they boarded a Huey chopper and lifted off for the designated area.

'Hey Gunner, what routine do you guys follow on an insertion like this?' one of Travis' Troopers asked.

'Well man, it's like this, we buzz over the jungle and swoop, hovering here and there like a bee sussing out where the nectar is. This throws Charlie off, and when we do insert you guys, he has no clear idea of where we drop you,' the gunner explained.

The choppers dropped them at a suitable spot and moved out quickly to avoid any enemy fire. This was the first time they had been on their own without the comfort or protection of their platoon or company. It was spooky, and Travis could feel the fear and apprehension of his squad. He whispered fiercely, 'Get a grip on your bloody knickers you daft bastards and let's rock and roll.' They grinned at him as he glanced around the anxious faces and waved them on.

The sun was starting to go down as the patrol moved, with great caution, to link up with their mates in the troubled patrol. Suddenly, the point man came to an abrupt stop and froze in position and signalled Travis forward. Looking into the face of the trooper, he was met with a horrified stare. The trooper pointed forward. They had found the patrol, or at least what was left of it. It appeared that the enemy had outflanked them, and had placed some kind of improvised explosive devices up in the trees. When activated, they had decapitated every trooper in the squad. The American weapons, ammo, grenades and the like had been stripped from the dead.

Travis, knowing that the VC had to be working from the tunnels nearby, warned his squad, 'Watch your arse guys, we are close to a whole mob of Charlies. Let's go and find a clearing where we can get in an airlift for our dead buddies.' The nickname for their Viet Cong enemies came from the radio phonetic alphabet, as in Victor Charlie for VC.

Travis' patrol moved out on a compass bearing until they found a suitable spot, where they hunkered down for the night in all-round defence and posted sentries. Next morning a second squad, accompanied by engineers to check for booby traps on the bodies of their dead comrades, was dropped into the clearing to help with the retrieval of the bodies for a 'dust off' or airlift by Medivac choppers. Travis' crew and the second squad were then airlifted back to base, under cover of helicopter gunships, without seeing an enemy soldier or firing a shot in anger.

As he lay awake that night, haunted by the sight of the butchered Troopers, drowning in his own sweat and pestered and bitten to lumps by mozzies, his mind turned to his Grand Uncle Philip Crorkan, a former policeman in the Royal Irish Constabulary. How in the name of all that's holy, in 1920, had Uncle Philip survived, let alone fought, in the West African jungles of the Gold Coast as a volunteer Police Inspector in the Great Ashanti Wars? Especially with antique clothing and weapons, and without the medicines and medical care we take for granted. At times, his nearest doctor must have been a native witch doctor and treatment by him would have been sudden death to a European.

Uncle Philip had been quite a hero to Travis as a young boy hearing about his grandmother's favourite brother. He recalled that at one stage, Philip, as part of the garrison, had been held under siege at a place called Coomassie by battling Ashanti warriors. What courage he must have had taking part in the epic breakout by crossing the Akwasbosh River under heavy fire. He remembered how Philip had been detailed, along with a small detachment of native police, to go to the village of Abuabugya to seize the Golden Stool of the Ashanti Nation. He remembered his grandmother telling him that the Stool had been hidden there by a tribal witch doctor who had buried it to keep it from the British Forces. The capture of the Sacred Stool, which was believed to contain the soul of the Ashanti Nation, by an enemy, would spell defeat in battle for the Ashanti. Uncle Philip certainly had balls, because on orders to take the Stool into custody, he set off with just a small band of native policemen. The seizure of the Stool in the middle of warring tribesmen had been one hell of a brave action. Its capture had helped to bring about an end to the costly war in that country.

But poor, brave Uncle Philip had never been able to enjoy the peace. Going up country to take over a station whose European Officer had died of a fever, he had caught the same infection and died from convulsions.

One day, Travis vowed, he would visit Philip's grave in the British cemetery in Kumasi. He shuddered as he tried to imagine what an 'up country station' must have been like back then, and wondered if he could have endured the same terrible conditions without throwing the towel in in very short order. He recognised, not for the first time, that he had good and brave military blood flowing in his veins. He just hoped that it had drowned out the cowardly blood of his father.

Travis' tour in Vietnam settled down for the most part, a dull if very uncomfortable routine made up of eighty per cent perspiration, ten per cent preparation and ten per cent sheer, mind-blowing terror. The VC tended to leave the Troopers alone on their daylight search and destroy missions and long-range patrols. The Troopers' aim was to try and engage them and destroy them, along with their supplies and weapons. It was also very important to collect any enemy documents they could find.

During the day, the enemy depended on a horrible array of booby traps and the odd ambush to take out Troopers and keep their colleagues' nerves on edge. Loaded down with gear, they were operating in 100 degrees of heat, hungry and bone-tired, trudging through some godforsaken area of jungle, then getting back to base camp to eat cold rations and sleep in the dirt and the dust. It was debilitating and mind bending, to say the least.

Charlie liked to hunt at night and he was bloody good at it. He could move in the dark without making a sound. Because he lived in the field, he knew where he was going, even when he couldn't see his hand in front of his face. This was his life, and he was well attuned to it. As night socked in, all the Paras could do was hunker down in the best positions they could find, turning them into prepared ambush positions, then lay out claymore mines to give all-round explosive protection and wait out the night. With two of the squad on sentry, the rest of the unit would try to sleep, not helped by the sounds of the night animals and insects, most of which operated like the fighter pilots of WW2, dive bombing any area of exposed flesh. To make matters worse, swathes of salty sweat ran from the soldiers' hairlines down into their eyes, making them sore and red raw from rubbing to stop the stinging and retain clear vision. This situation would be compounded by rain with the power and speed of an open sluice gate. All in all, it was a shit way to have to fight a war.

Short R & R breaks or stand downs of two or three days, where they could have a cook-out, were a welcome respite for the shattered Paras. While the mixed race squads mucked in together when in the field on operations, they tended to mix with their own race or ethnic group when relaxing. Not so with Travis and his buddies from boot camp, Chief, Doc and Frenchi. This was their best time, when they could get together and shoot the breeze. They would catch up on what was happening in the other squads and platoons and get rat-faced on chilled beer and good whisky, soaking up some rays and getting some sun on their backs before returning to the shit once again.

It was rumoured that they could be offered a few weeks R & R away from Nam, in some exotic place or places, at some time during their tour of duty. More in the hope than expectation, Travis wrote to Melissa and invited her to meet up with him for a short holiday whenever and wherever, should the rumours turn out to be true. He would pick up the tab for her air travel from Dublin and back. Melissa replied in great excitement, which Travis had to damp down in his next letter as he knew how unreliable Army rumours were. But lo and behold, halfway through his tour, he was offered a week's R & R at a range of top spots. He picked Hawaii. He could hardly wait to tell Melissa, and he rushed to the nearest phone to tell her the good news.

'Hi Babe, ever been to Hawaii?' he asked, knowing full well that she had only ever been to France and Italy.

'No darling, why?'

'Well you'd better see to booking your flight and packing your bikini because our trip is on.'

Squeals of delight from Melissa followed by, 'Did I ever tell you that I love you Patrick Travis?'

'Only because I'm bloody wonderful, that's all' he said, fishing for a compliment, but his hint fell on deaf ears.

Hawaii was all he had dreamed it would be, a romantic paradise. It was like another planet compared to Vietnam. Melissa, in her almost breathless excitement, looked incredibly beautiful as she pushed, face flushed, through the crowd of passengers from her flight to throw herself into Travis' waiting arms. They kissed passionately and held it for a long time, not caring what anyone thought, just lost in a cloud of mixed but happy emotions. At last they broke free and hailing a taxi, made the short journey to their hotel.

It had never been mentioned in their letters or phone calls, but by tacit agreement they shared the same room and bed. They had made love on their engagement night back in Ireland a lifetime ago and then once or twice when he had been home on leave from the British Army. Now the moment was fast approaching, they both felt wrong-footed and awkward about their first night together. However, after a sumptuous dinner and a fair few exotic cocktails, they wandered hand in hand to their room.

Travis stripped down to his cotton shorts and slid in between the satin sheets of the king-sized bed. In a little while Melissa emerged from the bathroom wearing an extremely flimsy, see-through, pink negligée. She looked stunning as she slid into bed beside him.

'Wow' exclaimed Travis. Words failed him. Melissa smiled in contentment. Sitting up, with the pillows fluffed up behind them, he reached forward and slid the straps of her negligee off her shoulders. The garment snaked down to her thighs to reveal her gorgeous, full rounded breasts. Her nipples, dark brown, were the size of orange halves, and they tasted sweet and scented as he ran his tongue in an ever widening circle around each one in turn. In seconds, their dam burst and they locked in passion, two becoming as one. Travis was moving swiftly to the top of his emotional and physical mountain when suddenly, the face of Antoinette superimposed itself over the face of Melissa. This was quickly followed by a kaleidoscope of the horrors he had witnessed in Vietnam. First he saw the headless squad, followed by other grotesque scenes he had witnessed, all flickering through his mind like the trailer to a horror movie.

Travis started screaming like a wounded animal. Just before he climaxed he saw the face of Melissa, bewildered and crying in shock. He flung himself away from her and curled up in the foetal position in a far corner of the bed, weeping uncontrollably. He felt Melissa's warm, silk-like skin against his back, her hand caressing his arm and shoulder, her other hand running softly and slowly through his cropped hair. She was crooning to him in a soft, low voice, sounding quite like his young mother. 'There now, there now, my darling, you're safe now, it's going to be all right, I'm here with you, I will always be here with you'.

Her voice was the last sound he heard as his sobbing subsided and he drifted off into an exhausted but peaceful sleep. The horrors he felt and remembered so vividly had been washed away by his scalding hot tears.

The rest of his leave was an exercise in first aid by Melissa as she tried to pour the balm of her loving gestures, kisses and words onto his raw emotions. All too soon it was time for parting, and their farewell was very subdued set against their meeting just five days ago. It was a much-troubled Melissa who waved her goodbyes one more time as she entered the doors to embarkation. As for Travis, he felt he had let her down, ruining her holiday, as he had lowered his guard on his feelings, the wrong feelings. He vowed that if he ever got the same chance again, that it would be different.

On his return from R & R, he was called to an interview with his CO and Executive Officer. He was offered a promotion to Staff Sergeant and the command of a Platoon as already, the Brigade was

175

starting to be stripped of officer and NCO leadership through combat casualties. He accepted and duly took over the control of No. 3 Platoon, whose Staff Sergeant had walked onto a pungi-stake trap and been flown back to the States for treatment to a badly-infected right foot and leg.

Travis' promotion was only days old when he was called to an 'O' (orders) group, to be told that his unit would be participating in the first parachute assault since the Korean War. Eight o'clock on the 22nd February found him and his platoon chuted and sitting in the bucket seats of a C-130 aircraft. This was to be their third jump in the skies of Vietnam, but the other two had been training jumps; this one was for real.

As the plane lifted off into the sky on its two-hour flight to the drop zone, Travis thought about Melissa. He wondered what she was doing right now; possibly still asleep. He could never work out the time difference. Anyway, he would probably be in action against the Cong while she was at work in the Irish Sweepstake offices. She might be thinking of him, but she would never guess what he was up to, thank God. He just hoped he wouldn't let himself down with his platoon. He had to stop thinking of himself now and start to think of them.

His thoughts were interrupted by an aerial photograph which was being passed around the Troopers. Studying the photo took his mind off his feelings of apprehension. It was entitled "Drop Zone Charlie", which appeared to be near a place called Katum. As he and his boys exited the aircraft they would have Cambodia on their left and South Vietnam below and to the right of them, with the jungles of Tay Ninh Province beneath them. The whole operation was to be a vast blocking and encircling manoeuvre called Operation Junction City, and its objective was to destroy the main HQ of the Viet Cong.

Finally, it was time. 'Green light on, go!' Once Travis was stabilized in his descent, he could see the coloured smoke showing him his assembly area. His well-trained unit reached the area intact and in full fighting order. As soon as a head count was taken, they got stuck in to clearing and securing the DZ. Then, secure in all-round defence, they watched the heavy drop come in with the light artillery pieces, mortars and vehicles.

The drop was successful, and it was time to take the fight to the enemy. Travis' platoon took the point as they moved towards their objective, designated by the planners as Hill 875. It was midday, the heat oppressive with the tree line at Trooper level alive with biting, sucking insects of every type and size. The men were not just sweating, they were leaking water, at an alarming rate.

They had just settled back into deep patrolling routine and were starting to hack their way up the heavily-jungled hillside when the VC mortars started to drop in. This was followed by an attack under the cover of their mortar fire. The attack was heavy, and Travis' platoon was in danger of being overrun. Their Platoon Commander radioed back that his unit was under attack by an estimated two companies of Cong soldiers, and requested covering fire and reinforcement. In reply, the American 4.2 inch and 81mm mortars opened up with a fierce barrage, joined by the HE (High Explosive) rounds of the 105mm howitzers. All available attack aircraft joined the fray, bombing and strafing the Cong positions. Reinforcements were now being heli-lifted into the area. This plan of action was speeded up and doubled when it was discovered that what had been thought to be two companies of enemy turned out be two battalions, which in short order was beefed up by the VC to a full regiment. On this new intelligence arriving at the American HQ, the command element committed a whole brigade to the battle.

On the ground, it was chaotic. Travis' platoon was taking heavy casualties. Command and control was difficult, even at the squad level. He had no time for fear, he had to look after his men. Mouth bone dry, aching for water, voice hoarse from shouting commands, ears deafened by exploding mortars, he was in a world of shit, but he wasn't thinking about that as he and his men fought for their lives.

As the reinforcements poured in they started to hold the enemy and then push them back under their own curtain of fire. It seemed a lifetime later when Travis and his few remaining men were pulled back to where they could rest and recuperate. In fact they just slumped on the ground in the rear echelon, huddled together like the survivors they were. They were numb; no one spoke. Travis, in a totally exhausted state, had to make a big effort of will to rouse himself, check his men and tend to their needs.

So ended Operation Junction City for Travis and the remnants of his platoon. Back at base camp, well rested, with a couple of beers inside him as he lay on his cot, he looked back over the recent operation and his performance in it.

I didn't do too badly I suppose. God, I was shit scared when those bloody mortars crumped in and the attack started. I was worried sick about getting my wounded guys back to the MASH post. In the end, I was too busy to be scared and I've come away from the experience a lot closer to the men in my platoon. I know I can still hack it, when needs be.

As soon as they were ready and back up to strength again, Travis' Battalion was airlifted to relieve another Battalion in a long-standing fire base, from which they mounted short and long range patrols. They were back in 'The Shit' as the Troopers had come to call it, and shit it was, with continuous enemy sniping at the base and along the jungle trails. The drenching rains and the high humidity drained the energy and will from the patrols as they moved through the mosquito-infested jungle. It was backbreaking work hacking a path through tangled undergrowth, continuously swatting mosquitoes and burning blood-sucking leeches from their bodies. The whole area was their enemy, from the animals and insects to poisonous plants and reptiles. Weeks of sleeping on the ground without a change of clothes, or a shower, added to the discomfort. The Troopers were in very poor shape with bad feet, faces with lumps and welts from mosquito bites, hands shredded from thorn cuts and stomach trouble which brought on bouts of weakening diarrhoea.

The patrols started to see signs of an enemy build-up in their area and the harassment started to escalate. The Battalion Commander issued orders for a complete overhaul of the base defences and stepped up supply drops of extra munitions.

Finally, on a moonless night, the VC struck. Trip flares went up, lighting an area east of the fire base then, 'Control...This is Tango 2, enemy setting up mortars 100 yards in front of our position'. As Tango 2 opened up with its M-60 and M-40 grenade launchers, the VC started their softening-up barrage prior to a human wave suicide attack. The Troopers, outnumbered at least two to one, were assailed by a withering fire in the initial onslaught, with artillery and mortar fire raining down on them without a break. Battalion Artillery were no slouches when it came to support fire and with the aid of STANO (surveillance, target acquisition and night observation), they, in return, poured a deadly cocktail of mixed ordnance from the Battalion's 105 Howitzers on top of the attacking VC. But once their attack began the enemy kept coming on, regardless of losses. They must be extremely brave or exceptionally stupid little bastards, Travis thought, as he opened up with his M-16, which he had set on automatic. As the almost paralysing fear left him, it was replaced by a form of madness as he screamed and shouted obscenities at the oncoming enemy soldiers. He hosed the attackers down as they approached the barbed wire entanglements, changing his twenty-round taped-together magazines smoothly and without conscious thought. The 5.56 mm rounds, which bounced and spun in flight, had a horrific impact on their human target. The initial contact blew the victim backwards as if by an unseen hand, and then the round bounced around the body, destroying everything it touched, to exit in a gaping hole out the back. The technicalities were of no interest to Travis; all he wanted was to stop this madness by killing or maiming the men who were attacking him.

The sounds of the battle were like some crazy symphony, orchestrated by a mad composer and led by an even madder conductor who had decided to play all his heavy brass instruments at the same time and all his percussion, bass drums pounding, amid the deafening clashes of symbols. His instruments were automatic rifle fire, hand grenades, grenade launchers, claymore mines, light and heavy machine guns and mortars. For vocals, he had the screams of the wounded and dying. This insane music was ear-busting and gut wrenching. The varied and vivid colours of light displayed a vision of Hell on earth. Travis was to have the sights and sounds of this night etched on his heart and tattooed on his soul for ever.

The area in and around the base was alive with swarms of enemy soldiers trying to break through the defences. A frantic call from Tango 6 - 'We're being overrun' the radioman screamed. Then the Special Operations Combat Control team sent out the call-sign 'Spooky' to bring an AC-47 gunship into the fray. This almost antique, lumbering, specially-converted aircraft was armed with a GUA-8 Gatling machine-gun, firing thousands of rounds of ammunition per minute. It had been christened by the Troopers 'Puff the Magic Dragon'. Extremely accurate, with the ability to place its rounds in a ten-metre area, 'Puff' mowed down the main assault group, chewing up everything in its path. Backed by gunships firing continuous discharges of 2.75 rockets, every round and rocket seemed to hammer another nail in the coffin of the attackers, to such an extent that they started to break off their attack, turning it into an organised retreat and taking their dead and wounded with them. For Travis, the main attack and fighting retreat left him believing that he had just looked through the gates of Hell.

The early morning sunlight revealed a scene of utter carnage, both inside and outside the fire base perimeter, with dead and wounded lying in grotesque and scattered heaps, friend and foe intermingled. The big clear up started, with the wounded as a top priority. The welcome sight of the UH-1A's Medevac choppers as they dropped down for a 'dust off' of the injured troops brought a greater sense of urgency to the task of recovering and trying to save the injured men.

Travis, his medic and the remains of his platoon were hard at it transporting the wounded to the helipad, lining them up on the ground ready for a quick transfer to the helicopters. As Travis returned with a loaded stretcher and placed it on the ground, he found himself looking into the contorted face of Frenchi, lying on the next stretcher and suffering from severe chest injuries. Travis could hear the sucking sound of the air as it entered and exited a punctured lung. His friend looked a mess. A medic placed a plastic bag over the lung and packed it with field dressings. Frenchi was going into shock as Travis knelt beside him. Holding his hand, he felt his friend's pulse; it was weak and rapid, his skin cold and clammy. The medic was now trying to stabilise him with a plasma expander.

Looking up at his friend, Frenchi said, 'I can't breathe, Pop.'

'Hang in there Frenchi, you can make it' Travis replied.

Then Frenchi pressed something into Travis' hand. Opening his palm, he saw Frenchi's trick glass eye nestling there. Looking down, he caught the glimmer of a smile from his friend. Then, wheezing with every word, Frenchi said, 'Keep it safe for me, it's my good luck piece.' As Travis opened his mouth to protest, Frenchi shook his head and closed his friend's hand over the trinket. Travis leaned forward and whispered, 'I'll keep it safe for you.'

Then he and the stretcher bearers were up and running with the stretcher. Travis gripped Frenchi's hand, carrying the plasma drip with the other. He just had time to shout, 'God bless you Frenchi' before the Medevac chopper lifted off in a cloud of dust.

Most of the Nam wounded who made it back to base survived their wounds, but not Frenchi, who died from massive internal bleeding and shock in the skies above Vietnam. The remainder of the Battalion, having been severely mauled, were relieved and airlifted back to the main base, where Travis was informed of Frenchi's death. It was a sombre trio who assembled in the beer tent to drink to their fallen comrade. There was very little conversation between Travis, the Chief and Doc as they remembered and drank to their good friend. They were all wondering how many more friends and comrades they would lose before this damn war was over.

Chief, good old Chief, honest as the day is long, the best guy in the world to have beside you in a fire fight, summed it all up when he quoted James Shirley's poem: 'There is no armour against Fate; Death lays his icy hand on kings'. 'I'll drink to that,' Travis said quietly, and three glasses clinked to acknowledge the wisdom of the words and the passing of a dear friend.

Travis was now nearing the end of his tour and far from winding down, he seemed to be spending more time in the thick of things. So it was that he found himself once again heading for combat, being ferried to God knows where and what. All he knew was that enemy activity had been reported around a certain village area, and it was believed that the site might be riddled with tunnels. The choppers swooped in for a drop-off in an area of tall grass. As they hovered just above the ground the Troopers bailed out, hitting the ground running, spreading out in all-round defence. When the insert was complete, the troops moved forward warily towards the suspected enemy position. They soon made contact with a strong force of VC and put down suppressing fire on suspected enemy positions, or when they could see muzzle flashes or smoke. In the main, they were unsure where the enemy positions were situated as the high grass obscured vision.

They called for gunships to rocket suspected areas. That done, the Troopers advanced at a very slow pace, on the lookout for any nasty surprises Charlie might have in store for them. Unfortunately, as he looked down to unclip the handset of his radio, the company radioman failed to see the large, Russian-made bounding mine or its trip-wire fuse. Although the Platoon was well spread out, when the Bouncing Betty mine with its omni-directional fragmentation exploded with a whitish-blue flash, it caused multiple casualties in 3 Platoon.

Travis, who was ahead of his unit and keeping in touch with his point man, took a massive spread of shrapnel to his back. It was like a blow from a sledge-hammer as the shrapnel pierced his flak jacket and helmet. Then there was merciful blackness before he felt the searing, burning sensation over his back, head arms and legs.

CHAPTER THIRTEEN

AMERICA AND IRELAND

As he came to his senses, Travis had great difficulty in focusing. The natural daylight made him squint as he tried to make out shapes and sizes. Then, as his vision began to clear, he realised that he was in a bright, white hospital ward with nurses and doctors fussing up and down, attending to their various charges. He was lying on his stomach with his head to one side, his eyes looking at a pretty nurse who was holding his wrist.

She smiled at him and said, 'Welcome back, Staff Sergeant Travis.' As she moved away, another person appeared in his line of sight; Melissa. He closed his eyes, thinking he had to be dreaming. But on opening his eyes again, he found Melissa was still there, now holding his hand and smiling that old smile of hers, the one that turned her from a pretty girl into a very beautiful one.

He tried to speak, but only a croak came out. His mouth felt as if it was full of feathers. 'Water' he croaked. Melissa held a plastic drinking bottle for him and he sucked a delicious gulp of chilled water through a drinking straw, the water clearing his mouth and throat.

'What happened, where am I, why are you here?' he asked.

'You've been in a coma for some time, before and after neurosurgery. The Army contacted the Leclercs as your next of kin, and told your gran. She told me, and here I am.'

'Thank you darling, you are a sight for sore eyes'.

'I've taken an unpaid leave of absence, and I intend to stay here in the States until I'm sure you're are on the mend. You've had a very bad knock, but the doctors tell me you should make a full recovery.'.

She was as good as her word, and the hospital authorities were very helpful in letting her come and go almost at will. From then on, with the help of Novocaine and other painkillers, Travis' recovery was rapid, and soon the time came when Melissa felt she could leave him and return to Ireland. On her last day at the hospital, she wheeled him down to the cafeteria in a specially-adapted wheelchair, with Travis half sitting and half lying back on air cushions.

Over a light lunch, Melissa told him about her family in Ireland.

'They're on the move again' she said. 'Canada was a non-starter, so they're looking at emigrating to England, where they hope my brothers and sisters will have a better future.'

Then Travis spoke of his plans.

'I'm still hoping to make my career in the Army, even with my injuries' he said. 'I want to go as far as I can promotion-wise'.

'I know Travis, I know.'

There was a long pause as they looked at each other, then Travis said, 'You know I love you very much'.

'And I love you, Patrick.'

'Just as soon as I get some sick leave I'll be home to see you. It shouldn't be long now.'

'I'll be counting the days, darling' replied Melissa.

That night she started the long journey back to the Emerald Isle. The thought of seeing her again was a great incentive to fight back to full fitness for Travis and, as soon as his healing could stand it and under doctor's orders, he threw himself back into training, starting off with light gym work. As soon as was fit again he was on his way to Ireland, on sick leave, to a wonderful reunion with Melissa.

'I've got a nice surprise for you' Travis informed her on their first night together, as they had dinner in a quaint little restaurant overlooking Dublin Bay. With its twinkling lights and moon-dashed waves, it was a highly romantic setting. 'I'd like to take you to France for a long weekend, or more, if you can arrange for some time off.'

'That would be wonderful, but I don't feel very well Patrick, I'm sure I'm coming down with something.' Travis' brow wrinkled up in a concerned frown at this statement. 'I'll make an appointment to see my doctor as soon as possible and see if I can persuade him to give me a sick note for a couple of days or so. What do you think Patrick?' She gave a huge wink. He finally got the message, and laughed out loud.

That night he placed a long distance call to Chalonne; Madame answered, as he had hoped she would.

'It's me Mama, I'm calling from Dublin' he said. You could hear the emotion in Madame Leclerc's voice as she said, 'How are you, mon cher? When are you coming home to us?'

'That's why I've phoned Mama, but also I want to have a few words with you and ask your advice.'

In his phone calls and previous conversations, he had never mentioned his relationship with Melissa, in an effort not to upset his in-laws. But now he felt he had to, and the time was right. He would never take any major steps in his life without discussing them with his French family. He loved and respected them very much.

There and then he told Madame Leclerc all about Melissa and his reawakened love for her. He told her that his short life with her beloved daughter had taught him that true, loving commitment to another person brings great happiness and that there was no doubt in his mind that love was a healing power. Melissa had been a part of his healing process, and now he wished to propose to her, but felt that he could not do so without the blessing of his French family.

'There is no need to ask for our blessing Patrice, you will always have that' Madame replied.

'Thank you Mama, but there is something more I want to ask', Patrick said. A long pause, then, 'I want to bring her home, I want you to meet her, do you think that you and Papa would be able to cope with such a trial?'

'I'm sure I speak for Papa when I say that your young lady is more than welcome to our home. When were you thinking of coming? The sooner the better.'

'We could come within the next day to two.'

'Very good. Please let us know your arrival time, and we will have Raymond on tap to pick you up.'

'Thank you Mama. Au revoir for now.'

CHAPTER FOURTEEN

FRANCE

It was love at first sight for the Leclercs. Melissa was like that. She was warm and loving, with a great natural charm that tended to captivate people when meeting her for the fist time. The Leclercs looked on her as a new addition to their family, a new daughter. Although Travis had warned them that he hadn't given Melissa any reason to believe he was thinking of marriage, the reaction of the Leclercs was all he was waiting for, and on the couple's first Saturday in France, he whisked Melissa off to show her around Paris. They stayed overnight in the capital, then on the Sunday evening as they were at dinner on the promenade deck of the Eiffel Tower, he emptied his glass of wine in one go, cleared his throat, and took Melissa by the hand.

'I think you know by now that despite all that has happened to me, the long periods abroad in dangerous situations and the wounds I've had, all I ever want to be is a soldier' he began. 'I'm selfish, I want more than I have, in every way, both in my career and in my relationships. I know that this may not be a very attractive package to ask someone to share and that it could be all in the short term with the continuing war in Vietnam. But this may be the only time we have, and if it is, then I feel we should focus on the present, on what we have right now and not on the future, whatever it may bring. I want us to enjoy today together, and every day that God sends us. I want to be truly with you now, I want to love you now. I don't want to put off loving you, in every way I can, for another day, or when we feel settled and secure.

'The point of all this, darling, is that I am selfishly in love with you and I want to spend the rest of my life, be it short or long, with you.'

Then, sliding off his chair on to one knee, he asked her for the second time, 'Melissa Brandini, will you please marry me?'

'For the second time, Patrick Travis, Yes, yes, yes!' she joyfully replied. At that, and much to their embarrassment, everyone in earshot on the promenade deck stood up and clapped, cheered and whistled. They could hardly kiss for laughing as they embraced to seal their promise.

Back in Chalonne, they had a special engagement dinner, a quiet affair with Anton, Madame and Raymond. The only other addition to the party was Chantelle. During the meal, Anton stood up, indicating that he would like to say a few words. The family sat back in their chairs, smiling at him in anticipation.

'As a family, we have been through a nightmare of loss and sorrow' he said. 'But we have held together, loving each other, consoling and supporting each other. As indeed it should be, in any loving family. Mama and I have been blessed with two fine sons in Raymond and Patrice, and now we are going to have a daughter to welcome to our happy family. A truly lovely and beautiful woman, who in a very short time has captured our hearts, none more so than this old soldier.

'Melissa, we salute your engagement to our son Patrice and accord it our every blessing. We wish you all the happiness in the world. Now Mama, Raymond, Chantelle, please, a toast to the happy couple, with our very best wishes for their future.'

Travis and Melissa held hands and kissed as the family raised their glasses in a toast and then resumed their seats. Everybody started to talk at once, filling the air with excited chatter, finally stopped by the sound of a dessert spoon tinkling on a large-stemmed champagne glass. It was Raymond. He looked remarkably happy but nervous as he drew himself up, standing tall, bracing his shoulders back, touching his bow tie and straightening his jacket. His left-hand was holding on like grim death to Chantelle's.

'I, we…' he started, 'That is, Chantelle and I, wish to make an announcement of our own.' Looking into the glowing faces of Raymond and Chantelle, the rest of the gathering all knew what the announcement would be.

'Papa, Mama, Brother Patrice, Melissa. Chantelle and I also wish to announce our engagement to be married. 'Chantelle has been there for me helping me through my sorrowful journey after the loss of my beloved sister Antoinette. She thanked me many times for my support for her, in the loss of her best friend, though there was no need. We have always been best friends, even in childhood, but now, wonder of wonders, that friendship has turned to love, a love we believe will last for ever. Papa, Mama, we ask for your blessing on our union.'

With tears of happiness in their eyes, Raymond's mother and father pushed their chairs back, then stood up to embrace their only son and his fiancée, followed by Travis and Melissa. When they were all seated again, with much dabbing of eyes with hankies and napkins, Travis then took it on himself to propose the toast to the happy couple. He spoke glowingly of his brother-in-law and his love and respect for him and thanked Chantelle for her loving kindness and compassion for Raymond, acknowledging her love and lifelong friendship for Antoinette.

Then Anton stood up once more. This time he looked grave

and somewhat lonely. Before he spoke, he reached out his hand to his beloved wife, then with a nervous cough said, 'I have one more toast to propose. It is to the absent members of our family, whom we know and believe are not really absent tonight because we can feel their presence here, in this room. It's a warm and loving presence, and I feel sure that they add their blessings to ours. My beloved family, please charge your glasses and be upstanding, the toast is Antoinette and her Little Angel.'

Although tears were shed at these words, they did not dampen the happiness of that special evening.

Now that he had taken the plunge, Travis wanted to have everything done and dusted in double-quick time. His leave at an end, he flew back to the States, reporting to the hospital for some rigorous health checks and an examination of his wounds. All was progressing well and he was returned to the Division on light duties, with regular medical check-ups. He arranged for an interview with his CO to request permission to marry, particularly as Melissa was not an American citizen. The interview went well, and he was promised a good leave period to allow them to get wed and go on honeymoon.

With that out of the way, the CO put Travis at his ease and asked his Executive Officer, who was also in the room, to take over. Major Garry started off by saying, 'I'm sure you know Staff that we have pressing needs for good replacement leadership for the ongoing conflict in Asia. So with regard to your military background and your previous commissioned status in the French army, we would like you to accept a commission in the Army of the United States of America. How do you feel about that?'

'I would be more than honoured, sir' was the prompt reply.

Major Garry then opened a small square presentation box, presenting it with outstretched hand to Travis. Inside were two gold bars, denoting the rank of First Lieutenant. 'Congratulations Lieutenant Travis' he said. Travis took the proffered right hand in a firm handshake, and was congratulated by the EO. Then, saluting his superiors, he about-faced and marched out, to start another chapter in his chosen profession.

Travis wasted no time in jacking up his wedding. It would be in Dublin, in Melissa's parish church in Bootherstown, which overlooked the sea in South Dublin. His first quest was to ask Raymond to be his best man. Then he booked hotels for his French family, including Chantelle. Chief and Doc, both back in the States unscathed at the end of their tour, were invited. The only Legionnaire not on active duty was Hamish, who was also invited. Melissa's and his own Irish family, with best friend John, would make up the bulk of a very large and happy group.

It all went swimmingly. Again dress uniforms were worn, sanctioned by Irish Army HQ and the American Embassy in Ballsbridge, near to where Melissa worked. After a sumptuous wedding breakfast in the Grosvenor Hotel, they had their wedding photographs taken in the lovely St Stephens Green nearby.

The next day, Lieutenant and Mrs Travis, flew off to Lake Garda in Italy for the start of their honeymoon. Then it was on to Florence, ending up in the eternal city of Rome, with a brief stopover in Capri. There they took the tram up the dizzy heights to declare their love to the world from the summit. Patrick shouting, 'Patrick loves Melissa!' Not to be outdone Melissa shouted, 'Melissa loves Patrick!' All a bit silly, but much in keeping with the daft but loving antics that honeymooners get up to.

So the happy days slipped past, with the couple adopting the old saying 'When in Rome do as the Romans do' as they integrated with the local population. Melissa's Italian was rudimentary, but well up to the task of making new friends and smoothing their way when necessary.

The days seemed to fly by and soon, too soon, it was time to return to the States. It was a big wrench for Melissa leaving her happy family circle, but she quickly fell into the role of a loving wife, concentrating on her new husband, one hundred per cent.

Within a month of their return to America and having settled into base married quarters, the newly-weds were back in France for the marriage of Raymond to Chantelle. Travis returned the favour and acted as best man for his brother-in-law. It was a short stay, as he had to get back to duty.

They were hardly settled back to their routine and married life when Travis was summoned once again to HQ. He was to be posted, as an Executive Officer, to Company Commander Hank Beech. He was 'Nam bound again.

CHAPTER FIFTEEN

BACK TO VIETNAM

Despite all the wonderful, exciting and loving things that had happened to Travis since his return from Vietnam, it felt as if he had never left the place as he stepped down from the plane after a long, boring flight from the USA to start his six-month tour. Soon, he was back in the thick of the action, with his responsibilities having grown out of all proportion to his former role as a squad and platoon leader. But he took to it like a duck to water.

The going was hard and dangerous at times and he once again welcomed the short seaside R & R breaks and, six months into his tour, a week with his beloved Melissa. They met in Sydney, Australia and settled into one of the city's top hotels. There was no recurrence of the nightmares he had endured in Hawaii.

On their first night together, they made love with great passion and then again with sweetness and gentleness. As they were lying naked side by side in the afterglow of their lovemaking, Melissa asked, 'Darling, please put your ear to my stomach and have a listen.'

Puzzled, Patrick did as he was bid.

'Hear anything sweetheart?' Melissa asked

'What am I listening for?'

'The sound of our baby's heartbeat, my darling' was the reply.

Travis, gobsmacked, looked up from where he was lying into the eyes of his proud and smiling wife. 'No!' he said in wonderment and disbelief.

'Yes' from Melissa. Then they were both whooping and screaming in delight as they almost hugged each other to death in their excitement.

It was however a worried and chastened Travis who went back to Vietnam after an idyllic break with his beloved wife and 'What's-its-name' or 'Win' as their baby was affectionately referred to. Now he was to be a daddy. It felt awesome, but he soon realised that trying to wrap himself up in cotton wool, as it were, was not the way of a professional soldier. He had to learn to compartmentalise his life and become two different people; the dedicated and, where possible, fearless soldier, and the soft and loving family man.

With some jiggery-pokery he had Doc move into Company HQ in his role of Medic, with the rank of Sergeant. He was unable to shift the Chief, who was now a Platoon Sergeant, also on his second tour. But whenever the chance came to meet up with his friends and to chew the fat, they took it, renewing their close ties.

The three friends were nearing the end of their various tours when the balloon went up on a very big operation. The enemy were starting to mass in one of the very vulnerable provinces and Travis' Battalion was sent in to bolster up the troops already on operations.

They did their best to settle into the Fire Base assigned to them. It was a miserable time of the year in the middle of the monsoon period and highly uncomfortable, with constant heavy rain turning their position on a ridge into a river of deep, sticky mud, making it difficult to dig further defences and bolster up the berms, or earthworks, on existing defence lines. With next to no overhead cover, it was a crap time for the Troopers, pestered by the damp and the ever-present mosquitoes. Officers and men shared the same conditions, as indeed was the unspoken order at all times.

The area around the forward base had been defoliated by Agent Orange and the poison left the remains of the trees stripped and black, looking like monstrous burnt matches which some giant had stuck upright in the ground to light his way. Bomb craters had left the area looking like the surface of the moon. The effect resulted in a good killing ground, with no cover for outgoing or incoming patrols, who had to run the gauntlet of enemy fire when they operated in daylight.

Intelligence and patrol activity pointed towards a full regiment of Viet Cong gearing up for an attack in strength which, when it finally came, was devastating in the extreme. It resulted in every Tom, Dick and Harry, whatever his rank or role, being detailed to defend the base, and in the case of the medics, to tend and defend the wounded. Massive air strikes were called in and Travis wondered at the feeling of the enemy soldiers as the Huey gunships, equipped with their four machine guns and rockets, wap-wapped their way into the fray. He had no idea how they felt, and he really didn't care. But that wap-wap sound scared the shit out of him, worried as he always was that they hit the right target. It would be a right bummer to be hit by your own ordnance.

Despite everyone's best efforts, they were beginning to be overrun, with enemy suicide bombers breaking through the lines and aiming for the command hooches and aid station. In the end, Command had no option but to call in air and artillery strikes on their own positions. This action finally broke the spirit of the VC, and they started to retreat.

They left behind the worse scenes of carnage Travis had ever witnessed as he began the rounds of checking for wounded survivors. His hearing was shot to hell, and he felt as if he was in another dimension, with the voices of his soldiers sounding faint and distant when they were standing right next to him. He felt giddy and light-headed as he stumbled around the remains of the Fire Base.

He went to the aid station first, as he could see that it had been attacked. The first image to present itself to him was that of his friend Doc, whose body he found draped over his patient, shielding the wounded soldier from whatever horror had entered the makeshift medical area. He had been hit in the back by a burst of automatic fire. The enemy soldier lay dead on the floor beside the stricken group, a French burp-gun still clutched in his dead hand. For his sins, the VC had also been shot in the back by a patient, who was now resting, eyes closed, still holding the Browning automatic pistol he had dispatched the attacker with.

As Travis turned Doc's head around to check his carotid artery, a faint groan escaped through his lips. 'Thank God' Travis intoned as he gently lifted his friend down and laid him on the ground, shouting, at the top of his voice, 'Medic, Medic!'

Much to his surprise, a battered and bruised medic answered his call and immediately started to work on Doc. 'Don't worry sir, he's going to make it', the medic stated, looking up at the officer.

'Thanks Corporal' said Travis. He would have liked to address the medic by name, but the soldier was unrecognisable, his face covered in so much muck and blood.

Travis, dog-tired, eyes red-rimmed and sore, moved his search to the outskirts of the Fire Base. It was a scene of absolute carnage, with bodies, body parts, equipment and weapons scattered all over the area. As he searched around, he started to hear a strange chanting, which got stronger as he went nearer. It reminded him of the Red Indian death chants he had heard in the movies when he was a young lad. He moved slowly towards the chanting figure, stepping gingerly over the dead and broken bodies of his command and their attackers.

The chanting soldier was a big man. He was in a sitting position and as Travis bent down to examine him, he saw that the soldier, an American, was suffering from an appalling stomach wound and was trying to push his intestines back inside his lacerated body. Travis rummaged in the soldier's clothing, finding his morphine syringe. He injected the dying soldier, hoping it would ease the pain. He wished the Chief had been there. Maybe he could have comforted this poor guy. The victim's face and hair were a mass of wet and dried mud mixed with copious amounts of blood.

Taking out his water bottle, Travis gently started to wash the stricken soldier's face, starting with his eyes, nose and mouth. The face, looking Christ-like in its pain, reminded Patrick of a scene from the Crucifixion. Then to his shock and horror, the face took on a familiar look. 'Sweet Jesus!' Travis muttered in due reverence as the face of the Chief, his Chief, emerged from the blood and grime. With the hot tears cascading down his face, Travis cradled his dying friend. He had never known if Chief was a Christian or not, but nevertheless he whispered the Act of Contrition in his friend's ear. Then he asked God to wash away any sins he may have and beseeched the Heavenly Father to take his soul to a place of light and peace where he would never feel pain again.

Travis sat in the mud and carnage, cradling his friend until they were separated by the gentle hands of the stretcher bearers, who, placing the Chief on a stretcher, carried him to the heli-pad, Travis trailing along after them like a lost soul.

The big Indian died in Travis' arms before he could be moved to a Medevac helicopter. Travis crouched beside his dead friend, holding his hand and crying his eyes out. He had seen death many times since his first stint in Vietnam, but this was so close, this was one more of his best friends. The only saving grace was that because of his terrible wounds, death had become an angel in disguise for the Indian brave.

Back on R & R Travis was alone, and that was just the way he wanted it. Doc was back in the States in hospital, so he had no close friends in Vietnam any more. He sat on the beach late into the night looking up at the stars. To him they looked like pinholes in the curtain of the night. Looking at them he thought, *I can feel God here.* Thinking of his dead and injured friends, he remembered an old priest telling him, 'You know Patrick, a good thing or a good person never dies. That is the core of our religion. But they do leave the world a little darker for their going'. Amen to that, Travis thought.

Before leaving for 'Nam, Melissa had picked out a star to be their own special one. *Maybe she's looking at our star right now,* he thought. *Wouldn't that be something. If you are, babe, I love you.*

CHAPTER SIXTEEN

AMERICA

Finally, his tour ended, Travis made his way back to the States and Melissa with hardly a scratch on his body. Feeling guilty that he was OK when his friends had been struck down, he was once again experiencing sleepless nights as he wrestled with his demons. In this, Melissa was the life-preserver who saved him from sinking into another black hole of depression. Without her, he wondered how he would have kept his sanity.

Melissa had a good pregnancy, with the exception of morning sickness and a massive craving for oranges. She finally went into labour in her due time. Travis, suffering from something akin to pre-jump nerves, drove her to the base hospital. Then the long wait, wondering would Melissa be OK and if 'Win' would be a healthy baby with all its fittings intact and in good working order.

He was in very mixed, but good, company in the waiting room. Here, rank meant nothing as soldiers from many different units supported each other.

Finally, as midnight approached, Melissa delivered a beautiful son. He was healthy, with a shock of auburn hair, not like the dark hair of his mother and father, but typically Irish. *Maybe it was all those oranges*, thought Travis. But no one could doubt who his daddy was. Even in this infant stage, he was the image of his father.

'Darling', Melissa began, 'before you say anything, I would like little Win to be called after your French father-in-law. I want him to be called Anton.'

It was a selfless and wonderful gesture to the father of his first wife, one Travis knew would make a dear and sad man very happy. For the life of him on this very special night in his life, he couldn't refuse this wonderful woman anything, and so Win became Anton Patrick Travis.

Travis' joy knew no bounds as he cradled his 7lb 14 ounces of cuddly love. This little mite was already helping to lift the darkness from Travis' soul. It was a joy to come home to his new family after duties; in fact for the next few weeks he felt he was walking on air. He couldn't believe he was a father and that he had helped to bring new life into the world, a new life that would forever carry his name.

His happiness was interrupted by a letter from his childhood friend John James in Dublin. They had always kept in touch by the odd letter and never missed sending Christmas cards, or getting together when Travis was home. Now John had some grim news to impart.

Dear Patrick

It is with great regret that I write to inform you that your father and your stepmother have both been killed in an accident. They were on a touring holiday by car, in the South of Ireland, when it happened. They were driving through the Knockmealdown mountains, with your father at the wheel, when it appears he had a heart attack. Their car went over the side of the mountain, dropping some 500 feet, and they never stood a chance. I know that you and your Dad were estranged, but I know you still loved him, and I am truly sorry for your loss.

Now, just one thing more, I am enclosing a cutting from the Irish Times, placed there by a solicitor trying to get in touch with you. It has the full details, address and telephone number. I think it would be a good idea for you to make contact with him and see what he has to say. That's all my news for now, but if you should get home, please look me up and we will have a night on the town, like the good old days. Meanwhile, my very best wishes to you, Melissa and little Anton.

Your friend, John.

Travis handed the open letter to Melissa. She read it quickly and reached out to take him in her arms.

'So darling, what do you think we should do?' Travis asked.

'I think you should put in for compassionate leave, go home and pay your last respects to your father. Then make a visit to the solicitor and see what he has to say. Baby and I will come along if that is OK with you, and it will be a great opportunity for my parents to see their new grandchild.'

Within forty-eight hours, the little family were on their way to Ireland. On arrival, they found that burial of the dead couple had taken place some days before, so leaving their newborn son with his delighted grandparents, Travis and Melissa visited Glasnevin Cemetery in Dublin, to see where his father and stepmother were buried. It turned out that they had been buried in the same grave as his mother and grandmother. It upset Travis that his cruel and vicious woman should be buried with his beloved mother. He was to find out that his step-aunt and her mealy-mouthed husband had taken care of the arrangements.

That night, lying in bed next to Melissa, he remembered how they had made the peace between them after that bitter and terrible row that had driven them apart, how they had rekindled their love and eventually arrived in the happy position they were in now. He regretted that he had never made contact with his father and tried to make it up with him. It was too late now, and he was sad that he had lost the chance to make peace between them.

In thinking about his father, he wondered if a person, however, long he lives, can live virtuously enough to justify the harm he has done. He doubted it.

The next day he went to see Noel Hegerty, his father's solicitor. Hegerty was a kindly, elderly man who put Travis at his ease straight away.

'Now then, Lieutenant Travis, let me get straight to the point. Your father has left his entire estate to you. That includes the house and all the goods, chattels and any monies remaining after burial, death duties and taxes are paid. But be advised that we have had vociferous claims from a couple I believe you would call your step-aunt and uncle, a Mr and Mrs Cahill. Now let me put your mind at rest, they haven't a snowball's chance in hell of getting their hands on your inheritance. That said, how would you wish me to proceed?'

'Well, first of all, thank you for all your work and your care on my behalf, Mr. Hegerty. But just for now, all I want is the keys to my father's house'.

The next morning, with the keys in his possession, Travis let himself into the old, dark Victorian house. All he was interested in at this stage were the family papers which had not been deposited with the solicitor. He found them in a square, battered biscuit box. At the bottom of the papers he found a sealed envelope. Opening it he discovered a wad of photos of his mother. The find gladdened his heart, as he knew then how much his father had loved his mother.

Going back to see Hegerty again, he told the solicitor, 'All I want from the estate are the family papers and in particular this envelope of photos, as well as any money left over from the settlement of the estate. I intend to put the money in a trust fund for my son and any other children my wife and I may have. The rest I wish to sign over to Mr and Mrs Cahill.'

'If that is your wish I will get on to it straight away. However you will have to attend along with the Cahills to sign the deeds over to them.'

Some days later Travis was given an appointment to visit the solicitor's office. On the fateful day he and Melissa were seated with the solicitor having morning coffee and biscuits when Margaret and Liam Cahill were shown into the office. Mrs Cahill greeted the solicitor with, 'What is this little bastard doing here Mr Hegerty?'

'Please Mrs Cahill, control yourself and watch your language' Hegerty said. But Margaret Cahill, ignoring him went on, 'You broke my sister's heart you little git, after all she did for you. Keeping a home for you, dressing and feeding you, pouring out all her love on you, and what did she get in return? Nothing but grief. You should be ashamed of yourself, but no, here you are scuttling back at the sniff of easy money. Well, we have something to say about that. You tell him Liam.'

Liam Cahill was a civil servant and a pretentious, cocky know-it-all. He was a bald-headed, Humpty Dumpty of a man who wore pince-nez glasses perched on the end of his nose. Pushing the glasses back into place, he spoke up.

'I have looked into this case and we know our legal rights, and if you think for one moment that you are going to wing your way back to America with part of our inheritance, you have another think coming.'

Throughout this unwarranted tirade Travis sat in silence, his right hand tightly gripping Melissa's, warning her silently to hold her tongue. He was cold with anger as he listened to the foul-mouthed Margaret Cahill. Travis remember the times when the fearsome duo had visited his home, when he would be turned out onto the street until they had gone. No ham sandwiches and fairy cakes for him. He remembered the time he had begged for a puppy or a kitten, only for Margaret Cahill to kill off any chance he had of getting a pet. 'That little brat will never look after any pet you let him have' she had said. 'The animal will run riot around the house pissing and shitting everywhere and you will be left to clean up after it, my sister dear.' She just couldn't stand the sight of her step-nephew. She was childless and to Travis' mind, it showed that God knew something about people.

As the memories came flooding back to him, he knew just what he wanted to do. Reaching across the solicitor's desk, he pulled the will towards him and taking out his pen, he drew up another codicil. He motioned to Hegerty to witness the new modifying clause to the will. That done, he gestured to the solicitor to bring the proceedings to order by signalling with his hand in a cutting motion across his throat. All this time Margaret and Liam were still going at it in the strongest possible terms.

'I think you have made you point, Mr and Mrs Cahill' said Mr Hegerty. 'Please allow me to get on with the proceedings.' In a silence broken only by Margaret's Cahill's heavy breathing, Hegerty started to read the will. 'I Henry Travis, being of sound mind and body, in this my last will and testament, bequeath my estate and all my worldly goods to my only child, my son, Patrick Travis.'

The reading was interrupted by loud protests from the Cahills. 'Please please, I haven't finished, there is a codicil as follows' Hegerty said. Again there was silence and the solicitor continued.

'Forty-eight hours ago a further codicil was added by Lieutenant Travis and witnessed by Mrs Travis and myself, in that the entire estate, less any moniés accruing after death duties and taxes, should go to Mr and Mrs Liam Cahill.'

The silence in the office was tangible as the shocked Cahills tried to come to terms with the new turn of events. Margaret Cahill's face started to soften as she turned to look at Travis. But then the solicitor, trying to suppress a smile, continued: 'In the last few minutes a further codicil has been added, which amended the will to read as follows. That the entire estate, less any monies accruing after death duties and taxes, to go to The Dublin Cats and Dogs Home.'

Margaret Cahill appeared to be having a minor stroke. Whatever it was, she had certainly been struck dumb. Her husband was shaking and trying to placate her, shouting, 'Margaret, Margaret speak to me, please speak to me!'

Hegerty poured a glass of water and handed it to Cahill. Meanwhile, Travis and Melissa stood up, quietly thanked Mr Hegerty, shook his hand and left the office to the solicitor and his shocked visitors. As the young couple left the building Melissa broke into gales of laughter, saying, 'You're becoming a sly old fox Patrick Travis, adding that codicil at the last minute, I didn't know you had it in you.' Travis joined in his wife's laughter.

His successful and happy visit to Ireland acted as a tonic to Travis' depression and aided in his recuperation. Another positive input to his mental health was his regular visits to the hospital and later convalescence, where his friend Doc was recovering well from his wounds. Each visit was a form of therapy for them both as they talked about and through their personal demons. They discussed the weird feelings they had as they moved around homeland America, after each tour of duty in the 'Nam. Things were so normal in the States, with people going about their business and social life, while thousands of miles away young men were dying in pain and squalor and others being maimed for life. It could well and truly blow your mind if you let it.

Then there was the 'Why me?' factor. Why am I alive and my best friends dead? Why did they survive, when others lost their lives? Was there any reason to it? Their personal input and confessions to one another were worth a mountain of time with the trick cyclists, as they called their psychologists.

However, despite all this therapy, Travis felt he needed something else, maybe another good beasting. He finally made a decision to try for Special Forces. He first talked it through with Doc, who told him, 'You know Pop, I was just thinking along similar lines. Lying in hospital and watching the good work going on here, I've have decided that if I survive Vietnam I want to study to become a doctor and later a surgeon. Just as soon as I'm fit and well I intend to go back to 'Nam. That's where I can best help my fellow countrymen, my buddies. So go for it Pop, and good luck to you'.

Next, Travis talked it through with Melissa. 'Darling, as you know I am still finding it hard to come to terms with all the happenings in Vietnam' he said. 'You also know I've always solved my head, heart and soul problems by heavy physical and mental renewal. So, it's my intention, if you agree, to go for Special Forces training and induction. If I make it, it would be another step upwards in my career.'

Despite her love for him, or maybe because of it, Melissa, remembering his pre-proposal speech in the Eiffel Tower said, 'Darling, I know you have always been driven by your family background, by your father, Lord rest him. But don't you think you've proved yourself many times over already? Surely there's is no need to carry on putting yourself in testing situations. Honestly, there are times I think you've been born with a self-destruct mechanism, that you're an engine with no brakes. But if joining the Green Berets is what you want to do, I won't stand in your way.'

The next morning he placed his written request for permission to try for selection to the Special Forces Green Berets. With the need for seasoned officers for the campaign in Asia, he had his request for Special Forces Assessment sanctioned and, after special security clearance, he was duly informed of his start date at the US Special Warfare School at Fort Bragg.

Selection started with a 23-day exercise during which he was tested in mental and physical stamina as to his suitability for the Special Forces Qualification and Selection Course. Along with his course notification came his promotion to the rank of Captain. During his first week at Bragg, he was interviewed by a psychologist to check out any lingering mental problems he might have as a result of his experiences in combat during his military career.

Having returned from his last tour in Vietnam fit and well and spending many hours in the gym to return himself to full fitness, he put up a confident front. The physical exercise had helped him with his bad moments when he slipped back into darkness from time to time. However, the biggest antidote and cure to his mental problems were his beloved wife Melissa, baby Anton Patrick and his friend Doc. By the time he presented himself at Fort Bragg, he was well switched on and positive about himself and the future.

Luckily his full medical report from the French army had never been forwarded to the US forces, so his depression following the death of Antoinette and their baby was not recorded. Travis could feel the hand of old Anton in that decision.

When it came to the physical fitness tests, he felt and looked like an old man alongside younger officers and NCOs in their early twenties for whom the tests were designed. It was hard going to march between 18 and 50 kilometres carrying a 50-pound rucksack and personal weapon and having to swim 50 meters in uniform and boots.

In his second week there was more marching, the distances and weights increasing during the course, along with a very demanding obstacle course to test the volunteers' upper body strength. Despite his fitness, he struggled with that one. Dropped into a remote area with field rations, map and compass, he was told to make his way to a designated map reference within seventy-two hours, without been spotted and captured. He could hack the land navigation course from a physical point of view, but he was never a whiz at map reading. On his own during this phase, he couldn't give the map to anyone else.

It was a long and lonely course to travel, with some of the toughest terrain the Army could find. This exercise was to test the student's ability to navigate, operate and survive in isolated and rough terrain, day or night, rain or shine, on their own. Next, it was working as a member of a twelve-man Special Forces Operational Detachment on exercise. So it went on and on, with regular Boards to identify soldiers for elimination or retention.

The training was arduous, relentless and sometimes hazardous, and there were many times when he was driven to the verge of tears. But Travis knew that this was what he wanted. He was finally getting his mindset right, he believed he could do it and started every day with that as his main thought and mantra. He had always believed his mind was his best weapon with his ability to cope with stress, both mental and physical.

That phase over, as an officer it was on to Phase Two, which covered a 15-week period of instruction in Special Forces missions and operations with the Special Warfare Training Group. Following this came a major exercise in unconventional warfare, designed to pull together everything the volunteer had learned.

Having completed the exercise, Travis and the few remaining students were awarded their Green Berets. On graduation day the inspecting officer, a fellow Green Beret just back from the Vietnam war, gave the following advice: 'Remember the code of the Samurai, that you live by your word, that your soul is as good as the steel of your sword. That you maintain a sense of loyalty to your beliefs and to your friends and comrades and those you work with, whoever they are and wherever they are. Protect your integrity, because without it, you have nothing. Now, go kick ass.'

The words certainly hit home with Travis, as every good soldier he had worked with unthinkingly adhered to those principles. He knew in his heart of hearts that he always had, and always would.

Next, it was on to training in advanced skills and the Special Forces Detachment Officer Qualification Course, followed by a posting to a twelve-man 'A' Team, ready to be inserted in to any country in the world that requested the skills of the Green Berets, either as advisers and trainers or for direct participation in combat operations.

Travis believed he had now reached his peak, as the best possible soldier he could be, and he was more than ready for what might lie ahead. He was soon to be tested to the extreme.

CHAPTER SEVENTEEN

VIETNAM

Travis was in no doubt where he would be sent, and after an extensive leave period, he was 'Nam bound again. This time he was posted to the 5th Special Forces Group, assigned to establishing remote outposts and organising local people into paramilitary units and self-defence forces, the CIDG, Civilian Irregular Defence Group. In his case, it meant working with Montagnards and Cambodian CIDG units who were housed in Special Forces 'A' camps, strung out along the Cambodian border. They worked alongside these indigenous units as quick reaction forces, mobile guerrilla teams and re-con teams. They provided medical care for the tribespeople and built schools for their children to attend. All hearts and mind stuff.

Along with this, they conducted clandestine operations on the war's edges and grey areas, denying areas like Cambodia, Laos, the DMZ (Demilitarized Zone) and North Vietnam, in order to disrupt the infrastructure and supply routes of the NVSA and VC forces along the Ho Chi Minh Trail. It was exciting and dangerous work, but once again Travis took to his new role in solid Legion fashion.

Three months into his tour he was called in for a pre-infiltration briefing, which was opened with an ominous statement: 'This will be a clandestine cross-border mission Travis. Your crew will not wear any markings or insignia or carry personal identification. Should you or any member of your team be killed or captured, the United States will disavow all knowledge of you'. The briefing officer carried on: 'Intel has pinpointed a large command post nestled in a jungle clearing on the wrong side of the border. It is believed to house some top brass, intel and artillery fire control officers. Your mission is to eliminate all enemy forces and destroy the complex'. The mission statement was repeated so that there was no misunderstanding of what was required of Travis and his team.

The group for the mission was for the most part Green Berets, but it included two Nung tribesmen and two Montagnards. The team were kitted out in jungle cam suits which had been dyed black. They were armed in the main with M16s and 12 gauge shotguns; the latter, as Travis knew from his tour in Cyprus, were excellent in ambushes. Grinning to himself, he remembered the great quote from the *Dragnet* TV series, where police Sergeant Joe Friday explained the fire-power of the shotgun: 'The first shot cuts you in two, the second shot makes you a crowd.' Way to go, Travis thought.

His team also included two Scout/Snipers, their weapons fitted with telescopic sights and sonic suppressors. The snipers also packed their own personal weapons. The tribesmen favoured their AK 47s, which they had captured from the enemy.

This was his first special mission, and Travis looked on it as another test of his nerve and most important, his skills as a leader and soldier. The next day, he and his team were slicked into the designated area by Huey helicopter at first light. It was a risky business, but the infiltration went without a hitch. Travis' main hope of avoiding contact with VC depended on the skills of his tribesmen, who knew the area and its inhabitants as well as they knew their own children.

Avoiding trails, they began probing in the direction of the border with Cambodia. In minutes the men were running in sweat, despite the fact that the triple canopy jungle blocked out most of the sun's rays. They were safe for the time being, so long as the VC were unaware of their presence. As they moved ever closer to the border the going got very rough, with the terrain running up hill and down dale and bamboo thickets, elephant grass and jungle creepers pulling and tearing at the team as they laboured through the tangled vegetation. The area was thick with leeches and mosquitoes, poisonous snakes and the odd tiger to contend with.

Halfway to their destination they stumbled on a small village. Having sent the tribesmen to recce it, they returned to say that the village appeared to have been untouched by the VC and that the elders would help the team in any way possible. Travis decided to spend the night there and question the elders on the terrain and any enemy forces between them and their objective.

Jack Deeko, his medic, started treating sick or injured villagers with penicillin and cough medicine. The rest of the squad set about a 'hearts and minds' programme, giving out tins of powdered milk, which were welcomed by the villagers. The kids lapped it up, especially the army rations and the chocolate bars. Travis had his own nursemaid, a girl of about sixteen who waited on him hand and foot. Her name was Blin and she was lithe, with delicate features and shiny, jet black hair. She wore a handmade, woven and embroidered dress, with bronze friendship bracelets on her wrists. She was a very beautiful young woman. Their visit was a very happy one, as Travis and his team had a lot of time for the friendly Yards and showed it, much to the delight of the villagers.

The next morning the head man of the village offered two of his best trackers to Travis for his team, and he gratefully accepted. They were armed with the deadly crossbow. The team was now fourteen strong.

On their second day out from the village, they came to a large clearing in the jungle, on the edge of which they hunkered down to observe before moving on. To their surprise, they spotted six Viet Cong crossing the clearing left to right of their position. He motioned to his two scout/snipers, Andy and Rollo, who adjusted their sights to deal with the range and the afternoon light that was softening into an early evening haze. Then, in a coordinated shoot, working inwards from front man and the tail-end Charlie and firing in unison, they started to dispatch the patrol. The only sound to be heard was the slight 'click-puff' of the silenced weapons.

As the two front and rear men went down, the other four turned to see what had caused them to fall over and as the next two enemy soldiers were hit, a look of horror and fear showed on the faces of the remaining two Cong. It was their last reaction on this earth before Andy and Rollo signed off with two head shots which left a pink mist where the VC heads had been. It was clinical but savage. The entire action, conducted in almost total silence, was over in seconds without alerting anyone else to their presence in the area. The team quickly moved the bodies and concealed them in the thick undergrowth before moving on to towards their objective.

Suddenly, they were there. That was the way it was in the jungle. One minute you are buried in the clinging humid confines of wall-to-wall vegetation, the next you break out into a clearing. It was so with the enemy position, which was almost the size of a village. It had four bamboo walls and an entrance with four manned watchtowers in the corners.

Studying their objective, Travis decided to send his two snipers right and left of the stockade to take out the watchtower sentries with their silenced rifles. He sent Mitch Jago, his explosives expert, to place a charge on the gate which would be blown on the successful dispatch of the sentries. Following the explosion, he and the killing group would rush through the entrance and discharge death and destruction on the inhabitants and their equipment.

As the encampment was in a small valley, Travis made his way to the high ground to observe the layout of the camp and assign his men to the various buildings earmarked for particular attention, like the barracks area and the signals centre and most important, the headquarters building. Then, plans made, he briefed his team, ending with the order, 'We shoot ourselves in, we shoot ourselves out. If in doubt when taking an officer, empty your mag into him.'

After the briefing, the team squirrelled away into cover and rested up for an attack at first light. Next morning, in semi-darkness, the snipers and the explosives expert crawled into position. In the stillness before first light, Travis counted the four barely audible click-puffs, followed by the explosion that blew the gate into matchstick-size pieces of wood. With that, Travis and his men charged through the gap, separating in twos for their pre-planned targets. Then, throwing grenades into the buildings, they followed up with weapons on full automatic, spraying the interiors with deadly fire. Travis and his two Yards ran towards the headquarters hooch, only to be confronted by some VC officers who burst out of the building. *Jesus, but the little bastards reacted fast,* Travis thought as he fired off a burst. His Yards were backing him up, but just as they reached the building, one of them was hit and fell beside him. Not stopping, he and the remaining Yard took up positions on either side of the door and lobbed in grenades.

Following the explosions they burst in, weapons blazing. Travis was shocked to see a wounded officer with an AK47 levelled at him, but his Yard companion let rip with a short burst and the officer was punched out through the bamboo wall of the building as if snatched by an unseen hand. The Mike Force firepower was sufficient and effective against the enemy defences, as their forces were concentrated into a very small area.

When the last of the enemy had been despatched, the assault group, having subdued if not eliminated the enemy, set about destroying all enemy equipment and weapons, setting fire to the bamboo houses and barracks. All material found in the command post was seized. The medic looked after their only casualty, the Yard who had been with Travis in the attack on the CP; luckily he was designated as walking wounded.

Travis gave the order to withdraw quickly and quietly, in case the enemy had had time to call for fire support on the compound. The whole action and move out, which was orderly and disciplined, was over in ten minutes.

It was reported by the snipers that a high-ranking officer and some of his troops has escaped through a gap in the rear wall of the compound. The snipers had taken out half of them, but the officer had made it to the cover of the jungle. Travis knew that as soon as the officer reached friendly forces, he would send out troops to track and attack his group. It was only a question of time before that happened, and the team had to make the most of it.

Apart from that, he was well satisfied with the success of the mission. His men had been aggressive and resolute in their determination to destroy the enemy and their installations. He hoped that this mission would affect the morale of the enemy soldiers. He hoped they would be thinking that if the Americans could attack them in an area like this, they could attack anywhere.

The team took off into the jungle, starting their return journey at a different point from their entry. Selecting a well-worn trail they moved along it fast, checking for booby traps and hoping to put as much distance as possible between them and any pursuit. Though it was early in the morning, the filtered sun rays shining through the triple canopy jungle added to the discomfort of the men.

At midday, Travis was told that his tail-end Charlie had picked up VC trackers on their back trail. That was bloody quick - or the enemy had a squad already on site, with extremely good radio communication. They would have to do something drastic, and quick, or they were in for a shellacking. The VC had some very good trackers, and it would be only a matter of time before they would close in on the team and hit them at a place of their choosing. Travis could not allow that to happen.

He gave the hand signal for a snap ambush and within another few yards, the team started to step off the trail to their right, one by one, and take up fire positions hidden in the bush. The VC were normally very coy about snap ambushes and rarely walked into one, but this time their leader was either too anxious, too stupid or too tired. The team let the enemy point man work his way along the track unhindered. When the six-man enemy squad were in the killing area of the ambush, Travis let fly with his weapon, and he was instantly joined by all of the team weapons. It was all over in seconds, and no one escaped the deadly hail of lead.

Travis and his team didn't hang around to check the dead for fear of a follow up by a bigger force. They left the track and carried on deeper into the jungle for almost an hour before turning and picking up the previous direction of march.

The next evening they stopped near the friendly village where their two guides hailed from. The two Yards wanted to press on to their home, but Travis held them back until morning. As the sun came up, he sent a small recon team along with the two Yards to check out their village. They returned to say that a strong force of VC had taken over the village and appeared to be waiting for them. Travis briefed his team.

'Right guys, listen up. There appear to be about twenty-five or thirty VC in the village, and it looks as though they are waiting for us. So let's not disappoint the buggers. I want the same game plan we used in our attack on the command post. Four right, four left and four in the middle. Let's get sorted out and on the move'.

The attack was swift and brutal, coming down to hand-to-hand fighting. The two Yard villagers fought like wild animals with no thought for their safety, and paid the price by being struck down from behind as they charged into the enemy. At the end of it all, there were no survivors among the VC. Travis had lost one of his Nung tribesmen and half of his men were walking wounded.

Village secure, they began to check the villagers. They found that the VC had beheaded the elders and cut off the breasts of all the mature females and the Achilles tendons of the tribesmen. The children they had used for bayonet practice. It was sickening, and his team struggled with their emotions as they dealt with the casualties.

To his great distress Travis found that little Blin was in desperate shape, disfigured for life and very weak from pain, loss of blood and shock. After swift medical attention by the team medic, Travis held Blin to him and they cried together at her pain, her mutilation, her lost innocence and the mindless brutality of the VC. His soldiers administered first aid around the village as best they could, with the medic attending to the worst cases. Any help had to be rushed as the team had to move on before Charlie closed on them, surrounded and annihilated them.

In the early morning they pushed on, hacking and forcing their way through virgin bush. Past events had proved that Charlie was good at tracking in this neck of the woods, and it would only be a matter of time before they picked up the team's trail again. Travis was worried for his men. He knew that they had to get out of jungle before dark, and he pushed and pushed his guys to make the most of the few hours of light to reach their previous LZ and call for extraction. He tried not to think of what could happen if they were forced to spend the night in the bush.

All too soon the VC were on their tail again, and a deadly game of hide-and-seek began, with death and injury the penalty for any form of contact with the other. The team drew on their considerable skills to kill or injure their pursuers. They backtracked and laid booby traps and finally doubled their pace, heading straight for the LZ leaking sweat from every pore, their throats hoarse from heavy breathing and lack of water. But they outstripped the VC troops, hitting the LZ before last light. By this time, the choppers were in the air and closing fast. Travis sent out a recce party to check the perimeter; it was clear. He called their chopper in. Just then, the Yard scout picked up the sounds of pursuit. With that in mind, Travis decided to change location for the extraction. He had already earmarked another location, in case the first LZ was compromised. Giving the co-ordinates of the enemy to air cover, the two Cobra gunship escorts laced the area with automatic fire and rockets minutes after the team pulled out. Again, setting out at the fastest pace possible for the tough terrain, they made it into the new clearing as the big Huey touched down to hover. The team, just a few feet from safety, were still far from safe. As they broke cover and raced for the chopper, they began to take fire from the tree line. Men started to go down as enemy bullets raked them. The rest of the team quickly formed into two, three and four-man groups and started a fire-and-manoeuvre retreat towards the helicopter, whose door-gunners added to their fire power, cutting up the enemy positions.

At last, the dead, dying, fit and wounded were aboard. The pilots, brave in the face of intense fire, waited for Travis as the last man. Then they lifted off and out over the jungle mass.

That day, mission accomplished, everyone went home for another much-needed leave break, this time in Singapore, where Melissa repeated the immortal words, 'Darling, would you please put your ear next to my tummy and listen?' Yes, another baby on the way.

Again it was a wonderful holiday, then back to the action, back to the shit again. Travis was still suffering from the loss of several fine members of his team who had died fighting their way to lift-off on their last mission. The brief holiday had helped, but it would take another incursion into the unknown to help take his mind off it.

Near the end of his tour, he had another surprise when a familiar voice shouted out, 'Hi Pop!' It was Doc, now a Staff Sergeant, having passed the Special Force course and won his Green Beret, coming through the Special Ops Medical Training Centre.

'Hello young feller, how the devil are you?' he said in a stage Irish accent. It was very funny, coming from one of the Brothers.

'I'm fighting fit and ready to rock and roll', was the reply. 'How the hell are you?' he questioned his friend, delighted at seeing him again.

'Fit as a flea sir.' Doc gave him a wide grin and a sharp salute.

'How would you like to join my team, Doc?'

'Got no bloody choice Bud, I've already been assigned to you,' he replied.

'Great stuff' Travis said, and both men bear-hugged each other.

So it was that by a strange coincidence, Doc was assigned as medic on Travis' final recon before his tour ended. Now in country again on another mission, the team arrived at a river which barred their way and they searched along its banks for a suitable crossing place. The Point Man finally found a narrow stretch where they could jump across, and he checked that there were no tracks or signs around that might be hiding a nasty surprise.

'Looks OK Boss' the soldier informed Travis.

'OK fellow, go for it,' he ordered.

The point man, a six-foot-two veteran from Texas, cleared the far bank with his running jump. Travis, at five foot eight, was next up. He made it cleanly, but nearer to the river on the far bank where, unfortunately for him, Charlie had laid a pungi-stake trap. The stakes were set at an angle and as his booted feet crashed through the camouflaged vegetation covering the trap, the stakes drove in through the sides of his canvas and leather jungle boots.

The pain was appalling and he clamped his rifle butt into his mouth to keep himself from screaming to high heaven in pain and alerting any VC in the area. The team were quick to assist him and Doc was there to tend to his wounds.

'Don't worry Pop, you're going to be all right' said Doc, after a quick examination of Travis' feet. 'You have the best medic in this man's army working on you'.

Now, with their leader crippled and unable to carry on, the team had to find a suitable and secluded area where a rescue chopper could land and extract their wounded officer. It was later established that the VC had laid traps all along alternate sides of the river. It was just sod's law that Travis had landed in one.

His wounds spelt the end of his operational tour, and he was shipped back to hospital in the States. Despite excellent medical treatment, his feet never fully recovered their former strength and he would experience intermittent pain from them when pushed on long walks or marches. This condition put an end to his assignment with the Green Berets. As he had hoped for another tour, he was crestfallen, but such is life. Having said all that, he was still sick to death with disappointment at losing his Special Forces status.

After his discharge from the hospital, he was returned to his parent unit by the Green Berets as not being medically fit for

Special Forces duty, and found himself back with the Airborne on boring admin duties. The brightest point in this period was the birth of his daughter Valerie, named after his French mother-in-law. To add to his joy, Raymond and Chantelle had produced twins, a boy and a girl. They had christened the girl Danielle and the boy Marcel after Chantelle's father. It was a time of great happiness for both families and for the children's besotted grandparents in France.

Back in the States, as the insatiable appetite for personnel in South East Asia knew no bounds, Travis was promoted to Major and given command of 'C' Company. He was reassigned to Vietnam. Although he didn't know it at the time, this was to be his last assignment in a war zone. He was happy again and steadily climbing up the promotion ladder, gaining valuable experience and a good reputation as a fine field officer. He loved his company, which stretched him to new limits of command and control, along with tactics and all the rest of the paraphernalia to do with fighting a war from his new perspective.

But he was on his own now, in every sense of the word, and he found that command could be lonely. He had no more friends, as with the exception of Doc all were dead and gone. He resisted the urge to befriend any of his subordinates, which was perhaps a good thing, for apart from his position and rank, he did not want the pain of losing any more close friends. It was bad enough losing Troopers from his command and having to write those dreadful letters to grieving parents.

His first major operation was to man a fire base in the highlands - *déjà vu*. He had this intuitive feeling of a large and imminent attack on the base, and his hunch was conformed when the recce team he had sent out that morning radioed in that a large force, possibly a regiment, was moving against the base. He had heard or read a quotation from some military sage or other that 'You are not a real leader until you have tasted defeat' Well sod that for a game of soldiers, he thought. He would always go for the win or bug-out before defeat became inevitable.

With that in mind, he had his men beef up the defences, using his hard-earned experience from the armies and fire fights he had been in. By now he was an astute tactician, a tough, battle-hardened soldier at the very top of his game. He knew what it meant to have real courage, and he could see it in the young men under his command. They were gutsy and determined and had no fear for the future. He had his men set up trip flares and claymore mines, hand-detonated mines with a hundred feet of wire. The mines, which were twelve inches wide and about eight inches high on little legs, held 600 steel ball bearings, with a one-pound charge of C-4 behind it, absolutely lethal in their application. They were laid to cover a large area of the perimeter. He had his mortar men vector in their 81mm mortars to fire high explosives and elimination with white phosphorus. In each front line bunker, he placed a 60mm lightweight company mortar for high-volume fire support, with the multi-option fuses set at point detonation, along with M79 grenade launchers firing 40mm, sharing with M60 gunners and riflemen. He placed a string of snipers across the base to pick off suicide bombers and enemy snipers. He had his gunners depress their 105s and ordered them to fire flechettes, small arrows approximately an inch long, at what would be near to point-blank range, barrels firing low at minimum elevation, level at the ground firing the beehive rounds. He told his men to 'shoot first and then shoot some more'.

Finally, with bugles blowing to encourage the human wave attacks, the VC struck. Travis' artillery batteries set down an impressive barrage, aiming to hit everything beyond the tree line.

They interchanged with the mortars in a walking barrage back and forth over the killing ground. Then Travis called in the fly boys with their bombs and napalm, followed by the Cobra gunships as the the 105s continued to walk their curtain of fire backwards towards the base, then reversed their fire plan to walk backwards to the tree line and forward again. They had to adjust their fire when they got too close to the concertina wire defence system.

The machine gunners and the riflemen rocked and rolled with all weapons firing on automatic, laying down a curtain of fire. A sniper's bullet grazed Travis' right arm at the shoulder, but before the enemy sniper could fire again one of his own snipers silenced him for good.

The air was filled with dust and smoke, making for poor visibility. Moments later the enemy were through the barbed-wire defences and into the front line trenches. The Troopers were now fighting hand to hand, and all was total and utter confusion. The VC made for the communications hooch, to cut off all contact with air and ground defence systems. With his command post under attack, Travis was conscious of fear when a VC attacker killed his bodyguard, but he was able to control it by emptying his Browning pistol into the attacker's face. Finally the VC broke contact, leaving a real mess behind, the outpost littered with countless dead bodies. The stench of burnt flesh and death was almost unbearable. When control was established, a bulldozer trundled forward to dig a trench for the dead bodies of the attackers.

Following the mass attack, 'C' Company were rotated back to the main base, where they licked their wounds, replaced their dead and wounded and had some R & R. However, with fighting troops thin on the ground, the Company were soon to receive new orders. They were tasked to secure one of the main roads between their base and the nearby city, keeping it clear of the enemy and open for the movement of supplies and troops. Frequent enemy ambushes and road mining made the route unsafe and sometimes unusable. It was during the hours of darkness that the Cong was most active in denying the roads to the Army. Travis used APCs, armoured personnel carriers, at times supported by M-48 tanks, to try to maintain control of the road and keep it open and safe.

One moonless night he was leading his company along the highway in a search-and-destroy mission. His companions in the command vehicle were his driver, his signaller and his bodyguard. Travis was standing upright using night vision glasses to scan each side of the road and the road ahead. It was then that his vehicle rolled over a rut trap, a rut or wheel track made of mud and filled with stagnant rain water. The rut and puddle concealed a square of tarpaulin to which a grenade was attached. In turn, the grenade was attached to a secondary explosion, housed in a large clay pot buried in the ground and filled with gunpowder and all manner of rusty scrap metal, bolts, nails, and nuts. Trap laid, the enemy would waited patiently for a military convoy to move along the road and trigger the rut trap before initiating their ambush.

The earth under Travis erupted, signalling the opening of a fierce onslaught on the Troopers. Travis was lucky - if you consider being blown up as lucky. Because he was standing at the time, he was blown straight up and on to the top of the banking at the roadside. His companions were not so lucky, and died in the mangled wreckage of their vehicle.

Travis' body had taken the full force of the explosion. He was a mass of shrapnel wounds, his face unrecognisable, and he had been blinded.

It was almost daylight before the company, fighting back, had secured the road again and begun to collecting their dead and wounded. At this stage, Travis knew nothing of this as he lay near to death in the sparse undergrowth at the top of the embankment. He was the last to be found as he hung on to life by the merest thread. Then, for the last time, his broken body was flown back to the USA after emergency surgery and treatment on board a US carrier in the South China Sea.

This time it was a very long haul before Travis turned the corner, having hovered between life and death. Then came the healing phase, which was to take many more months. Wonder of wonders, his vision returned and grew stronger with every day that passed. Physiotherapy was a nightmare of pain, sweat and tears of frustration, but one day he was able to go on his own to the gym and start the momentous task of getting fighting fit again. He progressed well, his health improved and his morale began to rise, only to be cruelly dashed by his doctors, who informed him that he would never soldier again. He was devastated, facing the end of his military career.

Unknown to Travis, things were moving behind the scenes, and he was eventually called to HQ for assessment and reassignment. There he received a very pleasant surprise. Because of his fluency in French and his connections in France and the French Army in particular, he was to be assigned to SHAFE, Supreme Headquarters Allied Forces in Europe, based at Brussels in Belgium, with the rank of Colonel. So a new and final chapter in his military career began for him, Melissa and his growing family.

CHAPTER EIGHTEEN

BELGIUM

The years that followed were good ones for the Travis family, the children growing up on the Continent and attending multi-national schools. As a family, they spent most of their holidays in Chalonne with their relations through marriage, Danielle and Marcel. The summer holidays were spent at a château bought by Anton in the South of France. The children loved it, running free, wild and safe in the countryside. Winter holidays saw them all skiing on the slopes of St Moritz.

Occasionally Travis and Melissa took the children to see their Irish families, but more often their Irish relations came to visit them in Belgium. Taking on German as a fourth language after Irish, English and French, Travis added a working knowledge of Italian and Spanish, picked up in the Legion and the US Army.

His duties were interesting and varied. He started as a Liaison Officer, dealing with Brigades and Regiments, Generals, Commanders and Deputy Commanders. Then he was involved in troubleshooting among the American, British, French and German troops. His main task was working with the GIs in the aftermath of the Vietnam War. In Europe, many of the American soldiers based there were drug addicts.

There was racial violence in the barracks, with officers and NCOs being physically attacked, the violence spilling out to the civilian areas. The chain of command had suffered badly from the loss through death and injury of its leadership during the war in Asia, and all areas of rank needed more training and experience in dealing with such situations. Travis was closely involved in restoring order and pacifying local officials. Enjoying and being fulfilled in his new position, he was also able to take part in and watch his children growing up into well-educated, charming and beautiful young people, the apples of their parents' and grandparents' eyes.

Back in Chalonne, Marcel followed his father Raymond into the family chemical factory. Danielle became a dentist, opening a practice nearby. On Travis' side of the family his boy Anton, who was half way through a university degree, approached his father about his choice of a future career.

'Dad, I'm thinking about becoming a soldier like you' he said. 'Maybe try and get into West Point Military College. What do you think?'

'Well son, as you know I have been a soldier all my life and I have had a great career' replied Travis. 'However, there is a dark side to all soldiers' lives, and that is the chance that they may have to go into battle. Whoever said war is hell knew what he was saying, and a bad stint on active service can have a marked effect on a soldier, one he will carry for the rest of his life. I have seen the horror of war and the cruel deaths of my friends. I have tried to compartmentalise it, lock it away in some dark corner of my mind, but every now and then, some of the shit I have been involved in still leaks out from time to time and pollutes my dreams with nightmares. I have learned to my cost that memories are something you can't kill.

'Then, in between the action you find lots of time is wasted in waiting. Some old sweat once remarked that soldiering is ninety per cent boredom and ten per cent mind-blowing, fear-ridden action. Some soldiers love the action and can't live without it, they thrive on the adrenalin rushes. Others, like me, do a workmanlike job and suffer in the night for the rest of their lives. Then there are the unlucky ones, who can't hack it and drink themselves to death or eat their weapons in suicide.

'However, the really sad thing about life is that you never know about yourself, or any given situation, until you try it, and most people are afraid to try. My advice to you, is like the old ice cream advert, suck it and see. So, if you feel that it's what you want to do, go for it and give it your all. You have my blessing, and if I can assist in any way, don't hesitate to ask.'

Young Anton entered West Point, where he excelled and on graduation as a newly-commissioned Lieutenant, he joined his father's old division. His first posting was as a liaison officer with the French *3eme Compagnie 1er Regiment de Chasseurs Parachutistes* (3rd Company of the 1st Parachute Infantry Regiment). They were stationed at Bir Hasen in the Ramlet al Baida area of West Beirut as UN peacekeepers and billeted in an apartment block in a sea-front residential area. Anton was seconded for the post, thanks to his fluency in French and the fact that he was a Paratrooper. He loved the posting and settled in quickly and was well accepted by his fellow Troopers. Travis was well proud of him, as indeed he was of his daughter Natalie, Anton's young sister, who became a medical doctor.

Their grandparents in Chalonne, now getting well on in years, were keeping in good health, being fussed and loved by everyone around them.

Unfortunately life was to deal one more tragic blow to Travis and his extended family in the shape of his beloved son Anton. Not long after six in the morning a yellow Mercedes-Benz water delivery truck drove into Beirut Airport, the home of the 2nd Marine Division of the United States Marine Corps. The unit was part of a multinational peacekeeping force, based in the Lebanon since the Israeli invasion of the country. The truck had been substituted for the regular delivery vehicle and packed with tons of TNT explosives. It turned into the access road and drove around the parking area. It then accelerated, crashing through the barbed wire fence, roaring past the sentry post, crashing through the main gate and into the four-storey cinder block building which housed the Marine contingent. The explosion that followed killed 241 Americans and wounded sixty others.

At his post in Bir Hasen, Anton, on hearing the explosion, which was just some kilometres away, rushed onto a balcony to see the smoke cloud raising from the bombed barracks. Fearing for the lives of his fellow American servicemen, he went back inside and prepared to rush down to the airport to see if he could help in any way. As he was getting ready, another suicide bomber was driving his truck down a ramp into the Drakkar building's underground car park and the home of the French Paras. The suicide bomber then detonated his bomb, levelling the eight-storey building, killing 58 Paras and wounding 15, among them Lieutenant Anton Travis.

News of the atrocity flashed around the world and Travis and Melissa were desperately worried, fearing for their young son. All too soon, they received the bad news that Anton was indeed a casualty.

Travis, Melissa and Valerie were waiting at the airport stateside when the military transport aircraft carrying their son and brother landed. From then on they hardly left his bedside as he lay in a deep coma after major surgery to save his life and limbs. Back in

Chalonne, Danielle hired a locum to run her dentistry and rushed to the States to be with the critically-injured Anton. They had always been close friends and it seemed that during a time of fear, sorrow or sickness or any upset big or small, Anton's comforting arm had always been around her. They had shared their innermost secrets from childhood to adult. Now she would be there for him.

It was touch and go for Anton. He was given the Last Rites of the Church on two occasions as the end appeared to be near. Each time he rallied and continued to fight for his life. The family all prayed for his survival.

Then early one morning, as Danielle slept in a chair nearby, he opened his eyes. Then he focused on her and whispered the single word 'Drink'. From that moment on he started the healing process and began to grow stronger every day. In time and with much encouragement and help from the hospital authorities and his family, Anton returned to good health and strength.

CHAPTER NINETEEN

FRANCE

One particularly beautiful summer, the families got together again in Chalonne to celebrate the 90th birthday of old Anton. It was one of those special summer evenings when all seemed right with the world. The family sat in the dining room of the old house, where happy conversation ebbed and flowed during dinner and many funny and touching toasts were proposed.

During a brief lull in the hubbub of conversation Lieutenant Anton Travis, US Army, got to his feet. His father noticed that he was holding Danielle's hand tightly. The young man coughed to draw their attention. When complete silence reigned, he announced, very formally, 'Papa, Mama, Grandpapa, Grandmama, Uncle Raymond, Auntie Chantelle, and family. I… we…'

At this, a lump started to fill Travis' throat as memories of Raymond and Chantelle flooded into his mind. To him the scene was a re-enactment.

The handsome young officer continued, 'That is, Danielle and I have an announcement to make.' The room suddenly went so quiet you could have heard a pin drop. 'Danielle and I are deeply and truly in love and we request your permissions and blessings to become engaged to be married.'

The silence held as the young soldier, face flushed with anxiety, gazed frantically around his elders. The young man's father and brother-in-law both looked up the table to where old Anton and Valerie sat. They were in tears. Travis' eyes began to fill up as speechless, he looked towards Raymond and nodded, his expression begging his brother-in-law to reply.

Poor Raymond was hardly up to the task, but pulling himself up to his feet he gamely replied. 'Speaking on behalf of your families, we are pleased to give you and your beautiful young lady our permission to become engaged, and we do so with every blessing and our very best wishes.'

Then all happy hell broke out, the youngsters dancing around hugging each other. The grandparents, Travis and Raymond just sat silently, lost in their memories, as their wives rushed to congratulate the young couple.

The wedding of Anton Patrick Travis and Danielle Marie Leclerc was another very special and wonderful day in Travis' life. He was surrounded by his French and Irish families, along with his army buddies. Hamish, now out of the Legion, was married to a Scottish beauty and running an outward-bound school in Inverness in his beloved Scotland. Doc was also married and now a brilliant trauma doctor in a top New York hospital.

As the wedding photos were taken, young Anton was handsome and resplendent in his Army dress uniform, Danielle looking beautiful and radiant in shimmering white. She was so like Antoinette that Travis had to pinch himself back to reality at the sight of her. There was one photo setting which involved the happy couple, flanked by old Anton and Valerie, and as Travis looked on with pride and joy, he imagined he saw his Antoinette in the background smiling and nodding in happiness.

THE END

About the author

Phil Tomkins was born in Dublin, Ireland and educated at CBS Westland Row, Dublin. In 2008 he was awarded a BA Hons Degree in Creative Writing by the University of Bolton, England, UK. An ex-elite soldier, his writing reflects his continuing interest in military history. He currently lives in the north of England, in semi-retirement with his wife Maree.

You may also like TWICE A HERO. From the trenches of the Great War to the ditches of the Irish Midlands.

The true story of hardship and horror in the blood and the mud as seen through the eyes of a teenage volunteer and his comrades in the forgotten conflicts of Salonika and Palestine, during the Great War, fighting for the freedom of small nations and in particular Home Rule for Ireland. Then his extraordinary courage in the Irish War of Independence, which ended 700 years of bloody struggle and helped establish a nation